LEAVE THE
LIGHTS ON

Also available by Liv Andersson

Little Red House

LEAVE THE LIGHTS ON

A NOVEL

LIV ANDERSSON

CROOKED
LANE

NEW YORK

Copyright © 2023 by Wendy Tyson

Published in the United States by Crooked Lane Books, an imprint of The Quick Brown Fox & Company LLC.

Crooked Lane Books and its logo are trademarks of The Quick Brown Fox & Company LLC.

Library of Congress Catalog-in-Publication data available upon request.

ISBN (hardcover): 978-1-63910-509-0
ISBN (ebook): 978-1-63910-510-6

Cover design by Heather VenHuizen

Printed in the United States.

www.crookedlanebooks.com

Crooked Lane Books
34 West 27th St., 10th Floor
New York, NY 10001

First Edition: October 2023

10 9 8 7 6 5 4 3 2 1

For Matthew. Keep believing.

CHAPTER

1

H IS SHIRT SMELLED of lavender. I held the French-blue linen to my face and inhaled, closing my eyes against an onslaught of unwanted emotions. Fury. Guilt. Acceptance. Warm cherry and clove from Josh's pipe wove around and through the fenugreek and cumin he'd eaten at lunch, but these scents, familiar and comforting, were only the backdrop to the cloying, fetid aroma of her cheap body lotion.

How could he not know?

I tossed Josh's shirt onto the laundry pile and closed the cabinet door. Maya would handle the laundry, just as she handled his calls and the cleaning staff and the groundskeeper, freeing me to do whatever I felt was important that day. Used to vague answers, Maya rarely asked about my schedule anymore. She simply went about her work, maddeningly efficient, giving me looks that somehow managed to be impassive and judgmental at the same time.

"Mrs. Wicker, will you be having lunch here today?" Maya asked, interrupting my thoughts.

I jumped at the sound of the other woman's voice. "No, not today." I turned, frowned. "Thank you. And please call me Beatrice." I'd been asking her to call me Beatrice for years. I knew nothing was going to change. "I'd really like that."

"Yes, ma'am."

My gaze strayed toward the closet, to the paneled door that hid the laundry basket. Maya's attention followed. I saw the unmistakable mauve lip prints on the bottom of a white Hugo Boss dress shirt and felt the flush of shame and anger on my face. Mauve. Lavender. In my mind, *she* was always shrouded in a haze of purple.

Maya pursed thin lips. "Extra starch for Mr. Wicker's shirts?"

"Please."

"Will Mr. Wicker be joining you for dinner this evening? We'll be having the chicken cutlets he likes."

I pulled a sweatshirt on over my T-shirt. Although it was early fall and the sun was shining, I could see the chop on the waves in the bay through the bedroom window. It was already a breezy day, windy and cool, with showers expected during the late afternoon. Over the past decade, I'd learned that the weather on the Maine coast was as unpredictable and unforgiving as its waters—and sometimes its people.

"Mrs. Wicker?" Maya said. "Should I set the table for two?"

"Beatrice." I forced a smile. *Should she set a table for two?* "You know his schedule better than I do."

Maya nodded curtly. She collected the laundry from the closet and left the bedroom. Despite her six decades, Maya's posture remained impeccable, and her loyalty to Josh was as straight and narrow as her spine. I watched the housekeeper's slender form disappear back into the hallway before allowing myself to sink down onto the bed. *Would* Josh be home for dinner? *Does he give a damn about chicken cutlets or starched shirts?* I had no idea anymore.

I lay down on the bed and stared up at the trayed ceiling. I could still smell the lavender. It trailed behind Maya, coating my nostrils and stabbing at my temples with relentless floral jabs.

I hated lavender. I hated her.

How could he not know?

*   *   *

"It's beautiful. Beautiful, but haunting." Seth Miller placed his camera bags on the ground and stretched his arms over his head, his gaze bouncing from the peeling main house to the meandering line of decaying additions behind it. Beyond the building, the steely blue of the Atlantic punched its way over the small island's southeastern rocky shoreline, spewing frothy cold water onto a patchy, browning lawn. A single seagull sat on a sagging porch roof, watching us. An old wooden rowboat leaned against the porch railing, it's bottom boards as worn and faded as the house's shingles. Seth's gaze locked onto the boat. "Where do we even start?"

"Wherever you want." I studied the building alongside him. It'd been love at first sight with the old inn and its ramshackle cottages, but I'd only been allowed inside the annex after a thorough inspection and after the Wicker Foundation had secured the purchase. Our first project was to finish one of the cottages, but the rest of the structures on the island remained largely uninhabitable. "The main building and the cottages will remain. The rest of the inn is being demolished."

Seth squinted, covering his eyes against the sun's glare with a well-manicured hand. "That's a shame."

"Wait until you see the inside of the annexes. You'll think differently."

"Can I see them now?"

"We'll need to be careful. The floors are rotted, and there's broken glass, mildew, and hazards everywhere."

"*Careful* is my middle name. Besides, we should capture the whole sad thing. The before and after contrast will help the Wicker Foundation raise money." He pointed to the house additions with their caved-in roofs and broken windowpanes. "There's not a lot to salvage back there."

"For sure." I wished they could save the entire building, but the cost of repairing and remodeling the three thousand square feet of additions was too much, even for Josh and the Wicker Foundation. I glanced up at Seth. "The Ross House evolved over time. I'm sure it'll survive one more new identity."

"I thought it had been in the Ross family for generations."

"It had." Researching the history of the island and the house had been my job, and discovering its roots had been a triumph. "It started out as a simple Puritan homestead. A small shack, some out-buildings, a pasture area for chickens and maybe pigs. There's even an old cemetery tucked away in the corner of the island."

Seth looked out on the fields between the Ross House and the cottages, which sat up on the hill around the perimeter of the island. The fields, now covered with scraggly meadow and weedy brush, had been fallow for decades. He said, "Imagine living here, at the mercy of the sea, and trying to grow your own food in this sandy, rocky soil."

"Every day would be about survival."

Seth's eyes darkened. "I don't know how they did it. Or why they'd do it. Why choose such a difficult life?"

I wasn't surprised by Seth's reaction. This place had that effect on people. Maybe it was the feeling of isolation, maybe it was the raw vulnerability of the land itself. "People don't always get to choose their path—especially back then."

Seth was silent a moment. "I don't believe that."

"You don't have to." I settled against the porch railing and held my face up to the ocean breeze. The pungent, briny smell of the sea never got old. "After that, it was an inn for a few years."

"And then a nut house."

I frowned at his choice of words. "Michael Ross, great-great-grandfather to the most recent owner, Miles Ross, was a wealthy man whose wife had mental health issues. These days doctors would probably say Michael's wife suffered from postpartum depression, but back then they labeled her with something uglier and more damning. From what I could tell, Michael Ross wanted to avoid the stigma of an institution, so he bought this place and created a so-called 'health sanctuary' for wealthy women. It was in operation until the mid-1900s." I shrugged. "After that, the Ross family handed this island down from generation to generation, using it only as a family estate."

"An asylum, huh? Sounds kind of creepy."

I had to agree. While the idea of a sanctuary was benign enough, based on the little I could find about the years the island had oper-ated as a mental health retreat, it was more like an unsanctioned psychiatric hospital, where doctors performed questionable therapies in private, out of the scrutiny of the public and professional eye.

"Wonder what kind of secrets this place holds." Seth's attention wandered toward the island's jagged edges, where the dilapidated cottages stood. They'd been made of proud white cedar once, but now their wood was as gray and washed out as the sky above. Only one cottage—our show model—had been renovated and stood fresh and ready for visitors. "The cottages housed staff for this so-called sanctuary?"

"Based on what I could find, yes, the residents lived in the main house and the additions, and the staff were put up in the half dozen cabins." I rubbed my hand over the porch railing, now chipped from the harsh winds and salty spray. White paint chips fell in a flurry to the porch deck below. "At first, only Ross's wife and one or two other women lived here, but the cool summers and soothing sea air attracted others. The main building grew in size over the years, with the rambling additions housing more residents, treatment rooms, and some staff."

"Must have been quite a family home once the retreat was closed."

I nodded. "Miles Ross, who lived here for seventy-three years—his entire life, really—let most of it sit empty." I thought of the old man, his penchant for suspenders and tartan caps, his annual trips into town, trips that had stopped in the last few years of his life. A direct descendent of those early Rosses, he'd lived in this eerie place alone for more than thirty years after his wife died. "Under Miles's eccentric and reclusive oversight, the family's fortune dwindled, and the buildings fell into disrepair."

"The old man died here?" Seth asked. "Also creepy."

"Passed away in his bedroom over eight months ago." I pointed to the upstairs right corner of the main house. "Up there."

Seth walked around the front of the building and stared up at the window. His distaste for the history of the island was painted on his face. "Rumor is this island's haunted."

I'd heard that too. The small cemetery inhabited the eastern end of the island, under a grove of old-growth oak trees. Some locals said the souls of those early, unnamed settlers walked the island. Others claimed it was women from the sanitarium who roamed the inn. On more than a few occasions, I'd felt a tingle on the back of my neck and down my arms while wandering around Ross House, but I chose not to think about any of that. What were ghosts, after all, but unfulfilled wishes and past regrets? *We all have those,* I thought.

Seth said, "There were no more Ross family members to take on the property?"

I unlocked the front door, recognizing the irony of trying to secure a building with so many holes. "Miles Ross's nephew, Eli Ross. But Eli has no interest in the island. He sold it to the Wicker Foundation. Happy to be rid of the liability, I imagine."

"Josh showed me the price tag. It was quite a find. Almost like Eli Ross couldn't wait to get rid of it." Seth's smile was tinged with condescension. "One man's trash and all."

"The island has potential, and if anyone can make something great with it, the foundation can." While I usually felt hopeful, for some reason, today a general sense of foreboding had settled over me. Forcing optimism I didn't feel, I said, "I'm sure you read the proposal. The main building will be an art studio and gallery, with offices and guest suites for visiting lecturers upstairs, and the cottages will be turned into individual artists' retreats and studios. The spot where the rambling additions are will become the courtyard and gardens. My vision—the foundation's vision—is to offer this island to artists as a place of inspiration and respite."

"An artist's sanctuary."

"Right." I watched Seth's face, looking for a sign that he shared our passion. I saw only generic curiosity and hunger for recognition. "I want young people to be able to come here too—teens who might not have a chance without the foundation's support."

Seth cocked his head in my direction, taking my measure with one long, appraising glance. In the year since he'd begun working as lead photographer for Josh, they'd become chummy, and he was now a part of the firm's inner circle. It was Josh who'd assigned him to this project, and it was Josh who ultimately oversaw Seth's work. The status had made Seth cocky, I thought, and I matched his appraising stare with one of my own.

Seth broke away first. He clapped his hands together and pointed toward the rocky cliff beyond the cottages. "It sort of feels like the ocean will just swallow the whole thing up one day."

"Really? I think the sea stands guard like a protector." I stared out into the waves. Occasionally seals would sunbathe on the rocks below the cliffs, and I'd witnessed whales hunting off the coast in May. "The ocean itself is a sanctuary, home to all sorts of creatures. Whales and seals and—"

"Mermaids?" The condescending smile was back.

I tilted my head and gave him a faint nod. "If you listen closely enough, you can hear them scream."

"Ah, another dreamer. Josh must really love you to have the foundation take this on." He flashed me a toothy grin, using his blow-dried good looks and a casual wink to try to soften his words. "Maybe even he's bitten off too big a mouthful this time."

"Josh makes the business decisions. He knows what the firm and the foundation can afford." I felt defensive of my husband, despite the lipstick rings and the nauseating scent of lavender. He wasn't a perfect man, but I loved him—needed him—in spite of those imperfections. Maybe even because of them. I glanced over at Seth. A man like Seth would never understand the breadth of Josh's vision. "Josh knows what's best for the firm. Like hiring you to do the marketing portfolios."

It was a subtle reminder of his place in the pecking order, one Seth ignored. He slapped the top of a camera bag. "On that note, shall we get started?" He lifted his chin toward the sun, which was just peeking from between the clouds. "Daylight is dwindling, and we'll want the natural light for the exterior photos."

"By all means. You're the expert. Shoot away."

* * *

It was well after five when we finished. The sun was sinking toward the horizon, and the wind had picked up, bringing with it a blinding gray mist that settled over the island. The short bridge to the mainland would be shrouded by fog soon. I eyed the rowboat, usually preferring to paddle back to the home I shared with Josh on Dove Street, rather than take a car, but with today's weather that was risky. Besides, I'd gotten a ride from the foundation with Seth—and I'd promised Grace I'd meet her for dinner.

Seth was packing up the last of his lighting equipment. He picked up his materials and aimed a shoulder in the direction of his car, which was parked in the weedy lot alongside the main building. "Ready?"

I let my gaze meander over the interior of the cottage we'd just finishing shooting. We planned to name it Mary's Cottage, after the artist Mary Cassatt. The cottage was small—just one room, with a bank of cabinets and a deep, narrow closet that would be expanded and made into a bathroom—and already I could picture some young artist sleeping here, painting here, creating here. I reminded myself that it was Josh and his money that would make it all possible. Despite everything, despite *her*, he did good things. He was a good man. This would be more proof.

"*Beatrice?* Ready?"

I followed Seth back to Ross House and to his Lexus. Together, we put the equipment in the back, and I climbed in next to Seth. Ross Island was connected to the mainland by a short, flat bridge that spanned the width of one car. Wooden and rickety, it was on Josh's list of things to repair. We drove over that bridge in silence. From the passenger seat, I watched the waves roll in, hitting the island's shoreline with a vengeance. Angry clouds were stewing overhead, and once the sun was down, there would be storms—a dramatic, wrathful deluge. For now, though, the shoreline and the ornery sky reflected my mood, and that gave me some odd sense of comfort. This place had become my home. Nothing would change that.

Suddenly sirens blared, startling me back to the here and now.

"Sounds like it's coming from the north end of town," Seth said.

That was where the foundation was located. I kneaded the flesh of my thigh, feeling that sense of foreboding return with a vengeance. What if something had happened at the Wicker Foundation? What if something had happened to Josh?

As we neared Route 1 and the foundation's offices, I saw police and firetrucks heading inland, toward town, away from Josh's business. I let out a long breath of relief. Whatever had happened in Cape Morgan, it hadn't happened to Josh.

"Look—I think that's smoke." Seth pulled into the foundation's parking lot next to my Subaru and killed the engine. He pointed in the direction of the town's only elementary school. "There must be a fire at the school."

Where there's smoke, there's fire. I heard *his* voice from another lifetime, clear and sharp and jarring as the screams of the gulls circling overhead when I was alone on Ross Island. My eyes closed of their own volition, and *his* face flashed before me. A shaggy mop of wavy brown hair, deceptively charming against chiseled cheekbones and hungry eyes, dark as the ocean at night.

"*Beatrice?* Are you okay?" Seth asked.

My phone buzzed repeatedly and loudly. I glanced apologetically at Seth and checked the screen. An Amber Alert—an eighteen-month-old boy missing. I showed the alert to Seth.

"Maybe they're related," he said. "The fire and the kid."

A fire *and* a missing child? "If they put out an Amber Alert, then the child is really missing—as in gone from the scene, not lost in the blaze."

"Either would be awful."

"Of course, you're right." My words had sounded colder than I'd meant them to, and I instantly regretted that. A missing child was terrifying. A missing child also meant a search party. Cape Morgan was a small community, and Josh was a local public figure, a hero of sorts. It was his architectural firm that brought jobs and attention to the town; his company's nonprofit arm, the Wicker Foundation, that had designed and overseen the completion of the rec center, the historical town office, and now Ross Island. He was an elder at our church, a speaker at local events, the first person called when the coffers were low at the veterans' home or the animal shelter or the food bank. Josh would want us to be involved.

I texted Grace, asking for a reschedule. And then I headed home.

*   *   *

I arrived to find Maya staring at the television in the family room. Her eyes were wide and moist, her hand was gripping the back of a chair. She glanced at me briefly before returning her attention to the screen. I joined her. It took a minute to decipher what the local newscaster was saying. An explosion at the school playground. A fire. Terrified children and parents. A missing boy.

"This doesn't happen *here*." Maya rocked back on her heels. I knew she was thinking of her own young grandson, Marcus, barely out of the crib and living on the other side of town. "People move to Cape Morgan because it's safe."

"Maybe the explosion was an accident. A fuel tank or a propane heater."

Maya's eyes flickered, hot and impatient. "What about the missing boy? No, no. They're not saying anything yet, but it sure sounds intentional. Like a bomb."

A bomb? Here? My stomach churned; bile rose in my throat. More sirens blared in the distance, their wailing fading as the vehicles moved north, toward the hospital. I watched as the newscasters milled about in the elementary school parking lot, stating the obvious and interviewing shell-shocked onlookers. One woman—her back to the camera, head bowed, shoulders heaving—caught my attention. The woman was surrounded by police. When she turned her head toward the camera, there were streaks of mascara like muddy train tracks running down her face. I saw a sharp nose and platinum hair and severely angled bangs.

I smelled the phantom scent of lavender.

A small boy. An explosion at the school playground. *Her.*

"Where's Josh?" My voice sounded weak and brittle, even to me.

"I don't know," Maya said. "He hasn't come home."

2

I T WAS A hair that first gave him away.

Such a little thing, innocent in its own right, but then I had been taught by the best to look for the little things. An inadvertent glance toward the object of guilt. Rapidly shifting eyes. A telltale flush.

The trailing scent of lavender.

The hair was long and platinum-blond, a stranger in a land of brunettes. It had adhered itself to Josh's new navy-blue cashmere sweater, right under the armpit, where perhaps he hadn't seen it. But I had. I'd pulled it off mid-hug, let it drift to the ground unnoticed by him, all the while cataloging the platinum blondes in his life. I couldn't think of a single one.

I let it go that day, shelved the incident away alongside other seemingly inconsequential moments. Occasionally it wormed its way into my consciousness, a splinter poking at my brain. I always dismissed it as residual paranoia—until the holiday party.

Wicker, Morris & Landing, Maine's premier architectural firm, founded by Josh, through its nonprofit, the Wicker Foundation, invested time and money in special projects like the Ross House artist retreat, the community boat house, and the youth recreational center. Every year, Wicker, Morris & Landing hosted a holiday party for its staff and the staff at the foundation. It was a festive event marked by a tasteful amount of locally prepared upscale food and enough booze to satisfy the college crowd in Cancun.

That year, the firm's management had decided on a whim to invite the staff from the newly unveiled rec center to the holiday gathering, so alongside Josh's colleagues and their families were a handful of teens and rec teachers and staff. Dressed in a cocktail-length black dress, heels, and red Santa hat, I had walked around the firm's reception area with my inner diva on full display. I'd been given a fresh chance at life, and by God, I was grabbing that brass ring and not letting go. Or so I thought at the time.

I'd been a fool. There were no fresh chances.

I'd looked up over my half-full glass of eggnog to see a platinum blond watching Josh from across the room. The woman was young—mid-twenties at most—with long hair and blunt bangs that framed a heart-shaped face. Round, red-framed glasses that were no doubt meant to be edgy gave her the look of a child playing dress-up, but it was the longing in her eyes that awakened something hard and bitter inside of me. Her eyes were at once worshipping and mournful. I understood those eyes all too well.

I walked over and introduced myself, engaging in the game of pretend I'd become so adept at playing. Those eyes widened in panic, but I remained cool as a Maine winter day. "Beatrice Wicker. Josh's wife." I'd held out my hand.

"Carly Baker," the younger woman said in a low, breathy voice. "I'm the childcare coordinator at the rec center."

The interaction took one minute. I made sure Josh saw us standing there together, haloed in the green and red glow of the Christmas tree lights. A frisson of alarm had reached his eyes before he relaxed. *She knows nothing,* his face telegraphed. *I'm safe.*

That was almost three years ago.

*   *   *

I lay in bed, awake, thinking about a kidnapped child and a bomb in Cape Morgan. Maya had been right: things like that didn't happen here. The Maine coast was safe, family friendly, and beautiful. Acts of terrorism were for other towns, other states.

Josh finally came to bed after three. I feigned sleep, avoiding the playacting that would inevitably come with being awake. Instead, I stayed still while he shuffled around the room, his breathing deep and harsh. Josh, fourteen years my senior, remained trim and athletic, but as a smoker, his breathing was always a little ragged, a little loud. Tonight, there was an added edge. He'd been crying.

Thunder boomed. A flash of lightning illuminated his broad back and slender hips. I closed my eyes against the storm, against the sad, hunched silhouette of his body. He slipped into bed next to me, onto his back, his body rigid. "Beatrice?" he whispered. His voice was a plea.

I kept still, hoping he couldn't hear the pounding of my pulse.

He rolled over, away from me. His body shook with tiny tremors, his breath came in short, sharp gasps.

It was a long time before he slept. I reached out and stroked his back, tracing a figure eight over and over again along the length of his spine. "I know it hurts," I whispered. "I'm here, Josh." By then, his sobs had turned to snores, the storm had moved out to sea, and the fiery-red glow of morning was streaming through our window.

* * *

On May 12th of the year before, Carly Baker had given birth to Oliver. He was a wee baby, as frail and gangly as a newborn fawn, with a shock of pumpkin-hued hair and squinty, forlorn eyes. I watched him through the hospital's nursery window, pretending to be a kindly, curious passerby admiring the newest additions. My gaze lingered on little Oliver—the way he clenched his long fingers, the way he waited patiently, tentatively while the other babies, the screaming babies, were tended to first. I'd felt a kinship with Oliver that day. If he remained passive, unwilling to demand his place in a harsh world, his would be a long, hard road. Maybe his father's genes would kick in eventually, and Oliver would learn to assert his will. But I didn't think so.

"Do you need help?" a nurse had asked me.

It was only then that I felt the wetness on my face, the thumping in my chest. I'd shaken my head and left, walking quickly through those callous, soulless halls.

Carly's pregnancy hadn't been a surprise. I'd noticed the baby bump one day in February when I stopped by the rec center, and I'd followed Carly's pregnancy from afar, ticking off the months like an expectant aunt. As her due date drew closer, Josh became alternately excited and distant. Maybe it was guilt. Maybe it was resentment. Three marriages, and Josh's only offspring was a secret love child whom he wouldn't be able to see without telling a host of lies.

I wanted to hate that baby, but how could I? Little Oliver was so innocent and vulnerable. Josh's flesh and blood—and the life I could not give my husband.

Would not give him.

The day after Oliver was born, Josh told me he'd be away for a few days. Urgent business, he said. I smiled my understanding, feigning belief. For three days, I pretended not to see Josh's Volvo parked outside Carly's little cottage on the western side of town. I chatted with him brightly when he called each night. It was only a few little white lies, after all.

And when it came to little white lies, I was the master.

* * *

The morning after the Amber Alert was issued, I ate breakfast in silence, my attention glued to the television. Our town was still on high alert. There were no suspects, and the child was still missing. A nationwide search was underway.

They didn't give the name of the child. They didn't need to. Eighteen months old. Red hair. Small for his age. A mother crying in the parking lot, a woman with a heart-shaped face and platinum hair.

It was Oliver. Oliver was missing, and my husband couldn't tell me, couldn't grieve, couldn't even acknowledge Oliver publicly.

"It was a pipe bomb." Maya's mouth pressed into an angry white line. She placed a bowl of granola on the table. "More yogurt, Mrs. Wicker?"

"Beatrice." I pushed my bowl aside, reached for a blueberry, and popped it into my mouth. "A pipe bomb?"

Maya nodded. "In a schoolyard, no less. What kind of sick person does that?"

A memory scurried across the recesses of my mind. I pushed it aside as firmly as I pushed back the stool on which I was sitting.

"Where are you going? Mr. Wicker is still asleep."

"To join the search for the child."

"Without Mr. Wicker? Perhaps you should wake him up, take him too?" Maya's eyes met mine, and in that instant, I saw an awkward cocktail of alarm and empathy. *She knows,* I thought. *She knows, and she's as caught up in this web of lies as we are.*

"You can tell Josh when he wakes up," I said. "He'll probably want to join the search as well. Him being a pillar of the community and all. But I'm not waiting for him. He needs his sleep."

Maya's straight spine slumped like she was a rag doll. "This is awful. What if it's not over? Until they catch this monster, our children aren't safe. Who sets off a pipe bomb? Who steals a *baby*?" Her voice trailed off.

I steeled myself against her fear. Fear, I knew, could be contagious. "Who indeed?"

3

G RACE MET ME at Briar Hill State Park, where volunteers were
gathering to comb the woods and beaches. Grace looked
shaken by the events of the prior night, her pleasant, round face
pinched with apprehension, and I had to remind myself that she
was barely more than a kid herself.

"You sure you want to do this?" I asked. "There will be
plenty of people hiking through the woods, Grace. You don't
need to go."

Her attention turned toward the large group milling about by
the building that housed the public toilets and showers. "I want to
do my part." She smiled shyly while pulling a gray cardigan more
tightly around her ample chest. "Anyway, I was hoping afterward
you'd come and look at my new pieces. I just finished it. If you're
not too busy, that is."

"I need to go to Ross Island after this. Come with me, and we
can swing by your apartment first and drop off your car. I'll drive.
You can show me then."

"That works," Grace ran a hand through her straight, purple-
edged hair and threw her chin up in a gesture I'd become used to
seeing when she was anxious. "I'm off today."

"Then it's a date."

That settled, we joined the large search group, which was being led by Henry Mackle, the head of the local PTA and an avid sportsman familiar with the park's dense woods and meandering trails. Mackle was explaining the process. He'd broken a map of the area down into sections and was going to divide the group into smaller teams, each of which would cover an area of the map.

"Walk slowly, side by side. Look down, pay attention," he said. "If you see anything unusual, tag it with the colored flags we have here. Take pictures too. We'll give them to the police."

Someone from the group raised their hand. "Aren't the police searching as well?"

Mackle said, "They were out last night and again at sunrise with dogs and helicopters. Don't worry; they know we're here." He panned the group before him, eyeing the crowd warily with sharp, emerald-colored eyes that seemed to pop from his weathered skin. "Just go slow and make sure you tag what you find. Don't touch anything. We can't go destroying or ruining evidence."

Grace and I were assigned to the beach area along with three men and one other woman. The woman was someone I recognized from the rec center—a colleague of Carly's. One of the men was the Wicker Foundation photographer, Seth Miller, and one was our local ophthalmologist. We introduced ourselves quietly, each of us, I was sure, mindful of the solemnity of the situation.

Len Kalchik, the stranger in the group, said his name gruffly. He was a thirty-something dockworker from nearby Portland. Tall, muscular, tattooed, with dark hair that clung damply to his forehead, he offered no personal reason for being there, but he'd come prepared, with a magnifying glass, tweezers, and baggies. "In case we find something in the surf," he mumbled. "Don't want it washing away while we wait for the damn cops."

Our group headed down the sandy trail, through the dunes, and onto the narrow strip of beach. We walked side by side, as Mackle had instructed, with Len closest to the ocean and Grace nearest the dunes. No one spoke. I turned toward the surf and caught Seth watching me. He had the decency to blush and turn away. When I'd first arrived, I'd seen a few surprised faces from the rec center and Josh's firm. *What do they know?* I wondered then. The question still plagued me.

Grace squeezed my hand. I squeezed back. A cool breeze blew from the ocean, spraying us with a light, salty mist. I pictured little Oliver—still small for his age, with glasses strapped to his skull by a black elastic band and a head of red ringlets. Had it been happenstance that Josh's son was the one taken from the scene of the explosion, or had someone chosen Oliver specifically? And if the latter, why?

Grace nudged me and pointed toward the dune, where a blue sock was lodged in the scrubby brush. We walked over to examine it up close. The sock was adult size and dirty, crisp from the wind and saltwater. It had been there for some time. Simultaneously disappointed and relieved, I plopped a red flag near it anyway.

Kalchik, the dockworker, joined us. There was disdain in his glare. "That's nothing important. You're wasting their time."

"Just in case," I said, pulling myself up straighter and pushing back my sleeves. "You never know what could be a clue."

"A little common sense would be nice." He stormed back to his spot.

"Asshole." Grace watched him leave. "Oliver's so young. Just a baby. That jerk is walking around, and a little boy is missing. Life's not fair."

The wind carried her words away from me, and I had to strain to hear. "Yeah, well, don't expect life to be fair."

"A little justice would be nice."

"Justice?" This time, the face that flashed before me was twelve years old, world weary, and hidden under a mass of greasy black hair. "Sometimes justice seems like a pipe dream."

* * *

We searched for over four hours, combing every inch of the beach and the eastern portion of the dunes. We found nothing other than that blue sock, a rusty necklace, and a pair of running shoes someone had tossed into the restricted area of the dunes. The police bagged all the items. I hoped maybe the sneakers would offer a clue.

When we got back to the parking area, I spied Josh standing in a tight circle with Henry Mackle and a man I recognized from our social circle, Detective Sergeant Thomas Rebelo. Near them, women from the foundation were chatting in an animated fashion, including a young, tall blonde who kept glancing back at Josh with unabashed admiration. I recognized her as Julianna Kent, Josh's latest intern. For his part, Josh's arms were flailing angrily, and his face, handsome in any light, looked distorted, frustration and anger coloring his skin red. He glanced over his shoulder, and seeing me standing there, watching, he stopped the flailing and waved. He seemed chagrined. Or maybe I just wanted him to seem chagrined.

"Stay here," I said to Grace.

I wondered what a wife who didn't know about her husband's affair and love child would do right now. *Join the group,* I thought, and forced my legs to walk in their direction. My body felt like lead, my breath was a boulder in my chest.

"What's going on?" I asked. "Have they found the child?"

"Not yet," Detective Rebelo said.

"Not even a ransom note?" I asked.

"I wish it were that straightforward," Mackle said.

"Well, you all look like you're pondering something." I glanced at Josh, who quickly looked away. "What happened?"

No one spoke for a moment. Sirens sounded in the distance, and our gazes trailed in their direction. Hope swelled, but it was quickly crushed by the tight, defeated look on my husband's face.

Rebelo said, "You can tell her." An acknowledgment that I was a trusted inner member of the community by virtue of a fortuitous marriage. Nevertheless, there was warning in Rebelo's tone. "It goes no further, Beatrice."

I said, "Of course."

"Something showed up at the boy's mother's house," Mackle said. He glanced at Josh. "The mother's name is Carly Baker. The kidnapper left an item Detective Rebelo believes is meant to taunt her."

I waited for Rebelo to elaborate. Josh wasn't just a figurehead in Cape Morgan; he was a leader, burdened by responsibility as much as he was privileged with information and respect. Unfair, perhaps—but it meant this group of insiders would share at least some of what they knew with me, whether they should or not.

Finally, Rebelo said, "A doll. A dirty, worn baby doll."

"Left propped up on a chair on the mother's back porch," Mackle said, eyeing me sideways, looking, I was sure, for a reaction. "Just that damn doll."

"A *doll?*" I felt my gut knot into a million little twisted ropes, my breath catch around the boulder in my chest. I fought to keep my expression neutral. "Nothing else?"

"Horrible, right?" Mackle said, ignoring my question. "To mock a grieving mother that way. *Bastard.*"

"The good news is that forensics is already on it. One piece of hair, one traceable carpet fiber, and we'll get this monster." Rebelo smoothed his thick mustaches with his finger, using it like a comb. It was a nervous habit. The longer we stood there, the more he rubbed at his upper lip. "I can't tell you all of the specifics, but trust me when I say the doll was grotesque."

Oh God, no. I clutched my stomach. I was going to be sick. Rebelo didn't need to tell me the specifics because I could picture the doll myself. Pink-peach plastic flesh mottled with mud and mildew. Vacant, round, lashed eyes—green or blue or maybe violet. Molded hair, the paint rubbed off in places. I looked over at Josh. His attention remained elsewhere, but I saw the bloodshot whites of his eyes, the helpless clench of his jaw. I longed to reach out to him, grab his hand—both to support him and to seek support. But I didn't dare.

Not a mockery, guys, I wanted to say, but my voice was on lockdown, my heart turbo charged. *Not a mockery—a warning.* And not a warning meant for Carly or even Josh.

It was a warning meant for Emma Strand.

It was a warning meant for me.

4

HIS NAME WAS Luke Webb, and he was twelve when I met him. A tall, gangly boy on the precipice of puberty, Luke had hollowed-out cheekbones, thick lashes, and prominent eyeteeth that together gave him a sulky feline appearance. I was introduced to Luke in his living room while we perched on a stained second-hand couch that sat slightly unbalanced on a water-stained wide-plank pine floor. The smell of mildew was faint but present, and I wondered whether anyone in the family had asthma. Luke's file had mentioned that his mother was sickly. Twenty-one-year-old me had wondered arrogantly if that was why.

"Luke, this is Emma," said his social worker, a kind elderly woman named Ann Fink. Ann was my boss. "She's here to help you with your schoolwork or anything else you need."

"I don't need anything." Luke hid behind his hair, but he glanced up at his father for approval, peeking through that mop with resentful eyes.

"Do what Ann says." The words cost Luke's father. I could tell by the way he spit out each syllable as though they were nails. Gabriel Webb was tall like his son, with the same sharp cheekbones and hungry good looks, but his eyes were calculating, his expression surly. An auto mechanic by trade, Luke's file had called Gabriel "unapproachable" and "disengaged." He definitely seemed it.

Ann clapped her hands. "Can Mrs. Webb come out as well? I'd like her to meet Luke's new therapist."

Therapist was a stretch. I'd dual majored in art and psychology in college, but I had no real experience. I saw my future self as an art therapist, helping to heal the wounded by tapping into their creativity. I happened upon Helping Hands during a job fair at our school. The organization was a nonprofit that worked with kids in rural areas, and it was desperate enough for employees that it was willing to hire college grads with zero work background. Helping Hands kids were considered "high risk," many from impoverished or abusive homes, and Luke had been referred because of suspicions of abuse and neglect. Although no abuse was ultimately found, the county had assigned a caseworker, and the caseworker had procured the services of Helping Hands.

My job at Helping Hands was straightforward. I showed up five days a week for two hours a day to go over homework, do some artwork, and provide emotional support. If the kid would talk to me, that was icing on the cupcake. Luke seemed the quiet type.

Luke said, "My mother is sick. She's sleeping."

"Wake her up," Ann said sharply, the kindly grandmother gone. "She needs to meet Emma, and we're not leaving until she does."

Luke looked about to argue, but his father held up an oil-stained and calloused hand. "Get your mother," he said softly, eyes locked on Ann. "Then these people can leave us alone."

Luke disappeared behind a broken wooden partition that led to a long, shadowy hallway. He returned a few minutes later with a disheveled woman in her thirties. Her hair was thick and golden and partially tamed into a messy braid down her back. Tall and sylphlike, she had a face that *wanted* to be beautiful but landed just north of plain. Her mouth sagged beneath the weight of the glare she was aiming at Ann.

"What do you want?" Elizabeth Webb put a bony hand on her hip. She wore a shapeless yellow sundress that hung like a feed bag from her frame.

"We're here for Luke," Ann said. "Luke is the only reason I'm ever here."

Elizabeth said, "Get on with it then."

Ann introduced me. Elizabeth's gaze was unwavering. She stared into my eyes with a stony defiance I'd only seen in bulls and teenage girls. I shifted uncomfortably.

Finally, Elizabeth shrugged. "Whatever," she said, and returned to that shadowy hallway.

* * *

"I think that was an actual vote of approval. Our last two therapists were rejected because the missus didn't like them. This was *after* I brought each of them to the house to meet her twice, and all four times she was 'under the weather.'" Ann jammed the car into reverse. "I wasn't about to let her get away with that nonsense again."

I nodded, but my attention was on the home we'd just left. It was an old farmhouse—imposing and rambling and run down, with shutters that hung cockeyed and a porch that looked ready to collapse. A barn stood behind the house, just one of several outbuildings, faded and peeling but still holding its own against the elements. The buildings were framed by a struggling, weedy garden, brown fields, and the green hills that rose up in the distance. Three chickens pecked around a sparse yard in front of the barn, their heads bobbing to an unheard beat.

Ann stopped the car by the mailbox before turning down the dirt road on which the Webbs lived. In a too-loud voice, she said, "Don't you let them intimidate you, Emma. They don't like strangers in their home, but who does? Elizabeth is the one to watch out for. Gabriel *seems* tough, but he won't bother you. You just need to win *her* over." She turned her head to glance at me before studying her short, trimmed nails. "You're how old? Twenty-one?" She smiled approvingly when I confirmed my age. "A young girl like you can relate to Luke in ways an older person can't."

"I guess."

"I *know*. You've had a rough start at the agency, but that doesn't have to define your career."

Ann was fumbling with her briefcase—pulling out more files to leave with me—while I continued to study the house. Even the sunny cheer of that late-May afternoon couldn't warm me. I'd worked for Helping Hands for two months already, and Ann was right—it had been a tough beginning. One child ran away under my watch, and another's family asked that I be removed from their son's case because I was too young and "too tempting." I'd swallowed those humiliations and persevered. But there was just something about *this* house and *this* family that unnerved me.

The house had two floors, and in one of the upstairs windows, I saw a face watching me from between stained, lacy white curtains. It was Luke, his feline features unreadable from that distance. Only I didn't need to see his expression to understand how he felt about me. His arm came through the open window, extended in my direction, and he was pointing his finger toward me like a gun.

CHAPTER

5

After the search for Oliver at Briar Hill State Park, I drove to Grace's apartment. She lived in a tiny one bedroom over a garage on a farm that was wedged against the interstate on the outskirts of town. The main house, empty nine months of the year, was a white two-story colonial that had been grand in its heyday, but now it needed a good scraping and a few coats of paint. Two barns sat unused on the side of the property that bordered I-95. The garage apartment, like the garage itself, was spacious but shabby and in need of repairs. Grace had done what she could to enliven its three rooms with thrift shop furniture and craft show art, and I admired her creative resourcefulness. Still, I knew the property owner from Josh's friend group. The landlord spent most of her time in Florida, and I doubted she would put any effort into maintaining the garage. Eventually, Grace's efforts would be overcome by her landlord's inertia.

I followed Grace into the garage and up the steep staircase and into her place. She'd woven fairy lights around the open rafters in the ceiling, and they came on when she hit the light switch, bathing unfinished wood plank walls in a soft, inviting glow. Grace took pride in her apartment—it was her personal space, after all—but I felt a wave of sadness whenever I was there. Maybe it was how hard she tried to brighten a space that others had left neglected for so long, maybe it was the traffic noise from the bordering highway, or maybe it was simply the bleakness of the interior. That melancholy weighed on me now.

Grace was astute enough not to press me on the shift in my demeanor. While she changed her clothes, I waited in her tiny living room, seated on a secondhand loveseat she'd covered with brightly colored sari material. Grace was fond of the color purple, and the throw ranged from eggplant to the lightest lavender. I ran my hand over its smooth sheen and sank back against the couch, still worrying about that doll.

Who would do that? And why now, after all these years?

When Grace reemerged, she was wearing jeans and a long-sleeved T-shirt, her hair swept back with a yellow bandanna. In her hands were two matted and framed eight-by-ten paintings, jewel-toned, abstract renderings of a mother and her child. In one, the mother was sitting on a stool, the infant in her lap, but the mother's attention was focused on an unseen view outside, through an open window. In the second painting, that same mother was leaning against a wall, watching the child as he slept in a bassinet, her arms crossed protectively across her chest. In both paintings, the mother's expression was pensive, almost fearful, the use of color and shadow lending a forlorn, anxious air. The second painting had a title—*The Silent One.*

"They're beautiful," I said, meaning it. I touched the edge of one canvas, running my finger along its spine. "Your use of color . . . breathtaking. Very unique, Grace. You have real talent."

"You really think so?"

I nodded. "You're wasting your time here. You belong in art school." I smiled to soften my tone. "There are scholarships, ways to afford it. I could help you."

Grace's smile was wistful. "Someday."

I let the subject go. I'd met Grace during a pottery class over a year ago, and I was taken by her quiet resolve to learn a craft that seemed beyond both of us. We'd chatted often during the class, laughed about our fumbled attempts to use the pottery wheel, and despite the twenty-year age difference, a friendship had eventually blossomed. Grace had once called me her mentor, but for me, it was more of a mother–daughter relationship, which is why, perhaps, the paintings touched me the way they did.

Grace placed the canvases on a shelf over a cheap box-store bistro table. "What do you need me to bring to the island?"

"Nothing," I said, and stood from the loveseat. "Just your artistic eye."

Grace smiled. "That's about all I have."

* * *

I glanced at my phone. Two missed calls from Josh, and one from Maya wanting to know how much food she should cook. I sent each a text message saying that I would be at Ross Island and not to expect me until later tonight. I was sure Maya was annoyed—she preferred a predicable schedule and clear communication. I figured Josh would be relieved.

* * *

The sun had emerged, and the day was unseasonably warm, so we chose to kayak across the channel from Dove Street to Ross Island. Grace wasn't as practiced at sea kayaking, and I followed her closely, making sure she didn't accidentally get pulled beyond the channel and out to sea. I'd seen it happen before—a young boy and his brother had recently wandered too far adrift and drowned—and I was wary. As Ross House came into view on the other side of the island's tall cliffs, my heart gave the same little skip it did every time I saw it. This would be my salvation. This would make it all worthwhile.

I tilted my face toward the sun, enjoying the warmth on my skin.

Grace said, "It's majestic. Or it will be."

"Someday," I said, echoing her earlier statement. "If the money doesn't run out."

The foundation had given me two years and a workable budget to complete the project. Over the fall, we would demolish the existing additions and get the exterior buttoned up. This winter, we'd start on the interior work on the main house, and next spring and summer we would tackle the remainder of the cottages. The following year would be for final interior work and landscaping. We hoped to open that next fall.

It seemed a long way off.

As I paddled, I pictured the final product. Regal, inviting, and vindicated—Ross Island restored and improved, its questionable past overcome. A larger wave splashed over and into the cockpit, and Grace laughed when I screeched. The water was *cold*.

"I'm not sure what you see in this," she called, panting.

"I'm not sure what you don't!"

Eventually, Grace paddled her kayak onto the small island beach and struggled out of the cockpit. She pulled the boat onto shore and waited for me to do the same. I led her up the rocky path toward the main house. Neither of us spoke. It was the first time Grace would see the interior of Ross House, and I was excited for her reaction. It took me two tries to unlock the cranky front door, but then we were inside.

Grace breathed in sharply. "Oh, Beatrice." She walked forward, her hands outstretched in front of her. "How . . . what . . ."

How will you turn this place around? What were you thinking? Grace didn't need to give voice to either thought—I could see the questions painted across her young face. I looked around, seeing the house through her eyes. Random-width wide plank flooring, marred by years of neglect and abuse, was dull beneath dusty furniture and outdated fixtures. The walls, once a pristine white, were soot stained, as was the ceiling. The period trim had been ripped off in places, bare wood showing like scabs beneath, and water stains snaked down and around the fireplace and several windows. A single filthy blanket sat crumpled in a corner—once the property of a vagrant, now fodder for mice nests.

I walked Grace through room after room, one worse than another, until toward the end of the ramshackle row of additions, only rotting wooden skeletons stood against time, their meager skin and sinew thick with grime and mildew. Despite the million tiny wounds that let the outside air in, the interior was thick with dust and something worse, something putrid.

"Beatrice, I don't know what to say. The main house is beautiful, but the rest of the rooms—" She scrunched up her nose. "It's going to take a lot of work."

"It sat abandoned for years. Even when someone lived here, he didn't care much about the place. He let it fall into ruin. Now I want you to see the place through my eyes. I want you to focus not on what's here, but on what *could be*." I'd made this speech a hundred times. First to Josh, then to the Wicker Foundation's board of directors and donors. I still meant every word. I wanted everyone to see what I saw. I wanted everyone to be a believer. "Come with me."

I walked her back through the main house and shared my vision for each room. I paused to describe the trim, the paint colors, the decor, and to share the function of each space. "We'll remove the last hundred years' worth of additions, replacing them with stone patios and gazebos and gardens overflowing with native flowers. Artists of all ages will be able to sit outside, listen to the call of the gulls and the rhythm of the waves. This will be a place unaffected by the hustle of everyday life, a place to create."

Grace listened attentively, nodding her agreement. I studied those eyes for signs that she thought I was delusional, but I saw no mockery, no doubt. When we arrived back at the front entrance, Grace placed her backpack against a wall.

"What can I help with?" she asked.

"Up for some cleaning and sorting?"

"Where do we start?" She placed her hands on her hips and tilted her chin upward. "I'm all yours."

"We'll start with the smallest room," I said. "Tiny wins will keep us going."

CHAPTER

6

WITH LUKE WEBB, tiny wins kept me hopeful.

The first half dozen times I arrived at the family's West Virginia farmhouse, Luke refused to talk to me. His homework would be complete and sitting on the kitchen table, ready to be reviewed. It was nearly always perfect—so perfect that at first I suspected his parents had done it for him. Then I would invite him to go for a walk or show me the chickens or share some treat I'd brought along. He would always refuse. His father would be at work, and his mother was typically sleeping.

"She's unwell," he'd say. "She needs her rest." Even at my own tender age, Luke struck me as a child far older than his years.

The second week in, I pulled my art supplies out of my bag. Watercolor paper, paint, sketch pencils, charcoal. I sat at that kitchen table alone and started drawing. I used charcoal pencils to sketch the apple tree on the far side of the scrubby yard, just visible through the window. I sketched the pile of math books on the coffee table, the broom wedged against the closet door. I sketched Luke while he sat on the couch, his eyes a storm of accusation and defiance.

And then I left.

I continued this for another week: homework, offers that were ignored, me alone at the table, drawing. In all that time, his mother only joined us once. She poured herself a glass of orange juice, looked over my shoulder, grunted something unintelligible at Luke, and disappeared back into the wherever from which she had come. Luke would stay on that couch, arms crossed, watching me.

I'd given up on any meaningful interaction with Luke—until the kitten showed up.

* * *

It was a hot June Friday afternoon. Outside, the sky was threatening rain, and inside the air was soup-like and stinky-stale. Luke was on the couch, wearing a pair of running shorts and a threadbare tank top. Sweat glistened above his lip and on his shoulders, and his black hair hung in damp ribbons around his face. He seemed particularly agitated. His foot tapped up and down, and he gripped and ungripped his hands as though he was just waiting for me to leave.

I'd gone through the normal routine, but on this day I just didn't have the energy to pull out the art supplies. I'd met a kid I couldn't reach, and it was time to admit yet another defeat.

"You're leaving?" he asked as I packed up my belongings.

I nodded and opened the front door. Luke was heading down that dark central hallway, when I remembered that I needed his mother to sign the form confirming I'd been there all week. I turned back around and called her name. Just then, a small black object darted from down the hallway door and beelined for the open front door, Luke in fast pursuit behind it. Seeing the panic on Luke's face, I caught the kitten before it scrambled outside.

It was a tiny bundle of fuzz, not more than seven or eight weeks old. It seemed healthy and well fed, and it purred when I held it to my chest.

Luke reached for the cat, eyes still wide in panic. "Give her here. Hurry."

I started to hand over the kitten. From behind us, I heard Luke's mother opening the door to her room. "Luke?" she called. "Is that woman *still* here?" Wearing a faded blue bathrobe and carrying a glass of water, she shuffled into the light and paused by the kitchen doorway to peer out at me and Luke.

Luke's eyes pleaded with me, and on impulse, I stepped outside and put the cat behind my back.

"No worries, Mrs. Webb. I need you to sign my form." Catching Luke's subtle head nod, I said, "But I can do that Monday."

"Yeah, yeah." She walked away from us, into the kitchen. I heard her rattling around in the cupboard. She emerged with a bottle of pills and her glass of water. "Luke, feed the chickens." And then she was gone, having disappeared once again into the bowels of the house.

Luke hurried outside and closed the front door behind him. His father's old Chevy was parked in the driveway, but Gabriel Webb was nowhere in sight.

"You're not gonna tell her, are you?" Luke asked. "Please don't tell her."

"Tell her what? About this little thing?" The kitten had been struggling against my grip, and my hands were crisscrossed with stinging, bloody scratches. I handed Luke the distressed kitten. He cuddled her to his chest, and she immediately calmed down. "Your parents don't want you to have the kitten?"

He swallowed and looked back at the house. "My mother said we don't need another mouth to feed."

"Ah."

"This one is the last of a litter."

"Where are the others?"

Luke glanced down at the cat. "They didn't make it." The flush that spread across Luke's face told me what I needed to know.

"Oh, man, I'm sorry." I patted the kitten's head. She was soft and sweet and clearly attached to Luke. Thinking, I said, "You can't hide her forever, Luke. Eventually your mom will find out. And then—" I let the words hang there between us.

"She only said we don't need another needy mouth to feed, so if I can feed her and she and my father don't need to do anything, what should they care?" Luke hung his head. "I have to try. It's not *her* fault she was born. What else can I do?"

"Do you think they'll come around?"

He shrugged, despondent.

I watched him standing there like that, holding back tears, that mound of fur safe in his grasp, and made an impulsive decision. "Let me take her. She can live with me, Luke. It'll be our secret. I'll bring her by when and if I can."

His expression hardened, then relaxed. He was just a child, and I knew I was asking a lot of him. I could understand the desire to keep the animal, especially in this unfriendly household, regardless of the consequences. Recalling the boy I'd first seen in the window, the boy in the shadows pointing a finger gun at me, I was relieved to see he had a soft side. Relieved—and a little scared for him. A sensitive child would suffer here.

"Take her," he said finally. "But promise me you'll keep her safe. And feed her well. She likes soft food, especially tuna and canned salmon and Fancy Feast, if you can get it. And sometimes she cries at night, real soft-like." His words tumbled out in a stream of choked syllables. I had never heard him utter so many words. "When that happens, she wants to be held."

I nodded, picturing Luke huddled in his room, clasping the crying kitten, trying to keep her quiet so Elizabeth wouldn't discover them. "You're doing the right thing, Luke."

"Then why does it feel so awful?" That hangdog head sank farther down, and he shrugged bony shoulders.

I mustered a gentle smile and turned to leave.

"Her name is Jamaica," he called after me.

I turned back around. "That's a lovely name, Luke. How did you decide on Jamaica?"

"It's warm and sunny in Jamaica." He shrugged again. "And far away from here."

*   *   *

Luke was back inside, and I was bringing the mewling kitten to my car, when Gabriel sauntered around the corner. He was carrying a shovel. His shirt was sweat-stained, and his jeans were streaked with mud. He nodded when he saw me, and then his gaze strayed to the kitten. His eyes rounded in surprise.

I hugged Jamaica protectively to my chest.

"Glad the boy decided to give her up." Gabriel's mouth turned up at the edges, just hinting at a smile. "Don't tell Elizabeth Luke was harboring her. She isn't too fond of cats."

"So I've heard." I slid into the car and placed the kitten on the seat beside me. She cried softly to be held, but I wanted to get out of there before anyone tried to take her back.

I needn't have worried. Gabriel watched me pull out of the driveway, his long, lanky body leaning on that shovel, his expression mildly amused. He didn't move until I drove away.

* * *

Pets were forbidden by my landlord, so I hid Jamaica in my apartment. Over time, we developed the kind of bond formed by fellow prisoners, each of us caught in a place and a situation we hadn't asked for. Jamaica ignored my long absences and moody behavior, and I pretended her soft meows were for me, not the can of Fancy Feast I fed her every night. Some evenings, she'd deign to crawl onto my lap, kneading her sharp claws into my thighs and purring insistently. On those nights, I'd sit on my living room couch with the cat on my legs and picture Luke in that drafty old farmhouse, alone except for his cold, angry parents. Even with the West Virginia hills between us, his loneliness enveloped me, seeped right through and into me, leaving me breathless. I wanted nothing more than to give the cat back. Luke should know her warm comfort.

But I could never send Jamaica back to live with Luke. His mother *would* have killed her. Of that, I had no doubt.

CHAPTER

7

IT WAS AFTER midnight when I finally crawled into bed next
to Josh. Lavender permeated his skin, the sheets, my pores. I
breathed the nauseating scent, embracing the penance, my mind
on little Oliver. Josh stirred, rolled toward me. I caressed his cheek,
my touch a whisper, my mind still replaying the week's events,
and watched Josh sleep. His face contorted into silent shouts and
hollow commands, restless and angry and taking charge, even in
slumber.

Guilt consumed me. I tossed and turned but couldn't get com-
fortable. What would coming forward about my past accomplish?
It would destroy my life *and* Josh's—and chances were, it wouldn't
help the police find Oliver. The Webbs were too good at hiding,
too good at running. I told myself that to say something now would
only muddy the waters, get me in trouble, and send the cops on a
wild goose chase. Let Rebelo, the FBI, and the local police do their
thing. They would find Oliver. My crazy story wouldn't help.

I told the universe that if Oliver could just be returned
unharmed, I would find a way to make this right. I couldn't go
back and change the past, but I could try to work things out with
Josh. I could finish the Ross Island project. I could help Grace get
into art school. I could still make a difference.

I told myself so many tiny lies that I finally fell asleep.

*   *   *

Josh woke up at three in the morning. He snuggled next to me and wrapped me in his arms. I wanted to pull away, but the touch of his skin against my back and his breath on my neck felt so good. For a brief second, I could pretend I was loved and wanted and safe. I didn't object when he slid his hand under my nightgown and caressed the soft skin on my belly. I didn't object when he hiked my nightgown up and my panties down. I didn't object when he climbed on top of me and thrusted away at his helplessness and anguish and rage.

I didn't even object when he opened his eyes and, seeing me, seemed surprised.

It was a while before he fell back to sleep. He remained curled around my body, his bristly cheek against my back, but I knew it wasn't me he was holding. When I heard his first snores, I climbed out of bed, got dressed, and went outside. I sat on the stone veranda, nursing a glass of chardonnay, and listened to the sound of the water lapping at the shore.

8

JAMAICA THE KITTEN marked a change in my relationship with Luke. Instead of sulking on the couch, Luke would sit at the kitchen table while we drew together or played chess. Some days, we'd even walk around the farm and talk about his plans for the future. I learned that he and his family had moved around a lot, and the farm was the first place that felt anything like home. His father, an auto mechanic, worked multiple part-time jobs to make ends meet. His mother had recently lost her waitressing job. Luke loved working with his hands. In the future, he said he saw himself designing houses or making furniture or maybe working as an engineer.

He told me all these things in little halting bits, as though he were tossing breadcrumbs to a timid chickadee. I snatched every piece of information up like that hungry bird, anxious to get to know this boy and happy he trusted me.

Little did I know where that would get me.

"Want to see a secret place?" he asked me one day in early June. School was out, and my job had become more counselor than teacher, but most days I was simply a friend.

"Sure," I said.

It was a hot, sticky East Coast day, the kind of afternoon that made you believe in air-conditioning and sweet tea and long naps.

I followed Luke outside, through the dusty courtyard, past the small garden with its varieties of lavender, some already in fragrant bloom, through the roaming chickens, and behind the big barn. Black flies swarmed my mouth and eyes, and mosquitoes stung my bare arms. I slapped them away, but it did no good.

"My mom says to rub garlic on you," Luke said. "For the mosquitoes."

I laughed. "Happen to have some?"

"No," Luke said, solemn. He glanced down at my sneakers. "Might want to tuck your pants into your socks." When I looked at him questioningly, he said, "Lots of brambles and raspberry bushes and ticks. Your ankles will get scratched up."

I eyed the crisscross of red welts on his calves. Now I knew the source. I did as he suggested.

We walked another quarter of a mile down a barely beaten path through the bushes and undergrowth. Rusty machine parts, old beer cans, slabs of metal roofing, and an ancient toilet had been tossed unceremoniously behind the barn at some point, and these items blended into the greenery, parts of them sticking up here and there like ghostly works of modern art.

"This was all here when we came," Luke said about the garbage. "My parents are too busy to clean it up. Anyway, my dad says it's not our responsibility—it's the landlord's problem."

I hadn't realized they were renting. "Who owns the house?"

If Luke heard me, he didn't let on. Instead, he just kept walking ahead of me, skipping nimbly over rocks and fallen tree branches. Overhead, the sky was darkening, and the wind was picking up. We had thirty minutes, tops, before a storm would be upon us. I thought about suggesting we turn back, but I kept my mouth shut. This was the first time Luke had shown a willingness to share his life outside of the house, and I wasn't about to ruin it.

"We're renting from the guy who owns the mechanic shop where my dad works," Luke said, answering the question I'd posed minutes ago. "Dad says he's a stupid, lazy asshole."

"Sounds like Gabriel doesn't like him much."

Luke shrugged. "Dad says the work pays the bills."

We finally reached a wall of trees that led to a state forest. Sugar maples, red oak, and black cherry trees were interspersed with densely packed Eastern white pines. With the darkening sky and the tight foliage overhead, it seemed like darkness had descended. Rain started falling, just drops at first, then a steady drizzle that pelted my face and clouded my vision.

I felt Luke's hand on my arm. "Almost there."

He ducked between the trees and into a small clearing. I saw it then—a tiny tree house that had been built into the branches of a short, sturdy red maple. The house was made of plywood and old barn siding; the roof, pieces of asphalt glued to more plywood. The front door was a soft blue. Blue bottles hung from the other tree branches.

"Come on. It'll be dry inside."

I eyed the rope ladder that led from the ground to the tree house. It looked like the kind you'd use to escape a house fire, and I questioned whether it would hold me. The rain was falling harder now. A bolt of lightning flashed in the distance, followed quickly by the roar of thunder. Luke scrambled up. I waited until he was inside before following. I wasn't so sure a tree house was the best place to be during a storm, but I went anyway.

I barely fit inside the fort, which was maybe thirty square feet. It had a low ceiling, and a worn welcome mat served as a carpet. The interior walls were painted the same blue as the door, and a baseball bat stood against one wall. A transistor radio, a notebook, and a pile of pencils had been lined up on the floor at the rear of the room. Rain pounded on the roof, but the inside stayed dry. Luke pushed the mat toward me.

"Sit," he said.

"You built this?" I eyed the structure in wonder. It seemed watertight and substantial. "How'd you get the materials?"

"It's mostly stuff I found around the farm. Crap in the yard, trash my parents pulled out of the basement—that kind of stuff. Figured no one is going to miss it, least of all them." Luke stared down at his hands, turning them over as though seeing them for the first time. "They're too busy to notice anyway."

Busy? I'd barely seen Elizabeth outside of her bedroom. "Did your dad help?"

"No," Luke said quickly, his face burning ruby red. His dark eyes pleaded. "He doesn't even know it's here. You can't tell him. *Please.*"

Another secret to keep from Luke's parents. "Don't you think he'd be proud of you? This is pretty cool."

"He wouldn't like it at all."

Strange, I thought. I didn't know Gabriel well, but he seemed like a man who respected hard work. Luke and I sat quietly for a few minutes, listening to the sound of the rain hammering the roof. My time with Luke was coming to a close. Helping Hands had been contracted for six weeks, just long enough to ensure Luke was on track and not at risk in his home. We only had a few sessions left.

"Want to see my codes?" Luke asked.

"Of course."

I paged through the notebook Luke handed me. He'd created a dozen or so codes, and the keys were written in painstaking detail in blocky black letters and numbers. It saddened me that the only person he could share his work with was a twenty-one-year-old therapist, a person paid to be here. As far as I knew, he had no friends his own age and saw no one other than his parents and me.

"This is amazing," I said. "You're very creative."

Luke flashed me a twisted half smile. "Maybe I'll be a spy one day. Who knows." The storm was passing, and the rain had softened to a loud drizzle. Luke cocked his head, listening, before glancing at his Timex. "Oh no. We should get back. Before . . . well, it's almost supper time."

I had a hunch Luke wasn't worried about supper, but I let it go. "Right. Thanks for taking me here. I had fun today."

Luke's ears turned red. "Come on—we need to head back to the house."

On the way down the ladder, I gestured toward the fort's door with my chin, afraid to let go of the slick ropes. The color was unusual—a soft bluish green reminiscent of the sea. "That blue— did you pick it out? It's very pretty."

"Nah. My grandma told me about it."

"Your grandmother told you about a paint color? Is she an artist?"

"Nothing like that. She just liked this color. You get it by mixing blue and a little green. I took some old paint my dad found in the basement and mixed till I got the right color. At least I think it's the right color. I guess I really don't know." He craned his head so that he was looking at the door. "It's called haint blue."

"Haint blue?"

He nodded. "My grandma said you paint your door haint blue so ghosts can't get across the threshold and into your home. It looks like the sky or water or something they don't like." He shrugged. "The bottles too." He pointed toward the dozen painted plastic and glass bottles hanging from the maple tree. "She used to hang them all around her yard. It was kind of pretty."

"You were close to your grandmother?"

"She lived all the way down in Louisiana. Didn't get to see her much before she died."

"I'm sorry, Luke."

"Not your fault."

I looked around the small clearing. "The color and the bottles protect you from ghosts? I guess I didn't picture you as a superstitious guy."

Luke laughed. It was nice to hear him laugh. "You don't really think I believe in ghosts, do you? No way."

I jumped from the last rung to the ground and waited for Luke to join me. The mud was slippery, and I was careful not to slide around the base of the tree. "If you don't believe in ghosts, then why go to the trouble of painting everything this special blue?"

I expected him to say the color reminded him of his grandmother or that it was the only paint he could find. Instead, a shadow passed his features, and he glanced around nervously. "I figure if it works for ghosts, maybe it keeps other things away too."

"What other things, Luke?"

But the boy was already running ahead, and I was left to follow.

*   *   *

When we got back to the house, Elizabeth was retching in the kitchen. Worry pinched Luke's features.

"You go to your room," I said. "I'll check on her."

By the time I joined Elizabeth, she was mopping her face with a wet towel. The inside of the house was hot and stuffy, and her skin was red and blotchy and covered in a fine sheen of sweat.

"Can I get you something?" I asked. "Some water? Medicine?"

"No, I'm fine."

"You don't look fine. I can call a doctor, or maybe your husband."

At the mention of her husband, Elizabeth threw her head back and gritted her teeth. "Don't bother him, for God's sake." She rubbed her temples with two slender hands, skin as chalky white as a glass of milk. "Where'd you and my son go?" she asked, emphasizing the words *my son*.

"Just for a walk."

"A walk where?"

"In the woods."

"Your job is to stay here with him, in the house."

"I don't think that's true," I said. "Nothing prohibits me from—"

"What did he tell you?"

"Nothing."

Elizabeth made a harumph sound. She plopped down on a wooden chair and put her head in her arms on the table. "He lies."

"There was nothing for him to lie about. We just went for a walk."

"Uh-huh." She looked up at me, her wide gray-green eyes locking onto my own. I felt trapped there in the moment, stabbed suddenly by a vague feeling of menace. "What did he tell you?"

"Absolutely nothing."

"Now you're a liar too." She shook her head. "Goddamn liars everywhere."

"Elizabeth—"

She let out a mean, low laugh—more like a growl. "I told Gabriel enough with these goddamn caseworkers and therapists. Luke doesn't need help. He's a teenager, is all. But who listens to me?" She slammed a hand down on the table. "No one."

I finally found my voice. "Luke is making progress. In fact, if you could just see——."

Elizabeth flew out of her seat, moving more quickly than I'd ever seen her. She hovered in front of me, face just inches from my own, and leaned forward so our noses were practically touching. I smelled the stench of cigarette smoke and bile mixing in her breath, lavender body wash wafting off her body in waves. I took a step back.

"Stop questioning him or I'll call that caseworker and report you." She shook a finger in my face. "Progress means talk. Talk means lies. The boy lies. That's no secret. And now you lie too. Words are cheap, and the words coming out of that pretty mouth of yours are the cheapest of all." She waved her hand toward the door. "Go home. Leave. He's almost done anyway. We don't need you here."

"You can't just——"

"Go away!" she screamed. "Go away now!"

I saw Luke peeking around the corner at me, his face twisted in fear. "Please just go," he mouthed.

I glanced from her to him and back again. She screamed at me once more, and I left.

CHAPTER

9

Elizabeth's words, the crazy way she screamed at me, the rage in her voice, and the wildness in her eyes, had chilled me to my core. I left that day and shared my concerns with Luke's caseworker, Ann. She asked if I had immediate reason to worry about Luke's well-being. I told her I did not. Elizabeth's anger, after all, had been directed at me.

I told her Luke didn't need me anymore. I'd done all I could do. The truth was, I didn't want to go back.

I couldn't sleep that night. I lay in my bed, restless and worried, Jamaica stretched out beside me. I stroked Jamaica's fur and pictured Luke huddled in his hideout, concocting secret codes and believing that a color would somehow protect him.

Protect him from what?

I knew firsthand that children could hold onto fantasies if it meant feeling sheltered. I also knew that sometimes there was no protection, and the very people who were supposed to keep you safe were the ones who couldn't—or worse, wouldn't.

My sleep was restless that night, and the next morning, as I dressed for work, I couldn't get Luke off my mind. If Ann determined that there was nothing else Helping Hands could do for Luke or his family, it was possible I'd never see him again. As I drove to work, the seedling of dread grew and spread like poison ivy until I couldn't untangle it from the weight in my belly. What if Elizabeth had turned that anger toward Luke? What if I had placed him in more danger? Who would ever find him on that farm, miles from town and alone on acres and acres of wilderness?

I pulled into the farm's driveway before eight that day, unannounced. It was another typical West Virginia late spring morning, hot and humid, the air saturated, so I was surprised to see the windows closed and the front door of the farmhouse shut. No cars sat in the driveway. *They must have left,* I thought, and put my Toyota into reverse. As I was getting ready to back up, movement in an upstairs window caught my eye. I saw a familiar mop of black hair, a sharp chin jutting defiantly upward. Luke was home alone?

With the resolute confidence—arrogance, really—of youth, I slammed my car door shut and beelined for the front entrance. It was locked, so I pounded and pounded until the boy finally answered. The eyes staring back at me were red from crying. The lips that formed "Hello, Emma" were split and cracked. Bruises like finger markings encircled his forearm. I swallowed a gasp.

"What did they do to you?"

Luke shook his head. I wasn't sure why I'd even asked. I knew perfectly well what had happened to him.

"You can tell me, Luke. I can help you."

Luke's hair was covering his eyes. He dipped his head further down and shuffled his feet.

"Come with me," I said. "Please."

"I can't."

"You can—you just need to get in my car. It will be alright. Leave with me, and you'll be safe. I promise."

Later, I would regret that promise. How could I have kept him safe? Me, a twenty-one-year-old who was lost as well. But on that day, I spoke the words firmly, calmly, with conviction. I would keep him safe in a way his parents never could. I would be his protector, his savior. I would be the adult in the room. Like that, my child abuse training kicked in, and I knew what I had to do, the assessments I had to complete, the calls I needed to make. But first, I needed this boy to come away with me before his parents got home.

"Luke, come on. No one will hurt you again."

"I'm fine. I don't want to leave."

"Luke, please—"

Luke backed away into the stuffy darkness of his house. I followed him. He ran down the hallway that led to his mother's room, me on his heels. I caught up as he was closing Elizabeth's door, his skinny arms thrashing about, a panicked snarl on his face. He was too slow and too slight. I stuck my foot between the door and the frame and blocked his action with a firm push against the door.

"No," he moaned. "Emma, please don't."

He looked suddenly terrified, terrified in a way I had never seen before, and all that confidence left me. My body froze with fear. I expected to find Elizabeth inside her darkened room, passed out on her bed. Or dead. Or maybe Luke *was* a liar, and I would find some unspeakable thing he'd done inside the recesses of his mother's bedroom. With a deep breath, I craned my neck to look beyond the doorframe.

This time, I couldn't contain the gasp. "Luke?" I whispered under my breath. "What the hell is going on?"

But Luke's gaze pulled upward with a violent tug, the terror on his face twisted into raw despair. A shadow rose up on the wall across from me, long and man-shaped and ominous. Before I could turn, before I could react at all, something hard and sharp came crashing down on my head, and I was swallowed by the darkness.

10

T HINGS SEEMED BRIGHTER in the Maine daylight.

During breakfast, Josh told me that the police had lifted some fibers off the doll. It was a big clue, he said, and they were certain they would find the boy alive within days, if not hours. For Thomas Rebelo to be so certain, there was more that they weren't saying, he said—he was sure of it. Josh said all this with a cheery smile, perhaps buoyed by the progress in the investigation, and I found it easier to nod encouragingly at his self-deception than to cast doubt. I knew who we were dealing with. They wouldn't be careless enough to leave damning fibers or fingerprints or hairs.

We sank back into silence. Maya bustled around the kitchen, chopping onions for whatever stew she was cooking for dinner, her face turned ever so slightly toward us, listening. This would matter to her, of course. It would matter to every parent and grandparent near Cape Morgan. While Maya had never seemed to accept me, I held no grudge. She'd been with Josh through his last marriage and the one before that. I was the newcomer, the interloper. And I was sure she wondered why I stayed.

Josh ate some cantaloupe, thanked Maya, and stood to leave.

"Will I see you later?" I asked. It's what a normal wife would want to know. I needed to act normally.

"I may have to work late." He bent down to straighten a nonexistent crease in his pants, avoiding my eyes. "If you get home before me, don't wait up, okay?" When I didn't answer, he said, "I'll call you later."

He kissed my forehead. I watched him leave.

"What will you do today, Mrs. Wicker?" Maya asked.

I'd been wondering that myself. "I'm going to work."

Maya frowned. "On that island?"

"On that island."

It was no secret that Maya believed the Ross House project was a waste of resources and time. She would never say it, but I could read her disapproval in every offhand comment, every dismissive wave, every dour look. She, like many in my father's generation, would remember hard times all too vividly, and in her mind, I imagined, art was a pointless luxury of the rich. And I was squandering more than my time—I was frittering away Josh's hard-earned money.

I ignored Maya's disapproval—disapproval she would never voice directly—and called Seth. I asked him to meet me at Ross Island. The contractors were set to work today, and Seth and I could plan the brochure for the upcoming fundraiser while the construction crew started demolishing the main house's additions. Today would be a good day to make progress. Any distraction was welcome. One that exhausted me was even better.

On my way out, the house phone rang, and I heard Maya answer it. She spoke softly, sternly, repeating, "Yes, Mr. Wicker," several times. I lingered by the door until she'd hung up.

"Was that Josh?" I asked.

"Yes."

"What did he say?"

Maya returned to her onions. "Mr. Wicker said he'd prefer pork loin tonight. The other cuts are too fatty."

She was lying. Whatever she was making, Josh wouldn't be eating it, even if he happened to come home on time—which he wouldn't. Food was the last thing on his mind. But it was easier to leave than confront her. Whatever information or request my husband had conveyed, it would stay between him and Maya.

Everyone should have someone so loyal in their life.

* * *

The sun was just starting to burn off the morning mist, which had settled like a heavy blanket over the ocean and shore, leaving Ross Island deep in shadows. The house, which stood watch over the ocean like a worn and forgotten sentry, was half consumed by fog. I climbed out of the car—the first one to arrive—and started up the stone steps that led to the house. A hush fell over the island, and as I neared the front entrance, the hairs on my arms prickled. Had I caught movement out of the corner of my eye? I stopped, stood still, and listened.

Tap, tap, tap.

It seemed to be coming from inside the foyer, on the other side of the door. Unable to see more than a few feet in front of me, I hurried the rest of the way across the porch, tripping over a broken step, and fumbled with the lock.

Tap. Tap. Tap. There it was again.

I pushed open the door. The inside was dark from shaded windows and the foggy morning. I felt around the wall for a light switch. *Tap. Tap. Tap.* My fingers finally found the knob, and I flipped it, letting out my breath in anticipation of what I would see. Only . . . nothing. The light didn't work.

Tap, tap, tap.

"What now," I mumbled under my breath. I reached in my pocket for my phone and turned on the flashlight app. Starting with the corner behind me, I aimed the weak light across the massive room and into the corners, going counterclockwise and walking carefully as I did so. My heart thumped wildly against my ribcage, and my throat constricted. *Tap, tap, tap.* The noise seemed to echo, mocking me.

And then I saw it. An old hanging planter, the skeleton of some long-dead houseplant sticking up in tufts above the bronze ceramic, was hitting the windowsill rhythmically over and over. *Tap, tap, tap.*

Damn it, Beatrice. I tucked my phone into my pocket and reached for the hook that held the planter, feeling foolish. That's when I realized I was cold—chilled to the bone, need-another-sweater cold. I watched the angle of the planter as it hit the wood. A breeze was blowing through the room. I followed the source of the cold air. The foyer led into a large parlor, and at the end of that room, one of the picture windows had been broken. Not just cracked—someone had busted the entire sheet of glass, leaving the room open to the elements, and spreading shards of glass all over the wood floors.

Maybe it was from a fallen tree branch, I thought. *Or a strong wind.* Only there were no tree limbs inside, and the weather and seas, while worked up today, had been calm last night.

It didn't take me long to find the culprit. An ax lay wedged between an old chair and a Queen Anne–style table. Someone had used it to smash the window, then flung it there for the police to find. Someone careless? Or someone sending a message?

I threw my head back and screamed.

* * *

"Someone flipped the breaker," the uniformed officer said. He was young and pimply, with cropped blond hair and a large mole over his upper lip. "Looks like they crawled in through here and made their way to the utility room."

"Maybe it was the ghost," Seth caught the look the cop gave him and threw me an apologetic smile. "Just trying to keep the mood light."

"Too bad they didn't cut themselves in the process," I said "Then we'd have some DNA. Can't you use one of those special lights? See if there's some trace of blood on the glass shards?"

The officer smirked. "This isn't a murder scene."

I said, "True, but a child was abducted in town. What if they're connected?" *Because the father of the abducted child owns this island.*

Seth said, "Seems pretty unlikely, Beatrice. This looks like your typical teenage shenanigans."

The cop nodded. "We see it more than we'd like. Bored kids, an abandoned building, a private spot to have some fun. This island is easy to get to because of the bridge, and even by boat it's a pretty quick paddle." He shrugged. "I'd say these were partyers."

"Only there are no beer cans, no used condoms." I glanced around the room. A shiver ran through me, and I wrapped my arms around my chest. The house, which until recently had felt like a place of possibilities, felt malevolent today, violated. *I* felt violated. "Wouldn't kids have left *something* behind?"

"Maybe they're neat kids. Or smart ones." The cop shrugged again. "Look, I'm going to take some photos so I can finish up this report." He waved his pen toward the broken window, which the contractors were busily boarding up. "Not much more that I can do, I'm afraid. You might want to invest in a security system."

I said, "It's on the list, but not in the budget."

"Maybe add it to the budget," the cop said. "Reprioritize."

"If only it were that easy."

"Think you'll find who did this?" Seth asked the cop.

"The truth?" The cop frowned. "Probably not. Nothing was stolen, no one was hurt. Not much of a trail. And even if they had stolen something, chances would still be slim."

Once the officer had disappeared down the hall, toward the utility room, Seth said, "Still up for some photos today? The sooner we get this brochure finished, the sooner you can fundraise and maybe add a security system to the budget."

He was being flippant, and I wasn't in the mood. "Let's do what we came here for."

"Great," he said. "Who knows? Maybe we'll capture your ghost on film."

I didn't smile, but that didn't deter him. The sound of his chuckling followed us back outside.

*   *   *

Frida's Cottage, as we'd decided to call our first remodel, sat nestled on the edge of the property, in the elbow of the woods that lined the cliff. It had once been a delipidated, cedar-shingled, one-room camp with small windows and a nonworking bathroom. As the first building we renovated, Frida's Cottage now housed a bedroom, a tiny kitchen, a small art studio, and a bathroom—and next year, a small garden of native flower beds and a meditation fountain would replace the shrubby bushes and weedy beds outside its front door.

The dying conifers behind the cottage had been taken down so that from the studio picture window, there was a clear view of the dramatic cliffs and the Atlantic beyond. The windows over the bed had been placed precisely so as to frame dramatic shots of the cliffs, the ocean, and the mercurial Maine sky. With pale-hued woods and white walls, Frida's Cottage was light filled, inviting, and connected to the island's environment. I loved it. And as a special bonus, Josh's team had designed the entranceway with a three-quarter wall that separated a small mudroom from the rest of the cabin. He'd left me this wall—an inviting white canvas—to paint as I'd like. I'd designed an homage to the women who had been housed here when this island was a mental health retreat. I thought Frida Kahlo would approve.

It was my favorite cottage, because of its views and the location. Frida's Cottage offered the most privacy, the best vistas. Back here, an artist could disappear into the surroundings if they wanted to. Back here, an artist could make the world disappear.

"This place is beautiful," Seth said. "What are you putting on the feature wall?" He pointed to the entryway.

"I'm painting a mural."

"Nice." He wandered around the interior of the cabin, pausing to look out the window at the cliffs and the ocean beyond. "Frida, huh? Are all the cottages being named?"

"Yes—after notable female artists."

Seth pressed his forehead against the picture window glass. "I can see why someone would want to stay here."

"I hope this gives you a better idea of our vision. What we've done here can be done to all of the cabins and the main building. I'd like the full potential for this project to come through in your photos, Seth. That's imperative."

"That's why I'm here." He tapped on the glass. "Josh's construction crew has their work cut out for them, though. I've said it before, Beatrice, and I'll say it again. I'm in awe of your vision, but holy hell, this will cost a pretty penny."

"Then you'd better get started on that fundraising brochure."

I left Seth in the cottage, taking photographs of the space and the view, and wandered outside. Seth's pictures would be juxtaposed against our computer renderings of the final project in the brochure, giving prospective donors a taste of what could—*would*—be. Seth was right, though. This *was* a massive undertaking. Last night's break-in worried me more than I wanted to admit. Even with the money Josh's business was contributing, existing grants, and the amount we expected to raise through our wealthy benefactors, we would have barely enough funds to complete the renovations. If we started having issues and word got out, it could hinder our success.

I stepped carefully over a stack of cut logs. The construction crew had reconstructed portions of the cottage's exterior, and to do that, they'd made a mess of the bushes and overgrown flower beds surrounding the cabin. I made my way through and around the chopped branches, stumps, and mounds of dead plants until I was standing in the small clearing by the cliff. The fog had dissipated, and the sun shimmered on the surface of the sea, which was deep gray and choppy today.

According to local folklore, at least three women had fallen or jumped to their deaths from this spot—residents back when the island was an asylum. I imagined those women. Had they been left here by concerned family members looking for a cure? Or had they been hidden here by family members embarrassed by their conditions? Had they suffered from mental illness, or were they women who'd had the audacity to have goals and aspirations and desires separate from their husbands'?

Had any of them run from a past they could never truly escape?

I edged my way forward until my toes were hanging over the precipice and I could almost—*almost*—hear those mermaids scream. One more step, and I would slide down the loose rock, onto the sharp shelf below. I closed my eyes and put my arms straight out from my sides, letting the cool wind buffet my face and torso. What had it felt like to jump from here? What would be so awful that it would compel someone to leap from this spot to their certain death? What relentless demons might they be running from?

"Beatrice! What the fuck are you doing?"

My breath caught, dizziness overcame me, and I stepped back shakily. "I'm fine," I called to Seth. Eyes open now, I steadied myself, regaining my composure and surveying the rocky shore below.

Who was I kidding?

I knew exactly what kind of demons could pursue a person right over that edge.

11

I CAME TO AT the Webb's farm, in an unfamiliar place, with a dry mouth and a head that felt crammed with spikes. The metallic smell of blood filled my nostrils. I gagged as a fresh wave of pain exploded in my skull. I remembered Luke's face and the tall shadow, but the rest was a blur.

"Lie still," came a familiar male voice from above me. "You'll only make it worse."

I blinked, trying to focus on the room around me, but all I saw were muted colors and shadows. I struggled to stand, and strong hands pushed me back down.

"Relax. You're safe."

I took a deep breath, trying unsuccessfully to calm my racing heart, and inventoried my body. Nothing seemed to be broken. My left hand felt sticky, and my clothes were damp with sweat. I closed my eyes, willing this all away.

"Where am I?" I managed.

"You're safe. I'm sorry for all of this, Emma. You needed to calm down before you risked hurting yourself." It was both Gabriel's voice and not Gabriel's voice—oddly kind yet commanding in a way I'd never heard from Luke's father before. "I hope to make you understand what's at stake. This goes beyond you. It goes beyond us. I'm not a monster. I feel awful for what you've been through. We all do."

"You hit me."

"I know, and I really am sorry. You'll understand, I promise. I'll help you to understand."

My mind reeled. I was confused by Gabriel Webb's change in demeanor, in tone. Even his vocabulary seemed more expansive. Why had he hit me? The image of that tall shadow in a strange room swam around the edges of my mind, and like that, I remembered what I'd seen in Elizabeth's bedroom. Sophisticated computers, flashing monitors, multiple televisions broadcasting silent news programs from around the world. What was an impoverished family from Sparrow, West Virginia, doing with sophisticated equipment like that? What were they involved in? What were they trying to hide?

"What is going on inside—"

Before I could finish my question, Gabriel put a cool washcloth to my head. "Shh," he whispered. "All in good time, Emma. All in good time."

* * *

Luke visited me some time later that day, waking me up from an agitated, painful slumber. He brought me a bowl of thin vegetable soup, a plastic cup of water, and some ibuprofen. I took the pills and swallowed a few gulps of water to force them down my dry throat. I didn't trust the soup. I didn't trust the water either, but my pain overrode my good sense.

"What the hell, Luke?"

Day had turned to dusk, and gold light seeped around the doorway. Best I could tell, I was in one of the outbuildings, my body resting on a lawn chair, a chamber pot and a roll of toilet paper on the packed dirt floor nearby. Otherwise, the room was empty. I wasn't restrained, but the door had been secured.

"Luke?" I asked softly.

Luke turned away. "You should have listened to me."

"This is kidnapping. Your parents could go to jail for a very long time."

"Gabriel is not my father."

Luke said the words so softly, I thought I'd misheard him. "He's not your father?"

Luke shook his head.

"He's your stepfather?"

"I guess."

"Is . . . is your mother here against her will?"

Luke shook his head vehemently back and forth. "Nothing like that. Gabriel's not a bad guy. You have to believe that. He's just . . . he'll tell you. Believe him when he does. He's telling the truth."

"He needs to let me out of here."

"After he makes you understand, he'll let you go." Luke chewed on his bottom lip, debating his next words. "The fact that you're here means he trusts you. Otherwise—"

"Otherwise what, Luke?" *Otherwise, he would have killed me?*

"Otherwise, we'd be leaving again."

"Leaving?"

"Moving, find another state, another house, like we do every time they find us. But he trusts you, so maybe we don't need to go this time." More quietly, "I don't want to go again."

I tried to comprehend what Luke was saying, but my mind was still fuzzy from pain and a probable concussion. *Every time they find us?* The family *had* seemed strange, but hadn't I worked with many strange families while at Helping Hands? Families came in all flavors, and I no longer had an expectation of what "family" meant. Still, Elizabeth's mood swings and anger, and Gabriel's bland reserve had made me feel empathy toward Luke. Now I wondered what was going on under the surface—and how much of what I'd witnessed had been playacting.

Luke's secret hideout. *Haint blue.* His fear of people finding them. Was that fear connected to this—whatever *this* was?

I said, "Let me out, and I won't tell anyone. I'll leave quietly. No one needs to know I was even here, and no one will come looking for me and causing problems for and your family." I lowered my voice. "Just leave the door unlocked, Luke. They'll never know it was you."

"They always know."

I pleaded, "Think of Jamaica, all alone in my apartment."

This seemed to move him. Concern shadowed his eyes. "Cats are resourceful. You told me you always leave lots of food and water out for her. She'll be okay for a day or two." He sounded unsure.

A day or two. "I can't stay here for a day or two, Luke. I have a job, appointments. People are missing me."

"Gabriel took care of that."

"How exactly did he do that?"

"He texted your boss. Told her you were sick."

I looked around for my phone. *Shit.* I'd been hoping Ann would remember Elizabeth's anger toward me and put two and two together. That wasn't going to happen. Iciness formed in my gut, spread downward to my extremities. I felt momentarily paralyzed. I had no family nearby, no one waiting for me. Ann had been my only hope. I was waiting for the cavalry to arrive, but there would be no cavalry.

"Luke, this is wrong. You know it's wrong. Help me."

But Luke was clearly done talking. He simply watched me from under that mop of hair, sullen and withdrawn, once again the resistant boy I'd met weeks ago.

* * *

Eventually Luke left me with the bowl of cold soup and a promise to come back. I heard the heavy click as he bolted the door from the outside. Night was falling, and there was no electricity in the outbuilding. I curled under a thin blanket on the lounge chair, rocked myself back and forth, and waited for whatever was next.

* * *

The crowing of roosters woke me up from a tormented sleep. My head still throbbed, my back ached, and I desperately needed to pee. I crawled off the makeshift bed and was in the midst of relieving myself in the chamber pot when the door to the shed slammed open. Elizabeth stormed inside with a rifle slung over her shoulder. She watched me finish peeing, her hands on her hips and her face unreadable, before nodding her head sharply in the direction of the house.

She ran a hand down the length of the gun. "Don't try anything."

"Where are you taking me?"

"Save your questions. Let's go."

I eyed my captor. She seemed especially washed out, her white-blond hair loose and cascading around bony shoulders. Her eyes were red and sunken, but they stared with beady contempt. Whatever was going on, Elizabeth was not happy. And she was most definitely not my ally.

I followed Luke's mother out into the courtyard. The sun had risen—a relentless, angry yellow disc in the sky—and I blinked against the sudden brightness. Furtive backward glances told me I'd been in the shed behind the barn, and as we moved away from the outbuildings, the house took on new dimensions of evil. Its closed doors and shuttered windows, the padlocked barn, the dead silence of the landscape other than the crowing of those roosters. What had seemed sad and worn to me a day ago now seemed creepy and threatening. How had I missed the air of malice that hung about the place like a noxious mist?

"Get going." Elizabeth poked my back with the end of her rifle. "He's waiting."

As we neared the front door, it opened, and Gabriel walked out onto the front porch. "Lizzy, put that thing down. I'm sure Emma doesn't need that kind of persuading. She's an intelligent woman, after all."

Elizabeth pointed the gun toward the ground and shoved me forward again, toward Gabriel. "You're making a mistake," she mumbled to Gabriel. "A big one. You can't trust her."

Gabriel smiled broadly, and dimples emerged on either side of his mouth. I'd never noticed them before—but then, I'd never seen him smile. Just as he'd sounded different yesterday, he *looked* different today. Same two-day stubble, same worn work clothes, but there was a brightness to his eyes and a confidence in his posture that hadn't existed before. He seemed like a totally different personality inhabiting the same physical form.

Elizabeth pushed me again, and I obeyed, as much out of curiosity as fear. In my gut, I realized, I felt safer with Gabriel than with Elizabeth. Despite the wound to my head, despite the kidnapping, despite the weapon still in Elizabeth's hand, I looked at Gabriel's friendly face and. as long as he was present, I didn't *feel* like I was in imminent danger. Elizabeth's erratic behavior terrified me.

"Come on, let me help you." Gabriel reached across the first few steps and supported my arm as I made my way into the house. His grip was firm but gentle. I followed him inside and down the hall, back to the room in which this craziness had begun. I hesitated.

"There's nothing to be scared of," Gabriel said softly. "I'm not going to hurt you. No one is going to hurt you again."

He took my hand and led me inside the room. Then he stood back. I felt unbalanced and bewildered. Instead of the computers and flashing monitors I'd seen the day before, the shelves were lined with stacks of old magazines, rumpled piles of clothes, and children's toys. A line of ratty, vintage molded plastic dolls sat across the top shelf, staring down at me with their ghoulish painted faces. The bed was unmade, and more clothes lay on the floor. The room smelled of sickbed and dampness. This was nothing but a bedroom.

"I don't understand," I managed. "I swear . . . yesterday there were computers and—"

"Are you certain?" Gabriel stood in front of me, his dark eyes alight with amusement. "I don't see anything but Elizabeth's mess."

"I swear. Maybe this is the wrong room—"

"Look at me, Emma."

He spoke with authority, and I turned in his direction. I considered pushing my way out of that room and out of the house, but I knew Elizabeth was down that hall with the rifle, and I hadn't seen my car parked out front. They'd taken my keys and my phone and hidden them. Even if I could get out, where would I go? I could never outrun them, not with this head injury and no car. They lived miles from anyone else.

"Emma?"

Gabriel's eyes softened. "Appearances can deceive, Emma. It may be cliché, but it's true. Look at the room again." He placed his hands on my shoulders and turned me gently toward the bookcases. In my ear he whispered, "Now *really* pay attention. What's wrong with this room?"

I studied those shelves. The wall to my left was covered by two floor-to-ceiling bookshelves, each flanked by a floor-to-ceiling cabinet with bifold doors. So what? Clearly whatever I had seen yesterday was a delusion, a trick of my muddled mind. I started to turn back toward Gabriel, to ask him to take me out of that godforsaken room, when it hit me: the shelves were too shallow.

"The shelves—they're hiding something behind them." Had I not seen the computers and monitors the day before, I never would have noticed.

I tried to run my hand along the top of a shelf, looking for a track of some type, but I couldn't reach high enough. Gabriel took my hand and led me away from the shelves. He opened the bifold cabinet doors on the left side of the one set of shelves. Inside was a broom, and he took this out before unsnapping and removing a false back inside the space. He repeated this with the other cabinet. Then he gripped the top shelf and moved it to the left until it abutted the folded bifold doors. He did the same on the other side.

"I don't understand," I said again. But soon I did. The room was made to look like a bedroom, complete with bookshelves and a bed. Behind those shelves was all of their equipment. It would only take a few minutes to hide everything, and anyone visiting the home would see a normal space. When I had forced my way inside, they hadn't been expecting me. Their guard had been down.

Yesterday, it had all seemed like something from a spy thriller, and here it was again today. I hadn't imagined a thing. Three computers sat side by side on a shallow shelf. Two monitors hung above them, and on one of the monitors, bright blinking dots were alight on a map of the United States. Along the bottom of this hidden space were drawers held securely with key locks and keypads. Everywhere, electronic gadgets pulsated in time with some invisible clock.

What the hell, I thought again. Why did a simple auto mechanic and his stay-at-home wife need three computers and blinking monitors and lord knew what other crazy equipment? What was going on?

"Who are you?" I whispered.

Gabriel's smile chilled me. He pulled the outer shelves back to the center, once again covering the computers and that blinking monitor, before placing the false backs inside the cabinets. He worked slowly, assuredly, a man certain the person witnessing this act could do nothing to intervene—or escape. I blinked back tears, felt the familiar twisting in my gut, that sense of fear and foreboding descending again.

Gabriel grabbed my hand and led me back into the hallway.

"Where are we going?"

Gabriel tugged me forward. His hand was cool and smooth. "To the basement."

CHAPTER

12

THE HOUSE FELL still. Neither Elizabeth nor Luke was anywhere in sight, and even the boisterous roosters were silent.
As I trailed my captor down the long, gloomy hallway toward the
basement door, I felt lightheaded, and my bladder seemed impossibly, uncomfortably full. Gabriel glided through the house like a
cat, heedless of my terror, the master of this hellhole. I thought of
ways to resist going down into the basement. Once down there, I
knew, there might be no coming back up. It was better to die fighting upstairs, in the light.

The door to the basement was locked. Gabriel let go of my
hand long enough to twist the key in the padlock. He pulled the
heavy door back, and the stench of damp and neglect drifted from
the blackness within. I took a step backward.

"Come on. You *can't* be scared. If we were going to do something, don't you think we would have done it already?"

"I'm not going down there."

Gabriel flicked a light switch on the wall, and the stairway was
bathed in a sickly yellow glow. "There is nothing sinister down
those steps, Emma."

I backed up, looking for a place to run. The basement door was
off the main hallway, near the kitchen. A back door led from the

kitchen to the rear yard. I could push Gabriel down the steps if I acted swiftly, then run for the rear door. My car had to be parked somewhere nearby—in one of the outbuildings or tucked behind the barn, maybe. But where were the keys?

"You're not going to push me, and there's no need to run away," Gabriel said as though reading my thoughts. "I want to show you the reason for what you saw in that room. The reason I had to take certain . . . measures yesterday." His eyes met mine for an instant, and he looked genuinely remorseful. "Please trust me."

Confused and dizzy, I stared down at my feet, avoiding his probing gaze, trying hard to center myself. At the mention of yesterday, the bump on my head began to throb. I rubbed it, and when I looked up again, I saw Gabriel fixating on something in the kitchen. He mouthed "no." I twisted around to look behind me. Elizabeth was there, that wild look in her eyes, the rifle in her grip.

"There is no need for that," Gabriel said to her harshly. "Emma was just coming with me. Right, Emma?"

I couldn't stop staring at the gun. My father had a rifle he'd slept with in his last years. As a teen, I'd sneak into his room and touch it, terrified it would go off and kill him or me but also intrigued by how such a simple device could cause so much devastation. A coward stick, my mother used to call his gun. It always enraged my father. I felt that same shaky quiver now—half fear, half excitement.

Gabriel started down the steep steps, and I followed. I'd take the basement over Elizabeth.

"Stay upstairs," Gabriel ordered his wife. "Go see to Lucas."

"She's going, I'm going. You can't—"

Gabriel stopped short in front of me. Shoulders squared, eyes straight ahead, he said, "Lizzy, I said go."

Those words, dripping with unspoken threat, forced another chill down my spine. I heard shuffling on the steps behind me, and then the door to the basement closed, leaving me alone with Gabriel. I waited for the unwelcome *clunk* of the padlock, but it never came. Gabriel started down the steps again, whistling as he walked, as though the encounter had never occurred, and he had no cares.

At the bottom of the stairs, we entered a low-ceilinged basement. Stains snaked along the cement floor, which had been swept clean of debris. An oil heater and a boiler sat on one side of the room, and the other was lined with old furniture and sealed boxes. A small doorway in the rear wall was closed, and bits of branches and old leaves had been swept up against the bottom of it. A broom stood propped against the wall nearby, next to boxes of latex gloves and other boxed cleaning supplies.

Gabriel pulled a cord that hung frayed and dirty from the ceiling, and a lightbulb came to life. "Stay there." He started sorting through boxes until he found one at the back of the pile marked "KEEP." This he opened carefully, slicing through packing tape in swift strokes using a pocketknife he'd removed from his jeans.

"Satisfied?" he gestured toward the room with the knife. "See? No monsters."

"What's in there?" I pointed to the small door at the far end of the basement. It was secured by another padlock, this one larger and thicker.

"That's the old coal cellar. I'm making it into my new research lab. I don't want Luke to wander in there and get hurt. It hasn't been maintained in years."

"Research lab?"

"You'll see."

I stood with my back to a wall, maintaining a wary eye on Gabriel and the steps. Standing there, waiting, I was struck by how very ordinary the basement was. Old, damp, and musty, perhaps, but filled with the detritus and memories of a family—not dead bodies or a torture chamber. I wasn't quite sure what I had expected, but it wasn't this.

"Ah, here we go." Gabriel handed me several photographs. "Go ahead—look through them."

They were ordinary family photos. In one, a younger Gabriel and Elizabeth were standing on a cliff by the ocean. Her head tilted upward, eyes adoringly focused on Gabriel, an easy smile captured on her then-pretty face. Gabriel was staring into the camera, those dark eyes brooding, stormy. It was this Gabriel, the commanding, confident Gabriel—not the halting, inarticulate Gabriel I'd known for the last month—captured in that photograph.

In a second photo, Elizabeth was standing with a much younger Luke by a small duck pond. A stately Victorian loomed in the distance, and a child's Big Wheel sat overturned on well-manicured grass. Elizabeth wore an ankle-length purple dress, and her long blond hair was pinned back, away from her face. She was smiling in this photo too, but the smile seemed forlorn, as though she were missing someone who couldn't be present. Luke had that same thick head of dark hair. Under the baby fat, a strong jaw and healthy cheekbones hinted at the preteen he'd eventually be.

"That's Elizabeth and Luke back in Michigan." Gabriel pointed to the Victorian. "We lived there. Luke loved that pond. When he was little, we'd catch him throwing his lunch into the water. I think he wanted to live with the ducks."

"Why'd you leave?" I asked, curious. The house was a far cry from the rundown farmhouse in West Virginia. "It was beautiful."

"Not voluntarily." He pointed to the third photo. "That's why."

I held the picture up to the light. It was larger than the other two and had been printed on thicker stock. In it, Gabriel was standing in what looked like a lab. He wore a white coat, protective glasses, and carried a clipboard in his hand. An ID card hung from his neck on a leather cord. The name was unreadable, but the photo on the ID card was definitely Gabriel.

"Okay—so what?"

"That was our family eight years ago. As you can see, a lot has changed. We lost our home, I lost my job, most of our money." He took a deep breath. "Luke has never been the same."

I glanced at the photo again. A sign on the wall was just readable, and I held the photo up to the wan light again, squinting for a better look. Most of the words were too small except for "Michigan State." I said, "I'm afraid I'm not following you."

"I worked at Michigan State University, in that very lab. Things were good—very good—until they took it all away.

"Who is 'they'?"

Gabriel's eyes searched my own. I looked for some sign that he was playing me for a fool, but I only saw bitterness and remorse and what seemed to be a plea for understanding. He glanced away, back toward the steps.

"Who is 'they'?" I repeated.

"The government," he whispered. "The goddamn government."

"I still don't get it, Gabriel. The government took your house and your job?"

"The government took my life."

13

GABRIEL LED ME upstairs, back through the hallway and dingy kitchen, and into the living room. Elizabeth was sitting on the couch, the rifle slung across her legs. The curtains were drawn, the windows shut; and despite the heat, she wore a light cardigan around her frail shoulders.

"Where's Luke?" I asked.

Elizabeth's eyebrows shot up. She looked at Gabriel.

"He's in his hideout." Seeing the surprise on my face, Gabriel smirked. "You think we don't know about every person who comes on this property? Every little thing that happens? It's the only way we've survived this long." He took my arm and led me toward the front door. Over his shoulder, he said, "Bring her some iced tea and something to eat. And maybe a change of clothes."

Once outside, he let go of my arm. They'd taken my watch and my phone, so I was unsure of the time, but the sun was directly overhead, so I figured it was close to noon. Black flies swarmed around us as we walked back toward the outbuilding. A dead chicken lay rotting on the side of the driveway.

"Goddamn fox," Gabriel murmured. "I'll get Luke to clean that up."

When we reached the outbuilding, Gabriel opened the padlock and pulled open the heavy door. Hot, musty air met us.

"I don't want to go back in there."

"Come on, Emma."

"I won't tell a soul about any of this. In fact, I'll quit Helping Hands. I was going to anyway. You never need to see my again." I shuffled backward. "You can't force me back in there."

Gabriel waited until I'd walked through the door, steely resolve telegraphed by the clench of his jaw. He shut the door behind us and patted the lawn chair.

"Gabriel, I—"

"I can't risk it, Emma. You'll get it, I promise you. Just sit."

I sank into the lounge where I'd spent the last night. As though plagued by muscle memory, my back and legs began to burn. I bit my lip, trying to hold back tears. I would not let them see me so vulnerable.

Gabriel nudged my leg over and sat on the edge of the plastic seat. He pushed my hair back with one finger.

"I promise, eventually you will look back on these few days with compassion and understanding. Just give me another day to help you see what we've been through." In the face of my silence, Gabriel said, "I can't risk my family. There is too much at stake."

"Just tell me now, then. Tell me what happened."

Gabriel frowned. Instead of responding to my plea, he said, "There's something damaged about you, Emma. Something deeply and sadly damaged. We're alike in that way, no?"

"We're nothing alike."

That same finger traced the single tear that had escaped my eye. "Let me guess. Absent father, dead mother, rural upbringing. I hear the littlest bit of a Midwest twang in your voice. Not a Chicago girl, so I'm guessing a farm? You don't seem afraid of the animals, and the heat and bugs don't seem to bother you too much, so I'm thinking dairy or cattle." His smile sloped sideways. "That sadness. You saw too much as a kid." He lifted his finger from my face, but the imprint of his touch still seared my skin. "Am I right, Emma?"

He was right about the dead mother and the farm—although it was corn and soybean, not cattle or dairy. My father had been absent, but only when he wasn't paranoid and controlling. And I wasn't afraid of the animals because our few goats and chickens had been my main friends growing up, at least once my sister, Jane, had left the house.

But I said none of that.

Gabriel leaned closer so his face was hovering just above mine. "I have a hunch you understand government interference."

I flinched. He'd done his own research on me and my family.

He said, "You lost your house. The one your mama raised you in. The one where she died." His tone was matter of fact, but those wild eyes shone dark and liquid with sympathy. "The state built a highway right through it. Gave your daddy enough money to buy that farm, but he was never the same. Lost the house, his sense of manhood, and his wife within a year's time."

I looked away, toward the plain wooden wall and its gouged surface. Everything Gabriel said was true. My father *had* moved me and my sister into an old farmhouse, not unlike the one the Webbs lived in, and he'd increased the size of his crops. Over time, he'd nurtured his anger at the government just as he'd nourished the soy and the corn, and that rage eventually spilled over onto the biochemical companies that sold him GMO seed, the buyers who underpaid him, even the school system that was turning his daughters into spoiled know-it-alls. My sister was allowed to graduate high school, but he'd homeschooled me in a room he'd built in the barn for that very purpose.

I'd daydreamed about playmates and oceans and faraway places. I'd had a lonely desk and a shelf full of books near a pulpit instead.

The schoolroom had been tucked next to the supply closets where my father stockpiled food and guns and ammunition for the cataclysmic end that was inevitably coming. When I wasn't actively learning, my job was to stock and clean and catalog those supplies. "You'll thank me eventually," he'd say.

"He died when you were twenty." Gabriel's voice was firm but kind. "By then you'd already been gone four years and were set to finish college two years earlier than everyone else. Smart girl. Couldn't wait to get out of that house, but in leaving, you left your daddy alone with his demons. When he died . . . well, that must have been devastating."

I closed my eyes against the truth of Gabriel's words. I hadn't spoken to my father for more than two years when he died. I'd wanted it that way. I regretted it now.

"He drowned his liver in whiskey," I said. "Whatever happened was what he'd intended. I didn't make those choices for him, and they don't impact me now."

Gabriel touched my hand lightly. "Oh, the lies we tell ourselves." Sweat beaded his forehead, and he wiped it away with the sleeve of his shirt. "Like I said, you're damaged, Emma. We're all damaged in one way or another. But together we can find peace. You'll see."

* * *

He left me there again. This time no one came until nearly dark, when Elizabeth walked in carrying a brown lunch bag, a thermos, and some folded clothes. A pistol was tucked under her arm. She placed the thermos on the floor by my chair and the bag on the chair itself. Gabriel had left me unchained, and I'd been pacing around the small space, trying to figure out a way to escape.

"Tuna sandwich, an apple, and some iced tea. I'd eat the tuna before it goes bad." Elizabeth held something up. "Clothes. Get changed and I'll wash yours."

"If you just let me go—"

"Give me your clothes." Icy tone. "Now, before it's too dark to see."

Reluctantly, I stripped down to my underwear.

"All of it," she said impatiently, touching the pistol.

I peeled off my underwear and bra, refusing to give in to the heat of humiliation warming my face and neck. I handed them to her. She took them, wrapped them in my shorts and T-shirt, and handed me a long, loose tan linen dress, which I slipped over my head. Elizabeth was taller and thinner than me, and the dress swept the floor and clung to my hips and breasts. It was sleeveless and light, though, and provided some relief from the heat.

"Eat," Elizabeth said. "Gabriel says you need your energy."

"This is a felony. You could go to jail. Think about Luke. What would happen to him if his mother was imprisoned?"

"Eat."

"Doesn't that matter to you, Elizabeth?" I studied her translucent skin, the dark circles under her eyes. Her arms and face had grown skeletal. "Let me go. Give me my car and let me out of here, and I won't tell anyone what happened."

Stony stare. "Eat."

I said, "I saw the pictures. From before. The beautiful house, Luke."

Silence.

"Do you always do what Gabriel tells you?"

Elizabeth's eyes blazed. "You don't know a damn thing about us or what we've been through."

"I know he said the government took everything away. Is that true?" I asked, eyeing the gun. "Are you running from the federal government? Are you criminals, Elizabeth?"

Elizabeth's eyes ignited in anger for a second before the fire died. The transformation was instant. She seemed to sink into herself, pulling her shoulders forward, hugging her chest, changing from the scary woman who'd entered the shed into a shell of that person.

"We're no criminals," she said. She left the room without another word, and I heard the thump of the padlock moments later.

* * *

None of it made sense. Not the government involvement, not the pictures of a prior life, not the computers, not Gabriel's shift in demeanor, and certainly not the kidnapping. I'd been hired by Helping Hands to give services to an at-risk youth who lived with his ill mother and disengaged father. It was a story we at Helping Hands saw every day. The home was always different—city apartment, shelter, farmhouse, dirt-floored shack—as were the actual adults involved. Couples, single dads, grandparents, aunts, single moms, older siblings. The average person would be shocked at the living conditions some kids had to endure, but those of us in social services grew used to these injustices—though rarely inured.

But this? This was different.

As I paced around my dark prison, I thought about Luke. What signs had I missed? How was he involved? What horrors had he witnessed? My mind wandered to that first day I'd met him. He'd been so withdrawn, so reserved. Had I mistaken rage for reticence? Duplicity for shyness? Perhaps that's why Elizabeth reluctantly agreed to have me as his counselor. She saw the young, naive girl I was—a poseur acting like a professional—and knew they could pull the linen over my eyes.

I had been a fool.

Fool me once, I thought. There wasn't much I could do in the dark, windowless outbuilding—I was lucky I could locate the chamber pot—but I knew the property. I could picture and plan in my mind, visualize an escape route over and over and over so that when I had the chance, my mind could access a map to freedom.

I fell asleep thinking about my apartment, my kitten. I'd never take home for granted again.

CHAPTER

14

Ross Island was my passion project, and the Wicker offices my second home.

"Tell me again what happened, Beatrice." Josh sat back in his chair and crossed his arms in front of his chest. "Don't leave out a single detail."

Seth had gotten to my husband before I had. He'd told Josh about the broken window and the flipped electric breaker in big, dramatic detail. Josh had called me at the Ross House and asked me to come to his office. I stood in front of him now, unsure whether he was worried about me or bringing me to task.

I went through everything again—my arrival, my plans for the day, the fog that had settled over the island, the feeling that I wasn't alone, the broken window and abandoned ax. Repeating these details only made me more anxious. With each telling, my certainty that it was no random act heightened.

"Did you see anyone?" he asked. "Anyone at all? Maybe a construction worker or even an unfamiliar boat moored on the beach?"

"No—no one and nothing. No boats, no cars, no tire tracks."

Josh frowned. "Where do you think the ax came from?"

"I have no idea."

"Did the police check for prints?"

I sighed. "I have to assume the police did their job. They certainly weren't asking for my opinion, Josh."

Josh spun his chair around so that he was facing the window that overlooked the firm's rear courtyard. Outside, Julianna, the intern, was a lone figure on the grass. She took long puffs of a cigarette, headed tilted upward, and let the smoke out in concentric circles. Josh watched her, his hands clenched together in his lap. It was a very long time before Josh turned around again, and when he did, it occurred to me that these last few days had aged him. Somehow, he'd gone from a young-looking fifty-eight to an old man in the space of forty-eight hours.

I thought: *You're wondering whether the break-in is related to the kidnapping of your son.* Instead, I said, "You're wondering whether the bomb and kidnapping and this break-in could be related?"

"Aren't you?" Josh picked up a pen and rolled it between his palms. "No note? No footprints? Nothing was left behind?"

No ransom note, Josh. No doll. "No, nothing. I even suggested they look for blood samples on the shards of glass. The officer pooh-poohed me."

Josh's jaw tightened. "That was an excellent idea. Who was the cop?"

I told him.

"I'll call Thomas. Maybe it's not too late to pick up some prints or blood splatter." He sneered. "That cop should have known better. He should have *done* something."

"The mess has been cleaned up already, so it's probably too late. As for the police, I'm sure they're stretched thin right now. The cop said he thought it was just partyers; nothing to worry about."

Josh shook his head. "Such bullshit. Given what's happened in this town, every crime is something to worry about. Every happening could be connected. We can't afford to sit around and wait."

I wondered what another wife might say right now. *Why are you so concerned about this when none of it has anything to do with you, Josh? Let the police do their job. Aren't you glad I'm okay?* Or maybe, *Why are you distracted to the point of obsession about another person's child?*

Instead, I said, "They'll catch this person. The community will be okay. That little boy, he'll be okay too."

Josh forced a smile that didn't reach his eyes. "The police *are* making headway."

"I know. They have a lead. You mentioned it this morning."

Josh stood, massaged his temples. "I wish they would get on with it."

"Can I do anything to help?"

Josh spun back toward the now-empty courtyard, but not before I saw raw anguish contort his features. "No, no. You've done enough, Beatrice." Then, in a choked whisper, "I'm sorry. About today, about the break-in. That must have been scary, especially with all that's going on."

Oh, how I wanted to say: *I know about Oliver, Josh. I know about Carly. I know your son is missing. I know it's killing you. Tell me the truth. Come clean and so will I. We can be a real family, you and me.*

Instead, I said, "I'll see you later tonight."

I am, and always have been, a coward.

15

COLD WATER FORCED me awake. I sputtered, spit, and coughed myself to a sitting position. *What the hell?* The only light was coming from the outbuilding's open doorway, and I squinted up to see who'd thrown water on me.

"Get up." Elizabeth pulled on my arm, dragging me off the lawn chair. "Put these on." She shoved my clothes at me, now freshly laundered, and kicked my sneakers toward me as well.

I crawled onto my hands and knees before standing shakily upright. My limbs felt like river reeds, and I needed to pee, but the chamber pot was gone, and so was the bag that had held my uneaten dinner. Elizabeth, the pistol in one hand, folded the flimsy lawn chair and leaned it against the wall while I dressed. She took the worn linen dress from me and poked me in the back with that pistol.

"Don't try anything," she hissed. "Do what we say, and everything will be fine."

"What's happening? Where are you taking me?"

"Just do as we say, and you won't get hurt." She leaned forward. "I mean it, Emma."

I'd never heard her say my name before.

I preceded her out into the sunlight, blinking against its callousness. My mind raced with the escape plans I'd hatched last night. Push Elizabeth down and run? My limbs were weak from disuse and hunger, so I didn't think I'd get far—and I still didn't know where they'd stashed my car. Push her down and steal the gun? Unlikely I'd win before one of us was shot. I ran through scenario after scenario, all the while walking in front of my captor, the good schoolgirl at the head of the line.

Inside the house, Elizabeth shoved me along the hallway until we reached a room I'd never entered before. The windows were shuttered from within, and large pieces of Styrofoam had been fastened to the walls. Three bean bag chairs sat in the middle of the floor, which, unlike the floors in the rest of the house, was covered by a thick wool rug. Boxes and boxes of tinfoil were piled in one corner.

Was this a quiet room? How had they explained it to Ann? As one hell of a time-out space? Maybe the Styrofoam and tinfoil disappeared the way the monitors and computers in the next room could.

Elizabeth gave me no time to ponder this before calling Gabriel to join us. He clutched my cell phone in one hand. My pulse raced at the sight of that phone. I hated how desperate I was for a connection to the outside.

Gabriel slid casually into one of the beanbag chairs, signaling for Elizabeth and me to do the same. He held out the phone, and when I reached for it, snatched it back.

"Not so fast. We need a favor." He looked from me to Elizabeth, to me again. "Your agency was here this morning, snooping around. Looking for you."

I nodded, afraid my voice would give me away. My insides were vibrating with excitement. Ann would find me after all.

Elizbeth said, "We said we haven't seen you in two days."

No. "They won't believe you. I'm not the type to just disappear."

Elizabeth's mouth pressed into an amused half smile. "No, you're not. But you're young and flighty, so you could fall in love with someone and run off, leaving your job behind. Or you could get frustrated at the pace of change and leave without notice." She shrugged. "Who knows why the young do the things they do, especially people with a background like yours."

"I haven't run off. They'll just need to go to my apartment to see that."

Gabriel extended the phone again, watching me closely, and said, "You will call your caseworker right now. You will tell her you're leaving the agency, that you've decided this isn't the path for you. You're quitting on the spot."

"No."

Gabriel nodded toward Elizabeth. She held up the pistol.

He said, "Look, Emma, we're not bad people, but we can't afford to be patient any longer. We don't want to leave West Virginia, but we can, and we will if forced to do something drastic."

Something drastic? I opened my mouth to speak, but my breath caught in my throat, and all that came out was a pathetic squeak.

"If you cooperate, we'll let you go." Gabriel held up a hand. "Eventually, that is."

"When?" I managed.

"Soon. Very soon—once you understand our predicament. In the meantime, we'll feed you and keep you safe."

"My apartment. My cat."

Gabriel said, "I've already boxed up your apartment. Make this call, and we'll retrieve your things and your cat. You can stay here for now. You'll be safe."

Safe from whom? I thought of the fate of those other kittens, of the fear in Luke's eyes when talking about his mother. She was pointing a gun at me, for God's sake. How could I possibly trust them not to kill me, whether or not I cooperated? They'd taken things this far. And even if they were somehow being honest, why would I ever want to live here?

"Call her." Gabriel handed me my phone. "No bullshit. If she doesn't answer, leave her a detailed message. Tell her you'll be hard to reach, that you're going away. Give her some realistic details. Put it on speaker."

I started to argue, but Elizabeth's glare shut me down. Hands shaking, I took the phone, flipped it open, and dialed my boss, silently praying she would pick up. She didn't, and on the fourth ring, her voicemail came on. I waited dutifully for the beep before opening my mouth. I planned to scream, "Help, the Webbs have kidnapped me," into the phone, and was sucking in enough air to do the words justice, when Elizabeth shot out of her chair and came around behind me. The point of the gun jabbed the center of my back just as I heard the click of the safety release. She poked my back, harder this time.

Deflated, with urine seeping through my shorts and down my leg, I said slowly, "Ann, this is Emma. I'm leaving Helping Hands." Gabriel jabbed me with his elbow, and I continued with as much convincing bravado as I could muster. "I don't want to do this kind of work anymore. I'll try to stop by the office if I can, but if not, just mail my last check." Elizabeth pressed the gun's muzzle into my spine. "I'm sorry for the abrupt notice. I know this isn't like me, but I've rethought things. I'm moving away." I clicked off the phone, biting back tears. "There. Happy?"

Elizabeth came back around so she was facing me and reengaged the gun's safety. Gabriel stood.

Gabriel said, "Excellent. A confused young person tired of her job. Who wouldn't buy that?" To Elizabeth, he said, "Tomorrow we'll go to her apartment and get her belongings and the cat. I don't want to go today in case they're watching for her. And tomorrow she'll write a letter to her agency stating that she feels Luke no longer needs intervention."

I said, "He was nearly done anyway."

Gabriel said, "You'll make sure no one else shows up."

Elizabeth sighed. "In the meantime? What do you want me to do with her?"

"Help her get cleaned up. Then move her inside."

*　*　*

Inside turned out to be a closet-sized bedroom upstairs, at the back of the house, but at least it had lights and a bed and a window. Gabriel nailed the window frame shut and placed a deadbolt on the outside of the door while Elizabeth put sheets on the mattress.

"You said you'd let me go," I said. "You promised."

"And we will." Gabriel tossed me my purse. "A show of good faith."

I dug around inside. My wallet was there, cash included, but nothing else. "The bag does me no good without my keys and phone."

Gabriel shrugged. "In time."

"Where is Luke?"

"This has been upsetting, so he's outside, playing in his fort."

I had no idea whether to believe him. Since the day he had caught me in their bedroom, staring at those monitors, Gabriel hadn't laid a violent hand on me, but Elizabeth's guns were an ever-present threat.

"Why am I here? Why are *you* here?"

Elizabeth had finished making the bed. It had a wrought iron frame and a full-size mattress, and she'd placed a faded star-pattern quilt on the top. An oddly homey touch for a prisoner, especially coming from her. Elizabeth left the room, and Gabriel patted the bed. I sat down, placing as much distance between us as I could.

"I know this is hard. I've felt displaced and uncertain. I don't want you to feel the pain that I've experienced."

I nodded, unsure how to respond to the man who was the cause of my pain.

Elizabeth returned with a box. She placed it on the bed between Gabriel and me and disappeared again. Gabriel opened the box and handed me several notebooks. Each was college ruled and filled with line after line of what appeared to be notes and equations. I recognized the handwriting from the signature sheets Gabriel and Elizabeth had to fill out each week: Gabriel's eccentric, left-slanted script.

"What are these?" I asked, suddenly utterly and hopelessly exhausted. *No more games.*

"These are the notebooks I was able to take with me. The ones I had when . . . when everything changed."

I waited for more, but instead of words, his explanation came in the form of another folder. This one contained letterhead and business cards for one Professor Gabriel Webb, chair of the Nuclear Physics Program at Michigan State. Also inside was a photograph from a news article. In it, Gabriel and Elizabeth were sitting at a large, round table at some type of reception. He wore a suit, she a simple green dress. The caption underneath identified the group as the Michigan State Science and Engineering Departments.

I held up the photograph. "What is this?"

"That was me, Emma. I was a nuclear physics professor in Michigan."

"And you had to flee because of the government?"

Gabriel nodded. A stray strand of dark hair covered one of his eyes, and he flipped his head back with an impatient gesture. He searched my face for some sign that I believed him, but all I could do was stare back at him, disbelieving.

I said, "Why would the government go after you?"

Gabriel tapped the cover of one of the notebooks. "Look inside."

I did, but everything looked like scribbled nonsense to me. "Sorry, but this is a foreign language to me."

"Have you heard of cold fusion, Emma?"

"Not really."

"How can I explain it in the simplest way possible?" He sighed. "Nuclear reactions, including nuclear fission and nuclear fusion, happen in things like atomic bombs and supernova. Cold fusion is nuclear fusion that occurs at a lower temperature. Theoretically, it has incredible benefits, like producing vast amounts of energy with minimal waste. Sounds good, right?"

I nodded, unsure what any of this had to do with my captivity or him and the government.

He continued. "Sounds good, but it's largely believed to be impossible. Until now. I discovered something in that lab that has the potential to change the world. Imagine clean power for every-one. No radioactive waste, no greenhouse gases." His eyes lit up like dawn on a Midwest horizon. "The US military has been studying it for years. Research is happening in other places too. Some have claimed minor successes in very controlled conditions, but nothing like my work."

I shook my head, not believing what I was hearing. "You discovered the secret to cold fusion?"

"In a manner of speaking."

My eyes wanted to roll, but fear kept them in place. "And the government stole your work?"

Gabriel opened his hands, palms up, in a gesture meant to convey honesty. "One day, I arrived at the university to find my parking spot gone, my ID nonfunctional, and my name removed from the faculty website. Our bank accounts had been frozen, and someone had changed the locks on our doors." His gaze was so intense, I had to turn away. He pulled my face back toward him. "They erased me, Emma. They took my work, silenced the university and my colleagues, and forced us to disappear. And now they want to kill us."

"Who is *they*?"

"The government."

"Why would the government want your work?"

"For their own use. And to keep my discoveries out of others' hands."

"How can they be trying to kill you, Gabriel? Even if what you're telling me is true, surely there would have been another way. They could have bought it. Or somehow confiscated it under some statute. Or made you sign a confidentiality agreement." I thought back to the way the state took our land. The government can do terrible things when it's convinced the ends justify the means, I reminded myself, but even the government has to follow rules. "Killing you seems extreme."

Of course, this was no highway going through a rural corner of Iowa. These were heady allegations. I stood up, my mind spinning. Did he actually believe this nonsense? Did he actually think the American government would steal his work and try to assassinate him and his family? Sure, the military had done some awful things, but that was in the past.

Right?

"I know this is a lot to take in, and you probably think we're crazy. That's okay. The government would want you to think we're nuts. That's their intent—force us on the run, make me look insane. But I'm going to leave the rest of this box here for you to look over." Gabriel tapped the box that was sitting on the bed. "You're an intelligent woman, Emma. Read everything in here, and then tell me we're crazy. I think you'll understand that our actions have been justified."

I watched him leave the room, heard the bolt slide into place.

Inside the box sat two folders full of documents: scholarly articles on nuclear fusion, papers on the future of energy and the climate, news clippings about the fossil fuel industry. And under all that, articles about families who'd disappeared.

I'd read through all of this, if for no other reason than to appease Gabriel and convince him I believed him. Maybe that would be my ticket back home and out of their lives.

*   *   *

By the next morning, I'd read all of the material Gabriel had left me. I'd fallen asleep sometime around dawn and awakened to the feel of Jamaica's fur against my face. Boxes from my apartment sat stacked against one wall. My place had been rented fully furnished, and these boxes of clothes, knickknacks, and photographs marked all of my worldly possessions.

Seeing the cat, I felt the first ray of hope I'd experienced in days. Perhaps they would be true to their word and let me go. I so badly wanted to believe they weren't toying me.

If Gabriel had been honest about Jamaica and my belongings, then maybe he could be trusted about other things too.

Like stolen nuclear fusion research. Like frozen bank accounts and threatened lives. The papers Gabriel provided did paint an ugly and suspicious picture. Families of prominent scientists and journalists falling over cliffs and dying in fires and small aircraft crashes. My rational side said *so what*? People died in odd ways all the time—sometimes alongside their families. That didn't mean their deaths were part of some grand conspiracy. Anyone could find events to support their worldview. Wasn't that how atrocities occurred? Convince enough people to ignore their better judgment, and you could get away with anything.

At the same time, I thought of my father, his distrust of officials, the years I'd spent holed up in that schoolroom, listening to him wax on about true freedom and prepping for the big showdown. He'd experienced firsthand what the government could take away when it felt justified. What if my father had been right? What if Gabriel and Elizabeth were examples of what could happen when a government had too much power?

I scanned the room, my gaze landing on the box of documents Gabriel had left for me. If he were lying, he'd gone to an awful lot of trouble to trick me. The notebooks full of equations, all the scientific journal articles explaining the theory behind cold fusion. Either he was telling the truth—or he was a hell of an actor.

That morning, with a purring Jamaica snuggled under my chin, I decided I'd talk to Luke. I still didn't trust Elizabeth or Gabriel, but I thought I could read their son. I'd watch him, question him, and only then would I decide what was real and what was fantasy.

I ate that morning: two scrambled eggs from the hens outside, some bacon, and a slice of sourdough bread. Gabriel brought me the food himself, and he sat beside me and watched me eat, a faint, satisfied smile playing on his lips.

I wiped that plate clean.

CHAPTER

16

GROWING UP ON a farm in the Midwest, autumn meant harvest time, which meant grueling work from sunup to sundown. It wasn't until November that my father would finally relax a little bit, and even then, he would start preparing the fields for the spring, weatherizing the barns, and in later years adding to his stockpiles in case disaster occurred over the long winter months.

In New England, though—especially along the coast of Maine—fall had a different feel.

Soon the leaves would be at their peak, and with those opulent colors came the leaf peepers, arriving in Cape Morgan and other coastal town in droves by car and by bus. The rush had already started. Restaurants were full, parking was limited, money was flowing, and nerves were shot. This would go on until mid-October. Once the last of the deciduous trees had lost their leaves and the final tour buses had come through, seafood shacks would close for the season, campgrounds would shutter, and Cape Morgan would take on a ghost town feel.

I couldn't wait.

For now, I braved the traffic along Route 1 and thought about Oliver. Where was he? Was he still talking, eating, walking in that drunken way toddlers did? Was he still alive? Was he being held captive in one of these mom-and-pop hotels that sprouted along the busy business corridor like so many weeds? Or had he already been whisked away to Portland or Freeport or south to Boston?

The cars in front of me inched forward, and I followed them. Every beach house, every business, every barn, every boat felt like a possible hiding place. Somewhere in this crowded corner of New England, Oliver's kidnappers were concealing him. Somewhere along the coast, Gabriel and Elizabeth were planning their next move.

In the quiet of November, they wouldn't be able to blend in quite so well. For now, though, they were just two more curious faces in a sea of tourists, waiting for the right moment to spring.

*   *   *

Maya was the only one home when I finally arrived later that night. The big house on Dove Street felt empty and dark, mirroring my mood. I tried to bypass the housekeeper, but she caught me in the center hall.

"What can I make you?" she asked. "Some soup? It's chilly out, and I have vegetable soup and homemade bread."

"I'm not hungry."

"You need to eat."

"I had something on the road."

It was another easy lie, and from the press of Maya's lips, it was obvious she knew it. I waited in the study until she was finished in the kitchen, and then I went out the back door, slipping unnoticed into the night.

Our home—Josh's home, really—sat on two acres of wooded bayfront. A gated, white clapboard historical behemoth, it had been in Josh's family for three generations. Pristine and stalwart against the volatile Maine weather, the house could have sheltered three families, and looking at it from the back—where the modern floor-to-ceiling windows Josh had added stared back at me reproachfully—I marveled at the path that had brought me here.

I was safe here. Or so I'd thought.

The wind howled. I pulled my sweater tightly around me and made my way, through the manicured rose gardens, to the back gate that led to the water. I punched in the code for the gate and slipped out into the marshy brush that edged the shoreline. Smooth stones paved the way to the small wooden dock Josh maintained despite his fear of water, but I didn't dare turn on the flashlight on my phone, so instead I fumbled through the sand and muck, steadfastly ignoring the rustling of night animals around me.

I found the small motorboat just as I'd left it, covered by a tarp, with my dry bag hidden underneath the seat. I climbed into the boat and dug through the dry bag until I found the makeup bag filled with powders and brushes and tampons—female items meant as decoys. At the very bottom of this bag were my safe deposit box key and my burner phone. I removed the burner phone and checked the battery. Then, satisfied, I dialed my sister's number.

She picked up immediately. Relieved, I said, "Jane?"

"Emma." Her tone felt as cold and biting as the ocean air.

"I wanted to see how you're feeling."

"I'm still here, aren't I?"

"How are the treatments going?"

A beat. Then, "Time will tell, I guess, but we both know this isn't a social call." Jane's voice was raspy and rough, as though I'd awakened her from a long, deep sleep.

Jane had been battling a serious lung disease for the last nine months. The doctors had given her a fifty–fifty chance at a cure, but each time I spoke with her—admittedly too infrequently—she sounded more worn down by the grueling regimen. Jane and her husband had chosen not to have children. If Jane regretted that decision, she'd never told me. But then, sharing her feelings had never been Jane's way. She had that in common with our father.

"No, I'm afraid it isn't a social call." In a rush of words, I told her about the child, the bomb, and the doll. I didn't need to tell her Oliver was Josh's son. The doll was enough. I heard it in the sudden quickening of her breath.

"*Oh,*" she said. That one word conveyed everything.

The water lapped against the shore, and the small boat, moored as it was, rose and fell with the waves, slapping hard against the water. My hair whipped behind me. I cupped my hand over the phone and listened for my sister's reaction. Ours had never been an easy relationship, but we'd forged a bond of necessity when our mother died, and then again over the last two decades. Jane was rarely kind to me, but she was resourceful, and I valued her opinion.

"You need to leave Maine," she said. "It's the only option."

I turned my face toward the wind, welcoming the sting. She was right, but it wasn't what I wanted to hear. For the last ten years, Josh and Cape Morgan had been my life. As Beatrice Wicker, I'd been able to forget Emma Strand and every iteration who came after her. As Beatrice Wicker, I'd come as close to the real me as I dared.

"Emma? Are you listening?"

"This could all be a coincidence."

"A bomb, the doll. It's not a coincidence." She coughed. "Be real. They've found you again."

"There's never been a kidnapping before. It makes no sense. Why start now?"

"Desperation makes people do desperate things. You, of all people, know that." Jane's coughing turned to hacking, and I reminded myself that she was twelve years older than me and not well. This wasn't her burden to bear, and I shouldn't have called her.

I said, "I'm sorry. This has nothing to do with you."

"Nonsense. That's never stopped you before. Leave, Emma. Go now. If you don't, everything there will come crashing down around you. Josh. Your job." She hesitated. "I can do this for you one more time. It may be your last chance."

Because I'm not going to be around much longer were her unspoken words. I let the boat rock me to and fro, contemplating my choices. Desperate people, indeed. The sky was cloudy, the stars hidden under their gray canopy, and the moon, barely visible, was just a hazy sliver overhead. How easy it would be to unfasten the rope and take off into the darkness. Josh was so preoccupied that it would be hours, maybe a day, before he'd notice I was even gone.

I'd done it before—left another town, another life—with Jane's help.

"I can't," I said finally.

"Think, Emma. If they're committing serious crimes now, you could be next."

"If kidnapping that child really was a warning and not some random act, as I suspect, then they already know where I am. They could have kidnapped me or killed me already if that was their intent. Why take a child?"

The laugh that erupted from my sister was deep and sharp and mean. "You know as well as I do they like to play with their food first. Things will escalate. You'll end up running. You always do. Do it the clean way, Emma. Go now while I can help you."

A ship horn bellowed in the distance. From the safety of the boat, I watched Maya's shadow retreat from the kitchen toward her rooms on the second floor of the house. Lights flashed on and off as she made her way through the downstairs, up the stairway, and down the hall. Josh must not be returning home, I thought. Maya only retired early when Josh was gone overnight.

Jane said, "Emma, I know it's hard, but don't be a fool. Tell me—what do you want me to do?"

I let silence settle like a shroud around me—punctuated only by the quiet lapping of the waves. I'd hoped Jane would have some great idea that would let me stay in Cape Morgan. Sitting there in the cold, legs hunched up under me, suddenly I was a kid again, squatting against the wall in our pantry on the farm in Iowa, the phone cradled under my chin, begging my sister for help. I was disappointed now—just as I'd been back then.

"Emma—" Jane coughed into the phone, a deep, rough, gurgling noise that seemed too loud and too wet and too raspy to have come out of her tiny body.

"Never mind," I said, feeling awful for involving her. "I'll figure it out."

"Let me finish, Emma. You've always been hardheaded and more like Dad than you'll ever admit. The only way to deal with what happened is to leave again. Find somewhere truly remote, and just blend in. Stop trying to form relationships or have a meaningful job. You can't have what other people have. Normal is not for you. Stop looking for it." She took a tortured inhalation, let it out with a gasp. "Unless you want to end up dead or in prison, run, Emma, and don't look back."

* * *

I untied the boat from the dock, removed my headlamp from the dry bag, and steered away from shore. The boat was too small to take out into the open sea, but I could use it to get to another harbor, another town. From there, I could access some of the money I'd squirreled away and let Jane help me create a new identity, find a new destination. Perhaps Mexico or farther south this time. If I were lucky, no one other than Josh would be looking for me. *And face it,* I said to myself, *Josh has other things on his mind.*

I lingered by the shoreline, letting the boat rise and fall with the tide, Jane's words echoing in my head. I *could* leave. I could steal away into the night with nothing other than my dry bag and the clothes I was wearing. I'd done it before. I could say a furtive good-bye to Cape Morgan, and head anywhere west, north, or south. It would, I realized, be easier than staying.

But I wouldn't go. Not yet. I knew deep down inside that regardless of what happened to Josh, to Oliver, to my marriage, and regardless of whether prison would be my last stop, I needed to stay. For once in my adult life, I wanted closure.

This time I would fight.

17

"So, the haint blue door was to keep out the government, not ghosts?" I asked Luke five days later. We'd been working side by side in the garden, pulling weeds and harvesting early tomatoes. Once the sun dipped below the mountains, though, we packed up our hoes and shovels, brought the bowls of tomatoes inside, and escaped to the tree house to enjoy some privacy before supper.

Luke set those fiery eyes on me. I saw a hint of amusement, an echo of Gabriel. "Maybe. Maybe not."

Luke turned from me to his code book, his face scrunched in concentration. Some days, he looked like a little boy. Other days, I saw glimpses of the man he would one day become. Today he twisted under the weight of my questions, a little boy carrying the burdens of adulthood.

I asked, "Do you believe all the things Gabriel says? About his work at the university? About the government stealing his research?"

Luke set down his pencil. "I lived it too, you know. One day I was a little kid in a big house with my mom and Gabriel, and the next day we had to run away. I left everything—toys, clothes, even my piggy bank—behind."

I recalled the photo of Luke with Gabriel and Elizabeth by the duck pond. Luke had been very young, maybe three, and I wondered whether he'd remember leaving his home, much less his piggy bank. His words sounded coached.

"What did the house look like?"

Luke described the big Victorian from the photo. "There was a duck pond in the neighborhood and everything." His mouth turned down. "I loved those ducks."

"Were you scared?"

"We all were."

"Where did you go after that?"

Luke's eyes narrowed. "An apartment somewhere, I think. I was young, so it's a blur."

Luke recalled the Victorian and the duck pond with perfect clarity but was unsure what happened next? It was possible to have memories from events that occurred at a very young age, but I was suspicious of the validity of these memories, especially because his most vivid memory involved a scene from a photo he could easily have been shown.

"Did your dad work after he lost his job?"

"He couldn't. The people who took his research blacklisted him. We had to run or . . . well, something bad could have happened."

"Like what?"

Luke picked his code book back up. "I don't want to talk about this, Emma."

"I'm sorry, Luke. Just one more question." Something else bothered me about Gabriel's story, and I decided to press. "If your family was so worried about the government, why did you get mixed up with child services? How could they let that happen?"

It was an unfair question to ask a twelve-year-old; I knew that. Still, I didn't trust the answer his parents would give me.

"That was my fault," Luke said. "I didn't listen when my mom told me to stay off the tractor, and I fell and broke my wrist. I had to go to the hospital." He glanced around the fort. "We never go to the hospital. We never even go to the doctor unless it's an emergency. Mom doesn't trust doctors."

"Did you actually fall, Luke?"

Luke chewed on a fingernail. Quietly, he said, "Yes."

"But the hospital staff suspected child abuse?" Likely with good reason, I thought, thinking of Elizabeth and her quick brushfires of rage.

Luke shrugged. "They asked me all sorts of questions about my life and my parents and my wrist. I got confused about what I could say and what I couldn't say, and I said the wrong things."

"Were your parents angry at you?"

His mouth twisted into a wry smile. "Wouldn't you have been?"

I remembered the wrist incident from his file. He'd been underweight too, and while neither the doctors nor the social workers had any proof, they'd suspected neglect.

I said, "When I met Gabriel, he seemed a lot less book smart than he does now."

Luke grinned. "That was my mom's idea. She said that caseworkers would be less suspicious if they thought he was kind of backward—that was my mom's word—and she was right."

I stretched my legs out straight in front of me, no small feat in the tiny space. The heat wave of the past few weeks had finally abated, leaving the earth parched and the air stale and dusty. A fine film of pollen had settled on the tree-house windows, tainting my view of the blue sky beyond.

"How about the computers? What are they doing with them?"

Luke gnawed at his bottom lip, something I noticed he'd been doing more and more recently. I'd also noticed fingernails bitten to raw flesh and collarbones as pronounced as the wings on a Thanksgiving turkey.

He said, "They don't tell me that stuff."

"You're a smart guy." I tapped my finger against his open code book. "What do you think they're doing?"

Luke shrugged. "Gabriel wants to prove what happened, okay? He needs to stay a step ahead of these guys in order to keep us safe, but the only way we'll get our lives back is to prove to the world that they stole his ideas."

"Ideas or research?"

"Aren't they the same thing?"

I crossed my legs under me and took a deep breath, choosing my next words carefully. "Don't you think that if the government had stolen Gabriel's work, they would be using his research by now?"

Luke held up his latest code project to the weak light streaming through the window and stared at what he'd written. A large spider hanging from the ceiling touched down on the paper, its legs scrambling for traction. I scooted backward, away from the spider, but Luke quietly and carefully scooped the spider up on his finger, crawled to the door, and placed it outside.

"Luke?"

After sliding back inside, he opened his code book again. "What makes you think they're not?"

*   *   *

By the end of the next week, we'd fallen into a routine. The door to my bedroom was no longer locked, and I'd wake up each morning to the enticing scents of breakfast—pancakes and bacon and oatmeal and occasionally Gabriel's cinnamon streusel muffins. Jamaica would find a sunny spot on a windowsill while I took a bath in the family's old cast iron tub, and then Luke and I would work in the garden, tending to the vegetables and herbs and the fields of fragrant lavender. Elizabeth was normally in bed before dinnertime, and in her absence, I'd begun cooking supper, usually some type of stew or soup with vegetables from the garden and fresh bread that Gabriel baked outside in the wood oven. Meat was scarce, but on day eleven, Gabriel killed a chicken, and we feasted on roast chicken for three days.

All the while, I waited. For what, I wasn't sure. Once the bolt was removed from my door, they never said I had to stay. I didn't have my phone or access to the internet, but I found I neither wanted those things nor needed them. I had my car for errands, but I rarely left the sanctuary of the farm. Helping Hands thought I'd quit and left town, but their office was fifteen miles away—and anyway, I'd never really socialized with the other counselors or staff. As the long, lazy days passed, I was surprised to find I was content at the farm in a way I had never been before.

Elizabeth remained in her room most of the time, and when she was out and about, she seemed as grouchy as ever, but she'd put away the guns, and she didn't complain when I moved around furniture or cooked in her kitchen. In my care, Luke thrived. His protruding bones were quickly covered by a healthy layer of flesh, and the sunken eyes and bloodied nailbeds disappeared. Even Gabriel seemed happier, whistling his way through his evening chores.

On the early evening of day seventeen, Gabriel received the news that Helping Hands had closed Luke's case. He found me in the garden, weeding the lavender beds, my body bent over the fragrant herbs. On her good days, Elizabeth used lavender to make soap and shampoo and even little sachets she sold to a yoga studio in town, and we all used the flowers to freshen bureau drawers and stuffy rooms. The smell was pervasive.

That night, Gabriel crouched down next to me and began pulling out plants. He'd changed out of his mechanic's clothes and into a clean T-shirt and faded jeans, and he smelled of sandalwood soap and peppermint shampoo. The sun had begun to fall below the horizon, and the sky was painted in brilliant bands of pink, orange, and gold.

"Looks better out here already," Gabriel said. "The garden, I mean."

I smiled. "Better was the only direction it could go."

"You have a green thumb. Luke's responded to your nurturing touch too."

"Luke's a good kid."

Gabriel picked several stems of lavender and handed them to me. Their purple flower spikes were soft against my fingers. I smiled.

"*Lavandula angustifolia.* Commonly known as English lavender. We have French lavender too—although my personal favorite is *Lavandula stoechas.* Spanish lavender."

"I never knew there were so many types of lavender."

"And they all have different growing seasons. When the lavender blooms, you know it's the long season of rebirth—from early spring into the start of fall."

I looked out at this sea of lavender. For these gardens to be so full, so large, they would have predated Gabriel and Elizabeth. There was something special about a plant that could endure so much neglect and still thrive. "What's so unique about the Spanish version?"

Gabriel smiled. "Everyone loves their silverish leaves. But me?" he traced a finger across the top of my ear, "I like the little purple ears that sprout from the bloom."

I smiled. "Is that so?"

Gabriel tossed a handful of weeds into the meadow behind the garden and stood up. He held out his hand, and I took it. While pulling me up beside him, he turned me around so that we were both facing the hills and the sunset to our west. His arm pressed against my shoulder. I could hear the soft rhythm of his breath.

"It's beautiful here, isn't it, Emma? A safe place to stay forever." With one finger, he pushed a stray curl back from my face, then ran his finger down the curve of my face. He laughed. "You look cute with streaks of mud along your jawline."

His touch was an electric jolt, and I stepped aside, shaken. The scent of the lavender was a heady elixir. I felt unsteady, almost giddy. When his lips touched mine, they were warm and sweet. I leaned into that kiss eventually, as hungry for companionship as I was for release. It was an embrace that only lasted a few seconds, but it broke my resolve at the same time it cemented my sense of belonging. It had been so long since I'd felt wanted and needed. I longed for the moment to last.

Drunk as I was on the warmth of Gabriel's touch, I didn't notice the willowy figure in the window, watching us, watching me, until it was too late.

CHAPTER

18

THE SHARP STING of frigid Maine saltwater startled me awake.
A hangover-worthy headache pounded the inside of my skull,
and a cramp threatened the tight, tender muscles in my left calf.
I uncurled my limbs painfully and slammed an elbow against the
unforgiving side of the boat. *Fuck.* At some point last night, I must
have fallen asleep. What if I'd drifted out into the ocean, alone and
unmoored? Panic forced me to sit up. Thankfully, I'd retied the
boat to the dock, but the sea had grown restless overnight, and a
few inches of water soaked the bottom of the boat. I let out a long,
choked breath. *Thank God I was still by the shore.*

I climbed out onto the dock, legs shaking, elbow and head
throbbing. Carefully, I recovered my wet bag with the tarp. The
sun was just starting to rise, so I knew it was after six, but the house
was still dark and silent.

I punched in the code for the gate and let myself into the yard.
I was about to enter through the back of the house when I stopped
to look out over the patio and gardens to the sea beyond. A mist had
settled over the ocean, leaving a gossamer-gray trail that only kissed
the shoreline. Most days, I would have thought the seascape pretty.
Today it frightened me.

"The view never gets old, does it?"

Startled, I turned to see Josh sitting on the stone veranda. He was tucked into an oversize cast aluminum chair, with a wool tartan blanket covering his legs. His winter parka stuck out from above the blanket. His watery smile seemed hollow, and his eyes glistened from the smoke wafting from the lit pipe he cupped in his hands. Had I been paying attention, I would have detected the familiar scents of clove and cherry in the brisk morning air.

"How long have you been out here?" I asked him.

"Long enough to know you never came home. Where were you, Beatrice?"

"In the boat."

"All night?"

"All night."

He stared at me for a long moment, and I held his gaze defiantly. Finally, he placed the pipe in the ashtray on his lap and put his head back against the chair. "Fine, have it your way."

"I'm allowed some time on my own."

"It seems like all you want is time alone."

My eyebrows shot up. That was a rich statement coming from him. "What's really bothering you, Josh?" I knew I was playing with fire. What would I say if he admitted that Oliver was his? If he told me that he was terrified that his only child had been harmed. His pain was unimaginable to me, and a stronger woman would have done something, said something, but my existence revolved around this unspoken quid pro quo. I couldn't give him the moral upper hand now; to do so would have been to sign my own death warrant. Still, some self-destructive impulse was pushing me that morning, and I said, "Are you worried about the child?"

"The child, the school, our town." He closed his eyes. "And I'm worried about you."

"You don't need to worry about me."

"You slept in a boat."

"I fell asleep in a boat. There's a difference."

Back on firmer ground, Josh's voice grew more determined. He opened his eyes. "Maya says you're not eating."

"Maya should mind her own business."

"Maya cares about you."

"Maya only gives a damn if it concerns you, and you know it. She thinks I married you for money, and now—" I let my voice trail off, unwilling to finish that thought. *And now she wonders why else I would stay.*

"What's happened to us, Beatrice?"

I stood there mutely. I couldn't help it. I wanted to say, "You fucked another woman and got her pregnant, Josh; that's what happened to us," but I knew that was only a half truth. When you really inspected this house of a marriage, it was obvious the foundation was rotten. It was hard to build an honest life on a platform of lies.

I turned to go inside.

"You need to eat." Josh sounded genuinely concerned, and I felt a familiar, unwanted ache in my chest. Once upon a time, he would have said that and then gone inside to make me an omelet. Now he sat there under his blanket, retreating from me—from life—like an old, broken, bitter man. And I let him.

"Grace is at the diner this morning. I'll get some breakfast before I go to the island."

I was reaching for the doorknob when Josh spoke again. "If you knew anything about that little boy who was kidnapped, you'd tell the police, right, Beatrice?"

I couldn't bring myself to turn back around. I didn't want to meet those sunken, grieving eyes. "Of course," I said, and darted inside.

*   *   *

"Beatrice Wicker, imagine seeing you here." Seth slammed a hand down on a scarred wooden table. "Care to join me?"

I glanced around the diner, hoping to see another friendly face, someone who could save me from having to sit with Seth, but most of the tables were full of tourists. "Sure, why not." I slid into the booth across from him. "I could really use some coffee."

Grace saw me from across the room. She smiled and waved a menu.

"Don't need it," I said as she got closer. "Two scrambled eggs, American cheese, sourdough toast, dry."

"OJ?"

Thinking of my cramped, restless night in the boat, I shook my head. "Just coffee. Lots of coffee."

Seth followed Grace's progress back toward the kitchen. Grace wasn't a particularly tall woman, nor was she very broad, but she tended to hunch when she walked, as though doubling in on herself to make her body seem smaller. Despite her self-consciousness about her size, it wasn't the first thing I'd noticed about Grace when we met. I'd noted her shy smile and the earnest way she'd approached the clay, as though she wanted to do right by it. If I was honest with myself, Grace's downcast demeanor reminded me of myself at her age. Like Grace, I'd faced the daily torment of wanting my life to matter but also waiting for some cosmic permission to act on my dreams.

And look where that approach had gotten me.

Seth said, "Our waitress—I see her here a lot. She in college?"

"She's saving for college. Wants to be an artist. Maybe even an art teacher someday."

Seth frowned. "Is she any good? At art, I mean?"

I thought of Grace's latest pieces—the saturated colors, the abstract depictions of everyday events that made one feel just a little bit uncomfortable, like a voyeur watching an intimate scene. Her work was disjointed, anachronistic—like the artist herself.

"Quite good, but I'm afraid Grace has a quiet talent that will go unnoticed unless someone helps her."

Seth took a long sip of his coffee, his attention moving to the back of the diner. "Well, I'm glad she's good at art, because she's not scoring any points as a waitress."

I followed Seth's gaze and watched Grace serve two men wearing orange safety vests. Unlike the other waitresses who worked at Casey's Grill, Grace didn't engage in easy, flirty banter with the customers. She came across as reserved, and shyness in this environment could be mistaken for snobbery. "Where's Evette?" one of the men asked Grace. His whiny tone made the question an insult. I felt a sense of sisterhood. *Long live the awkward introvert.*

"Her name is Grace, and she's just finding her way as a waitress and an artist. In fact, she's exactly the type of person who will benefit from the Ross Island Artist Center when it's up and running."

"Ross, huh? You've decided to keep the old name?"

"Part of the sale stipulation. Eli Ross sold it for a pittance, but he wants the name kept alive."

Grace returned with coffee for me and a refill for Seth. When she was gone, Seth said, "How'd you two meet?"

"Me and Eli?"

"You and the waitress."

"*Grace.* At pottery class."

Seth smirked. He had thickly lashed, intelligent eyes that conveyed either scorn or amusement—very little in between. Josh had given Seth the Ross photographer assignment without consulting me, and I was still sore over the slight. The Ross Island project was my baby, and I should have had the final say. Nevertheless, I could never quite decide whether my dislike for Seth had more to do with having him thrust upon the project or his actual personality.

"What's your story?" I asked him now. "What brought you to Cape Morgan? Most people don't just happen upon our town. They come here for a specific reason."

"Work. What else?" He shrugged. "Spent a few years trying to make it as a photographer in New York City. Did well enough, but I realized my heart wasn't in it. Not a fan of city life. I wanted to be somewhere quieter, cheaper."

"From New York to coastal Maine. That's quite a change of pace."

Seth broke into a slow smile. "I told you I wasn't a city boy. What was your reason for coming to the Cape?"

The front door opened, and an elderly couple ambled inside, their arms linked. The man was leaning on a cane, and he gripped the woman for support. Watching them, I said, "Love."

Seth's eyes crinkled in amusement. "Awfully cliché for an artist like yourself."

"Maybe, but it's true. I came here for Josh."

"Where did you meet him?"

"Aren't you the nosy one today?"

Grace returned with my scrambled eggs and an egg-white omelet for Seth. She set the food down and left to take care of the elderly couple. Seth stabbed at his omelet, but his eyes never left me.

"Come on, Beatrice," he said between bites. "Where'd you meet him? Let me guess. A fundraiser for the Wicker Foundation. You seem like someone who would frequent high-end fundraisers."

"If I didn't feel generous today, I'd think you were calling me a gold digger."

Seth laughed a little too heartily. "Not at all. With all the work you're doing on the retreat, I figured nonprofits were your thing."

I put my fork down and sat back in my seat. "Fate had Josh and me sitting next to one another at a concert in New York City. I was living there at the time, and he was visiting friends. Total happenstance. Neither of us enjoyed the concert, and we both snuck out, bumping into one another again by the bar, which was, of course, closed."

"Knowing Josh, he took you out for a drink elsewhere."

"He did, indeed."

Seth chuckled. "Brought together by bad manners."

I smiled. "You could say that."

"And now?" Seth raised a glass of water to his lips, but he didn't take a drink. His sharp eyes studied me, the amusement gone. "Are you still slinking away for stolen moments, or has the love worn off?"

"That's an awfully personal question, don't you think?"

I realized I'd spoken loudly and sharply, more so than I'd intended, and a hush fell over the diner. Suddenly, Seth let out a bellow of a laugh, cracking the tension. He pulled his wallet from his pants pocket, removed three twenties, and threw them on the table.

"I'm just messing with you, Beatrice. Lighten up." He stood. "Breakfast is on me."

When he'd left the restaurant, Grace came over to clear his side of the table. "Asshat."

"I can't decide what I think of him."

"I don't trust him, Beatrice. I got a weird vibe when I met him during the beach search party, and that feeling has stayed with me. It's reinforced every time he eats here."

"Weird vibe? What do you mean?"

Grace shrugged, thinking. "Everything about him is too much. His laugh is too hearty, his suggestions too forceful, even his tips are too big. It's as though he's playing a big part in some stupid play the rest of us don't realize we're in."

Fake, I thought. *He seems fake.*

"And I don't like the way he is with you, Beatrice. Condescending. Too familiar." Grace shook her head. "Aren't you sorry you asked what I meant?"

Grace walked away, and I remained at the table, watching customers come and go and nursing three more cups of coffee. I thought about Seth and his ignorant questions. *He knows,* I thought. *He knows about Josh and Carly, and he wants to know if I know.* Part of me desperately wanted to have him removed from the Ross Island project, but what reason could I possibly give Josh? The man had done nothing wrong, and my suspicions couldn't be shared without going to a place I wanted to avoid.

"Would you like anything else?" Grace asked, breaking my reverie. "I'm heading home soon, but I can get you whatever you need before I go."

A glance at my watch told me it was almost eleven. "No, I'm good. Sorry for hogging your table."

Her smile was sweet and forgiving. "You have a lot on your mind, I can tell."

I placed another ten on the table and left. I walked the half a block to my car, still distracted by thoughts of Seth. So distracted that I nearly missed the black GMC truck and the man sitting inside it, watching me. Dark hair, thick neck marked with tattoos, cross expression. He looked vaguely familiar. I waved, and he started the engine and pulled away without waving back.

CHAPTER

19

IT'D BEEN TWO months since I'd first met Luke and his parents, and almost three weeks since Gabriel had kissed me in the garden. In a twisted way, I'd found a family. The boys had come to depend on me, and Elizabeth, while aloof, largely ignored me. She and I rotated around one another like moons revolving around the same planet. Her self-removal from the everyday of communal living had become complete, and while I did some of the house chores and kept up the garden, she'd moved into the quiet room. Its walls were now covered in tinfoil, and a bed had been placed against one window. Elizabeth rested in there most of the time, reading books and listening to classical music CDs.

One evening in early July, Gabriel finally emerged from the basement and invited me into his bedroom after Luke had been sent to bed and Elizabeth had retired to her tinfoil sanctuary. I watched as Gabriel searched the internet, flagging the whereabouts of politicians, lawmakers, and military personnel involved in nuclear research. He unveiled his intricate tracking system, explaining that the pulsating red dots represented radioactive "hot spots" across the country.

"I thought cold fusion produced no radioactive waste," I said.

"Ah, you were listening." He grinned, clearly pleased. "It wouldn't produce long-lived radioactive waste, but it would produce tritium, which is a radioactive form of hydrogen that has a short half-life. Tritium is also a byproduct in nuclear reactors."

"Then this is basically a map of the nuclear reactors in the US?"

"More complicated than that, but from a practical standpoint, yes."

I watched the screen, mesmerized by the visual symphony. "What do the yellow dots represent?"

"The whereabouts of federal government offices."

I noticed a few yellow dots in nearby Charleston, West Virginia. "And the green dots?" There were only a few of them, but some overlapped with the offices, and unlike the red and yellow dots, a few even moved about on the screen.

Gabriel hesitated. "They're mostly politicians."

"Why are you tracking them?"

Gabriel sighed. He stood and turned off the monitors. "Let's take a walk."

It was warm and sticky outside, and I told him I'd rather stay inside.

"Come on, Emma." Gabriel leaned down so that his face was cradled against my neck. He breathed in deeply. "Hmm. Lavender. Lovely." He ran his hand along my side, skimming my waist and lingering on the curve of my breast. "It's hot and sticky in here, but outside it's beautiful and clear. The stars will be visible. Let's get out of here."

And so I followed Gabriel into the night. The air smelled of lavender and wisteria and summer phlox. A blanket of stars shimmered overhead. An owl hooted somewhere in the distance, and even farther away a coyote howled. I shuddered. It was easy to feel small and inconsequential here in the hills.

Gabriel took my hand, and I didn't pull back. We walked past the garden, through the beds of lavender and herbs, down the path that led through the outbuildings and beyond the barn, to the thicket of wildflowers and thorny hedges that edged the western side of the property. I lay down on the soft grass, and Gabriel joined me. We stayed like that for some time, staring up at that impossibly vast sky.

"There's the Big Dipper," Gabriel said, pointing.

"Hmm."

"And part of Orion's Belt."

"Nice."

Gabriel rolled toward me. "Do you want me to kiss you?"

I nodded.

This time, we didn't stop with a kiss.

* * *

Even as a teenager, I wasn't the type of girl who romanticized sex. I wasn't the type of woman who condoned sleeping with another woman's husband. I wasn't even the type of woman who pictured herself having a long-term partner of her own. But there I was, naked and breathless and covered in sweat, my head on the chest of the married man who just weeks ago had knocked me out cold.

I pondered this while we gazed up at the stars, our breath riding the same spent rhythm. Shame, I knew, was galloping right behind contentment, but in that moment I only felt a lazy sort of satiety and a strong sense of curiosity and wonder about the man beside me.

"You can help me and Luke, you know," Gabriel said. "You have a gift with people. You can ask questions, make some calls." He strummed his fingers gently along my arm and the sensitive skin of my lower back. "There's a man I've been talking to. I think he can help. I just need you to get a package to him."

"Why not send it?"

"Because of the nature of the documents inside. If the wrong person gets hold of it, the results could be catastrophic."

"You mean nuclear—"

Gabriel put two fingers to my lips. "Don't even say it aloud."

"What do you want me to do?"

"I want you to make a connection so that when you give him my papers, he takes them seriously."

"Why can't I just go in there and tell him your story?"

Gabriel's laugh was rough-edged and bitter, a tonic to the surreal sweetness of the night. "He won't believe you. Politicians need coddling, and a pretty face doesn't hurt." He kissed the top of my head. "Will you do that for me?"

"I don't know what 'that' even is."

"I work on this man's car. His wife told me he's looking for a new intern. Someone to run errands, do paperwork. Someone young and interested in politics and graduate school." He kissed me again. "Someone like you."

"I don't want to be an intern."

"You don't even need to get the job. You'll interview, make a connection, and leave something behind by mistake. A purse or a wallet or briefcase. Then when you go back to retrieve it, you can give him my papers. By then you'll have a rapport, and the papers won't end up with some low-level receptionist."

"Won't he feel used? It seems to me it would be better for you to set up some time with him, Gabe. Tell him what happened to you, and ask him directly for help. You know his wife. Maybe he'll be willing to go to bat on your behalf."

"Ah, the naivete of youth." Gabe's hand moved from the small of my back down lower. He was excited again, but for me, the magic of the moment had worn off.

"Is that why you're following the whereabouts of politicians on the monitor?" I asked, unwilling to let it go. "To get close to them so you can plead your case?"

Gabriel sighed just as he had the first time I had asked about the green dots, but instead of trying to distract me, he said, "They're people with some power, people with an interest in the project I was working on. I need them to understand what happened to me." He lowered my face to his and kissed my nose. "Just like I made you understand."

I smiled, despite my misgivings. "I hope you don't take the same approach with them."

Gabriel moved me off his chest and sat up. "This is serious, Emma. I'm asking you for your help. For the sake of our family."

Our family. "Do you really think any of them will admit to what happened, much less help you get your life back? If the government's implicated, they may be too scared to do anything."

"I'll make them help me."

The tone of his voice chilled me. I moved farther from his embrace. "You have a beautiful family, a business. This farm." *Me.* "Why not just let it go? Rebuild on your own. The hell with these men."

"Could *you* just let it go?"

I thought of my father, of all the nights he'd spent prepping for the big American showdown only to drink himself to death before the fight ever came. If he'd had the chance to let it go, would he have? Would he have traded the time spent planning and building his stockpiles for more time with me and my sister? If he had a do-over, would he have exchanged the hatred for a new romantic relationship, maybe even a new lease on life?

I had no way of asking him.

But even as a child, I'd known that the hatred and paranoia that consumed my father were more about my mother's death—the unspoken anguish, the blatant unfairness—than the house and the highway and his beef with the government. He'd nurtured that anger just as someone would feed a flame to keep it alive, hid it away in the darkest part of his soul, preferring the gunmetal taste of rage to the utter helplessness of grief and despair. The rage gave him purpose.

And even as a child, I'd wanted to help my father. Only I couldn't. And now, looking at Gabriel's handsome, tormented face, I knew I couldn't help him either.

But I wanted to. Oh, how I wanted to.

CHAPTER

20

IT WAS A nice day for sea kayaking. The wind had died down, the sun persevered, and the bay was all gentle ripples. Still thinking of my encounter with Seth at the diner, I paddled across the inlet, from the Dove Street house to Ross Island, with my duffle bag and purse in the vessel's small cargo compartment. I was scheduled to meet with Josh's intern, Julianna Kent, to review our plans for the main gallery. Julianna was providing services to the project gratis as part of her internship with Josh's firm, and he'd assured me that he would personally oversee her work. I was anxious to get started.

It was far later than I'd intended to arrive, and the construction crew were on site demolishing the rear part of the building. The foreman, a kind, burly man in his fifties named Louis, gave me a quick wave as I exited the boat. I waved back, secured the boat on the small, rocky beach, and hiked up to the house. The white Prius in the parking area suggested Julianna was already here, and I took a deep breath before entering the inn. Time to shift gears.

The house was empty. Julianna wasn't waiting for me in what would eventually be the gallery area—only her bag was there, on one of the antique library tables. I called her name while wandering through the halls, but she was nowhere to be found inside the main house. Outside, I asked Louis whether he'd seen a young woman on the property.

"Tall, blond?" When I nodded, he said, "About ten minutes ago. Saw her walking back toward one of the cottages like she had a beef to settle."

"Did you catch which cottage?"

"The one you told her to go to, I guess."

Confused, I said, "That *I* told her to go to?"

Louis had been pulling sheathing away from rotted framing, and he returned to his task. "With that note you left on the door. Said to go to the cottage by the cemetery immediately."

"Louis, I didn't leave a note on the door."

Louis froze. He pulled his work gloves off, one after the other, and squinted at me. "I saw the note myself, Beatrice. You told her to go right to the cottage closest to the cemetery. The note was hanging on the front door when we arrived early this morning."

"Someone else must have left that note. Was it addressed to Julianna?"

Louis shrugged. "I can't say. I figured it wasn't for us, so I just ignored it."

I took off in the direction of the cottage, running as fast as I could manage on the tough terrain. A note on the front door? From me? I could hear Louis calling after me, but I ignored him. Either someone was impersonating me—or that note was meant for me. With everything that had gone on lately, the kidnapping and the break-in, neither option was comforting.

As I neared the cottage, I thought I heard a woman's voice, but I couldn't make out what she was saying over the noise of my own panting. I stopped and forced my breathing to slow down, listening. There it was again: "Help!" and then, "Please, someone."

Another fifty yards and I was at the front door. The cries were louder now and coming from the cliff side of the building. I jogged around to the back, weaving through woods. That's when I saw Julianna kneeling on the ground.

She noticed me and let out a sob of relief. "Thank God! Do you have a phone? I left mine in the inn."

Hesitantly, nervously, like the person arriving first on the scene of an accident, I pushed myself forward, toward Julianna and whatever was on the ground. I waved my phone to let her know I had it, my eyes straining to make sense of what was happening.

"Call 911," Julianna said. "I was afraid to lift him."

"Him?" I whispered.

But she didn't need to explain. I recognized little Oliver's shock of red hair. He lay nestled in a bed of leaves, half wrapped in a plastic tarp. His eyes were closed, his cheeks pale as Mount Washington after a snowstorm.

"Tell me he's still alive," I said as I punched numbers with trembling fingers. Blood throbbed in my ears. *"Please tell me he's alive."*

"He is," Julianna replied. "He's breathing."

21

O UR SLEEPY LITTLE community snapped awake when there was trouble, and now the people of Cape Morgan rallied around Oliver and his mother, Carly. Within the hour, Oliver had been rushed to Portland, where he remained in stable condition and under police protection. Detective Rebelo and his officers were camped inside the Ross House, questioning me, Julianna, and everyone who'd been at the construction site that day. The afternoon slipped away as we each waited outside for our turn to be interviewed. When I was up next, Rebelo asked me for the minute specifics of my day again and again.

"You saw nothing when you arrived? No other boats or cars?"

"Just the construction crew and Julianna's Prius."

"Why did you choose to come by kayak today?"

I waved up at the blue sky. "Why wouldn't I?"

Rebelo, whom I had known for years, simply grunted. There was something different about his demeanor that afternoon, something that tugged on the rock in my belly. While other officers swept the island for clues, Rebelo and two others had set up three stations in the largest room of the main house, and they took turns grilling each of us, hoping, they said, to elicit some tiny detail that would aid their case. I was happy to help, but the more Rebelo questioned me, the more distant and surly he seemed to become.

"How about the message on the door?" Rebelo held up a plastic case containing the brief note that had been tacked to the front door. *Meet me at the cottage by the cemetery.* "What can you tell me about that?"

"What more can I say, Thomas? I already told you—I didn't write it."

"And you have no idea who did?"

I clasped my hands together in front of my face. "No, I have no idea who did. As I told you, I call that cabin the Georgia Cottage, as in Georgia O'Keefe. Anyone who knows the project knows that, so whoever left that note was either feigning ignorance, was actually ignorant of the project, or they meant the note for someone other than me—someone who wouldn't know it was named Georgia."

"What can you tell me about Julianna Kent?"

"She's Josh's intern."

"And she was here before you?"

"Yes. She found the boy." I saw his eyebrows shoot up, and I said, "Seriously? She's barely out of her twenties, Thomas. What reason could she possibly have for kidnapping Oliver?"

Rebelo tilted his head. "Who knew you were meeting Julianna?"

I stared at the detective, willing myself to be patient. I reminded myself that he was only doing his job and that making me answer the same questions three times probably had some logical purpose. "My administrative assistant, Joan. Our photographer, Seth. Josh." I shrugged. "And anyone Julianna or any of them might have told."

Rebelo rubbed the back of his neck. He was a short man in his sixties, with wavy, graying hair, and a paunchy stomach that contrasted with his bony arms and stick-thin legs. He leaned forward in his chair, pushing the table toward me with his abdomen. "Julianna said you were late. Where were you before you came to the island?"

"Casey's Grill."

"Who can verify?"

"At least half a dozen regulars, the waitress, my colleague at the foundation." I gave him Grace and Seth's names and numbers. "Before that, I was home. Josh can verify."

One of the other detectives called for Rebelo, and he stood. "Tell me again why you boated to the island today, Beatrice."

I didn't like the rudeness of his tone. "It was nice out. I needed time to think. What does it matter, Thomas?"

Rebelo bent over so he was eye to eye with me. "By car, there is one way onto this island—that stupid, rotting bridge. You drive across the bridge and into the parking area and that's it— everyone knows you're here. By boat . . . well, there are many places to land ashore unnoticed, like the entire backside of the goddamn island."

My face burned hot at what he was insinuating. "Not unless you want to rock climb up the cliff. You think I kayaked here, pulled ashore along one of the ledges, and then free-climbed up to the cottage with a toddler in my arms?" I stood, and he straightened to maintain eye contact. "My God, Thomas. You've known me for a decade. Why would I do that? *How* would I do that? I'm as likely a candidate as the intern."

"Calm down, Beatrice. I didn't say you did it, but it is possible that *someone* arrived by boat, not car."

"That's not what you were implying, and you know it."

Rebelo closed the distance between us with one large step. He was my height, and his breath smelled of tobacco and mint, his aftershave was cloying and cheap. I wanted to step away, but I made myself stand there and hold my ground.

Rebelo said, "This is a difficult case. We have a distraught mother, an injured child who suffered God-knows-what, multiple agencies involved, and"—he glanced away—"*others* we must answer to. The baby was returned here unnoticed, but whoever did it wanted him to be found. They left a note on the front door, for Pete's sake. The paramedics say he was drugged, but he's alive. He was cold, but the dry leaves acted as insulation, so he didn't freeze. His kidnapping and return were calculated to hurt the parents, but not kill the child." Rebelo's stare was stony. "I ask myself, Beatrice:

Who would go to that trouble? If you're feeling defensive, maybe that says more about you than it does about me."

Rebelo walked away, leaving me no opportunity to respond. What could I say anyway? He was right. Who would go to that trouble? And where the hell were they hiding?

*   *   *

Bad weather was brewing, and by early evening, the winds had picked up. pushing the investigators to finish their work before the storms set in. I stayed at the Ross House, watching the officers, ensuring no additional harm was done to the buildings. Mostly, though, I didn't want to go home.

The police were finished combing the area around Georgia's Cottage by five. I wandered up the hill to Frida's Cottage and went inside the small cabin. We hadn't furnished the interior yet, but the contractors had left two folding chairs in the living room, and I pulled the sturdier of the two toward the window. The sea was roiling now, and it would be for the next few hours. I'd missed my window to kayak back to shore. I either needed to get a ride or walk across the bridge in the driving rain and wind.

I'd wait it out. I wanted to be here in case whoever was behind this returned. Plus, as happy as I was that Oliver was back, I had no desire to see Josh. What would I say? How could I behave, knowing that inside he'd be flooded with relief but would have to hide his true feelings from me?

Watching him manage that dance would kill me. Managing that dance would kill him.

No, I'd stay here and go home once the rains had passed. Better for us both.

The sun was beginning to set. The orange and pink glow coming from the clearer skies in the west reflected onto the stormy clouds and sea, painting a moody watercolor backdrop for the gulls circling overhead. I opened a window to feel the cold, moist breeze coming off the ocean.

There was a sharp rap on the cabin's front door. Startled, I looked outside before opening it, and was relieved to see Rebelo standing outside. I'd thought he'd gone, and I was alone on the island.

"The last of us are heading out, Beatrice."

"Thanks for letting me know."

Rebelo shuffled his feet, patted his mustache. Dark circles shadowed his eyes. "If you think of anything, anything at all, or find anything on this island, call me."

"Of course."

He looked over my shoulder and into the cottage. "Are you staying here all night?"

"Probably not. I'll wait out the storm, and maybe cross when things calm down."

"Why don't you just leave now. I'll give you a ride. Kayaking at night like that isn't safe."

I pointed to my art supplies, which were lined up in front of the dividing wall. "I'll stay and work on the mural for the cottage. If it's not safe to cross, I'll wait here until morning. I promise."

Thomas didn't look convinced, but he nodded anyway. As he turned to leave, I reached out and touched his arm.

"How is the little boy?" I asked. "Oliver." His name felt strange on my tongue.

"Okay, I guess. Docs don't think he suffered any abuse, at least at this point. They're still running tests, and they'll have him see a child psychologist."

"Was there anything on him or with him that might be a clue?"

Rebelo didn't answer right away. "Too soon to tell, but if there is, the forensic team will find it."

"How about the fiber on the doll? Josh mentioned you found something. He seemed hopeful it would be the big break you needed."

Rebelo eyed me warily. "Dead end. Matched the mother's welcome mat, so we think it was picked up when the doll was left on the back porch."

I nodded mutely. "I'm glad he's okay." And I was. In my heart, I was thankful Oliver, my husband's only child, had been returned safely. "Do you know why he was left here, Thomas? On this island."

By the way Rebelo avoided my gaze and took a step backward, I knew he was thinking the connection was Josh. Whoever took Oliver wanted to get to my husband, the boy's father, and choosing the island the foundation had recently purchased was a way to target him further. Thomas Rebelo, a man Josh had known for decades, wouldn't come out and say any of that—even though he was surely aware of the connection. He was trying to spare my feelings—and Josh's wrath. I wanted to know what he knew, though, and so I was testing him.

Rebelo settled for, "Who the hell knows, Beatrice. You and Josh are leaders in the community. Maybe someone has an issue with Cape Morgan or the planning committee. Maybe they didn't get help from the Wicker Foundation when they asked for it. Maybe the island was just a remote place to leave the kid, giving the kidnapper time to escape."

I nodded silently.

"Don't worry, Beatrice. We'll find who did this."

"Thanks, Thomas. And before, during the questioning, if I seemed—"

Rebelo waved his hand. "No need to say anything. This is hard for everyone, and we're all on edge. First the break-in, now the child. It must feel like the deck is stacked against this project."

I watched Rebelo recede into the deepening darkness and closed the door behind him. Thunder boomed in the distance, and the first spatters of rain hit the roof. I knew I should go down to the main house and grab some flashlights, but I didn't want to leave the cozy safety of the cottage. Instead, I lit some candles we had stored in the kitchen cabinets and began organizing my art materials. I would begin the mural tonight. With the operatic background of the storm playing outside and the dancing light of the candles, I would finally begin to paint.

22

I RARELY PAINTED ANYMORE while at the farm. I'd found more practical activities to keep me busy, and my art supplies stayed packed in the box Gabriel had moved from my apartment all those weeks ago.

On this particular day, rain spattered against the window. The sound blended into my dreams, a persistent drumbeat driving my surreal walk through endless lavender gardens. I was painting in my dream—vast canvases of lavender stems, echoes of Van Gogh's sunflowers.

"Get up." Elizabeth knelt over me, a leg on either side of my torso, and hissed into my face. The scent of lavender wafted from her body, enveloping me. I coughed and struggled awake.

"Get the hell up, Emma. *Now.*"

"Why? What's happening?"

"Gabriel says it's time. You're to go to the senator's office about that internship. The man wants to see you today."

That stupid internship. Gabriel had applied in my name. Apparently, it had worked.

"There's an outfit on your dresser. Wear that." Elizabeth took my face between her hands. Her touch was icy cold. "Don't fuck this up. He's counting on you. We're all counting on you."

My impulse was to push Elizabeth off me and off the bed, but she seemed so pale, so weak, so bloated, that I couldn't bring myself to do it. I'd been urging her to see a doctor, but my urgings had been met with scorn. She hated me—that much was clear—but I doubted she'd go, even if Gabriel commanded it.

"Get ready," she said, sliding off the bed. "And wear some makeup. You've let yourself go since you've been here."

I watched her leave my room, a ghost of the woman I'd met just two months before.

I bathed, then put on the short plaid skirt, white blouse, and purple cardigan Elizabeth had laid out for me. The clothes somehow made me look even younger, but it was what Gabriel wanted, so I did it. Gabriel and Luke were outside in the yard, waiting for me. The morning rain had slowed to a drizzle, and their hair was damp from the mist. Luke seemed fidgety. Gabriel told him to wait inside the house until he got home. We climbed into my car.

We'd driven two-thirds of the way to the senator's office in Charleston before Gabriel pulled over by a Burger King. He opened his car door.

"It's all yours," he said. "Fetch me on the way back. But don't pull into the lot. Park here, on the side of the road."

"Aren't you coming with me?" I asked, panic setting in.

He kissed me tenderly. "It's best if you go alone. Remember—win him over. Only you will be able to help me make my case."

*   *   *

The interview was short. The senator, a bespectacled forty-something with a receding hairline and a bland, placating smile was cordial. He asked me all of the typical questions—Where did I go to school? Why did I want this role? Would I be satisfied with a job that didn't pay?—and I lied my way through the exchange. As instructed by Gabriel, I propped my heavy leather briefcase against the leg of the chair in which I was sitting. Gabriel said inside was a fake résumé, a few books, and some other official-looking documents and files he had created. He'd assured me that nothing contained my real name.

The entire interaction took twenty minutes. After that, I left—conveniently leaving my briefcase behind, as instructed.

As soon as he saw me, Gabriel walked around the perimeter of the Burger King parking lot before meeting me on the road. He seemed happy to see me—almost maniacally happy. "Good girl! Thank you. Now scooch over. I'll drive."

"What next?"

"We wait. When his office calls to tell you that you forgot your briefcase, you'll offer to come and pick it up."

"And I'll bring your papers then?"

He grinned and squeezed my knee. "That's right, Emma."

"And what if they don't call?"

"Then you have a handy excuse to stop by again anyway."

I nodded, thinking. I didn't like the frenzied look in his eyes. "What did you say was in that briefcase?"

"Emma, you're doing a good thing." He leaned sideways and kissed me so hard it hurt. "The world will finally know what was done to me and my family, and all because of you."

Gabriel's joy should have been infectious—he and Luke were going to get some help, after all—but the anxiety stabbing at my chest wouldn't let me relax. I stared out the window on the way back to the farm, watching the city turn to farmland and thinking of my father and his prepper's paradise. Why did some people seem so far away, even when they were right by your side?

* * *

The call came later that afternoon. I answered with the fake name we'd agreed on and listened while a tired female voice told me I'd left my briefcase in Senator Leffert's office. She would keep it at her desk, and I could pick it up from her at my leisure.

Gabriel seemed agitated. Clearly, he'd been hoping the senator would seem more anxious to hand me my briefcase himself.

I said, "Why does it matter? One way or another, I'll have the chance to stop by again."

"There's sensitive information in the packet I want you to give him. I don't want it left with some secretary, Emma. For God's sake, I could have done that myself."

"I'll ask to thank the senator personally," I said. "I'll go back into his office, and I'll give him your documents."

Gabriel brightened. "Great, perfect. You'll just have to be your most convincing self to get past the front desk. You can handle that, right, Emma? You're a smart girl."

Elizabeth and Luke had been standing near us in the kitchen. With Gabriel's words still echoing in the room, Elizabeth turned and stormed off. Luke seemed torn—follow his mother or stay with us?

"There may be a role for you too," Gabriel said to Luke. He gave him a mock punch to the arm. "Can you handle that, big guy?"

Luke squared his shoulder and nodded. He tried to hide his smile with his hand, but I could see the pride in his eyes. We glanced at one another, both of us waiting for more.

* * *

The *more* came the next morning. Once again, there was an outfit laid out for me on my dresser: this time, it was jeans, a low-cut cream blouse, and a pink blazer. A note on top of the jacket said, *Get dressed and meet me outside. —Gabe*

It was late July, and the day was clear but broiling. Gabriel was already in his car, with the air conditioner on. When he saw me, he climbed out and embraced me tightly. In his hands were a heavy, thick manilla envelope and a large box of Godiva chocolates. The envelope was tightly sealed with industrial-looking tape.

"Remember the plan. Ask for the briefcase, then request to see him personally. Tell his secretary you have a thank-you for him, and you'd like to give it to him in person. Tell her he's expecting the documents. Look pretty, smile. Flirt a little. Leave the chocolates, the envelope, and the briefcase."

"But—"

"You'll arrive just as the office is opening up, so she'll be busy. It will be easier to let you through. He's there—I confirmed that already—and you can tell her you're just going to slip in and give him what he needs."

"I don't think she'll just let me—"

"Emma!" Gabriel took me by the shoulders. The sudden gesture caught me off guard, and I stepped backward, nearly knocking the box of candy out of his hands. "I'm sorry, Emma, but a lot is riding on this. I need you to hand him that box and those papers and then get out of there. Don't worry about getting the briefcase. Do you understand?"

"Why does he need the chocolate? Wouldn't it be enough to leave the papers with his admin? The chocolates seem over the top. You could place the documents in something more secure, if you're worried about security—"

Gabriel took a deep breath and tilted his head up toward the sky. Eyes closed, he said through gritted teeth, "Just do as I ask."

I glanced from him to the house. My hands and arms felt tingly, my head throbbed. It was as though every neuron in my body was firing in warning at the same time. Luke was watching us from an upstairs window, his forehead pressed against the glass.

Gabriel opened the trunk of the car. He handed me the chocolates to hold while he placed the envelope in a milk crate in the trunk. I glanced at the chocolates—a two-pound box, but it felt heavier than that. While Gabriel was organizing the crate, I opened the corner of the box. There was no plastic wrap.

Instead of candy, I saw wires, pipe, and something that looked like an altered cell phone.

"No," I said, thrusting the box at Gabriel. "No fucking way."

Gabriel took the box, looking momentarily bewildered. "No what?"

"I won't blow up that man or that office or anything at all."

"Emma, it's not a bomb. Just a bunch of wires. It's a scare tactic."

"No. *No way.* I don't care what it is. I'm not scaring anyone, and I'm not going to prison."

Gabriel placed the box in the trunk and closed it. Calmly, he took my wrists in his hands and pulled them down by my sides, tugging me gently forward as he did so. "You won't go to jail. By the time you give him that and he opens it, you'll be long gone. We'll be long gone—packed up and out of Dodge." He smiled. "You and me and Luke. Don't you want that, Emma?"

When I looked up toward the window again, Luke was gone. My mind raced with the implications of what Gabriel was saying. He wanted me to hand-deliver a box that contained a bomb—or at least the appearance of a bomb. Even if the senator waited until I was gone to open it, they'd all seen my face. Senators must have security, so they certainly had me on camera. I thought back to the day before, how Gabriel had made me drop him off near Burger King. He'd gone into Burger King, making sure, no doubt, to be viewed on their security camera. Establishing an alibi.

But how would Gabriel even know the senator was at his office. The green dots on the monitors. *Of course.* He had worked on the senator's car, so placing a tracking device inside the vehicle would have been simple enough. It was early in the day, the senator was in his office, and the building was relatively small. That bomb could be real—and could be enough to do some serious damage.

If it was, I would be the lone perpetrator. But why do that to me?

"You're the one who wants to set the record straight," I managed. "Why send *me* in?" But even as I said the words, I knew the answer. I was expendable. He couldn't send Elizabeth. Sick or not, he wouldn't risk her life. But me? I was the young, gaga fool who would do his bidding. I was disposable—a useful idiot.

"This was never about getting help," I said. "This was always about revenge, and I won't do it. I'll turn you in, Gabriel."

"Go inside," Gabriel said, his face crimson. "Go to your room."

"I'm not a child."

Gabriel whacked my face with the back of his hand. I fell to the ground, stunned. The warm, romantic, misunderstood Gabriel I'd come to love over the past month had disappeared. This Gabriel was calculating, cold. Violent. This was the Gabriel who could hit a woman on the head and knock her out. This was the Gabriel who could blow up a government building.

"Go," he said again. "I'll deal with you later."

This time, trembling, I obeyed.

23

Frida's Cottage lost power sometime after midnight. Thunder roared, a flash of lightning followed, and then I heard the cracking and fall of a tree. Sparks flew outside the window before the room went dark.

I looked down at the paintbrush in my hand and laughed, an eerie sound that cut through the silence like a knife through Jell-o. My phone was nearly dead, the candles were burned to stumps, and now the power was gone. Soon I would be entombed in darkness—other than the momentary glow from the lightning strikes.

I would have to brave the storm and get the flashlights from the main house while I had enough cell charge to get down there. I put my brushes in water, pulled on my jacket, and slid into my shoes. I had no umbrella, but I found a piece of cardboard the contractors had left in the bedroom, and I held it up over my head as I stumbled down the path that led to the main house, the watery light from my phone leading the way. Lightning and thunder were rapid fire now, and I walked as quickly as I dared, avoiding the big trees and anything else that could attract lightning. The wind howled around me. I told myself I was fine. This was just a storm, and I'd endured worse.

The power was out in the house as well. I fumbled with the key and finally unlocked a back entrance into the kitchen. Inside, the rain and wind were just light background noise to my own ragged breaths. I felt myself hyperventilating. I forced shallow gulps of air. Panicking would only make things worse.

I tried to remember where we'd stored the emergency gear. I'd originally put it in the kitchen cupboards, but the contractors had moved everything while prepping for demolition. I shined my light around the laundry room and inside the supply closet—both were empty of supplies. Same with the one working downstairs bathroom.

Damn. The interior of the house was pitch black, and the pathetic light from my phone was just enough to create a spooky tunnel of illumination. I felt my way along the spine of the house, through the living areas and massive kitchen, and into the servants' hall, which led into the first of the linear additions. Because the roof over this part of the house was still intact, the contractors had left their tools in neat piles, covered with plastic tarps. This add-on had once housed examination rooms and "therapy suites" back when it was an asylum, but under Miles Ross's ownership, the rooms had served as storage units, each containing a hoarders' worth of boxes—the relics of one man's life. We'd thrown out most of Miles's belongings in this part of the house, but the sagging floors and water-stained ceilings left behind after years of neglect had proven to be beyond redemption. This addition, like the additions that followed behind it, was scheduled to be destroyed. I was glad. I hated this part of the house.

My phone died. Panic gripped my chest, squeezed my throat. The last thing I wanted was to be left here in the dark. Thunder shook the addition down to its rotten foundation. A flash of lightning illuminated the room I was standing in, and I heard another crack and then a crash. Another tree down. *Boom.* More lightning. The storm was right over us now, and the cycles were coming faster. It had become a house of horrors disco.

And that's when I saw it.

Tucked behind the workers' tools. Tall, human-shaped, headless. A scream caught in the back of my throat, gurgled its way to the surface. I choked it down, then moved closer, not daring to breath, and waited for the next flash of lightning.

It was a dress form, the kind used for fittings. How the hell had it gotten in here? We'd spent weeks removing Miles's old papers and household goods from the additions, and a dress form seemed an odd thing for contractors to bring in. Maybe it was a joke. Maybe we'd missed it, and the workers had placed it there. Maybe I was losing my mind.

I needed to find those flashlights.

I took advantage of another round of thunder and lightning and ran to the next room. No supplies. I repeated this—moving when the storm gave me light—until I finally found my emergency kit—two flashlights, flares, spare batteries, a first aid kit, a pack of waterproof matches, and a half dozen candles—on a shelf in a rear utility closet, way back in the bowels of the first addition.

Thank God. Tears of relief stung my eyes. I packed everything into a stray plastic bag and started to head back toward the main house. I'd find a few blankets and spend the evening in Frida's Cottage. But something called me back to that dress form.

Carefully, reluctantly, I walked around the piles of tools until I could shine my flashlight beam directly on its skeleton. I blinked, speechless. It *was* only a dress form, but I recognized the outfit it was wearing. Plaid miniskirt. White blouse. Purple cardigan.

* * *

Only three people could have known about that outfit: the short A-line plaid skirt, the frilly white blouse, the tight sweater. Two of those people had chosen it for me; the other was merely another victim.

I tore through the rest of that addition, ran back into the main house, and flew out the rear entrance, back into the night. Once outside, I threw my head back and howled into the wind, letting the driving rain wash away my angry tears. I could almost pretend Oliver's kidnapping had nothing to do with my past. I could almost believe that the doll was a coincidence. But that hideous outfit? Someone was warning me. Someone wanted to take every safe place in Cape Morgan away from me. Someone wanted to drive me mad.

I jogged the length of the path and let myself back into Frida's Cottage, slamming the door shut behind me. I flew between the rooms, tearing open doors and cabinets to make sure there were no evil surprises. Satisfied, I sank down on the floor in the studio and let myself sob. So many years of running. So many years of worrying. So many years of not daring to trust a soul, and there I was, back to square one. Worse, now I had people I cared about, a project I loved, and I was set to lose it all.

I stretched out on the floor, hugging my knees to my chest, and rocked back and forth. I couldn't tell Josh. I couldn't tell anyone— least of all Rebelo. To share my suspicions was to sign my own arrest warrant. Whether it was the government who'd get me or the Webbs, it didn't matter. I would be toast.

I'm not sure how long I lay there, rocking on the hard wood floor like an infant. Could have been an hour, could have been three, but eventually the tears stopped, and all that was left was a white-hot, searing rage. It was bad enough those fuckers had taken my name, my past, my freedom, but now they wanted my sanity too.

I crawled across the floor on my hands and knees until I found the flashlights and the candles. I lit the candles, placing them in the small foyer near the mural wall, and I set a flashlight up high so that it illuminated the studio. I pulled my brushes from the water jug, refreshed my paint, and started working. I was heavy handed with the primary colors: rich ruby reds, deep majestic purples, opulent golds, and bottomless black, slashing away at that wall like it was a body and I was the serial killer. When I was finished, the sun was up, and the rain had stopped. I stepped back to look at my work.

Mermaids, holding hands in a circle, surrounding the floating body of a dead man. They weren't the sexualized mermaids of Hollywood. These were strong, ruthless, brazen creatures whose hooded eyes shown with intelligence and cunning—and anger over the rape of their oceanic home. These were mermaids bent on justice and revenge.

I shook my head back and forth, in awe at what I'd done. Never had I painted something so raw and violent.

Never had I painted something so good.

CHAPTER

24

WHAT HAD *I done?* I suddenly saw my last month at the farm for what it was: a prison, with me as the willing prisoner. Not a sanctuary, as Gabriel had promised, but an encampment where I'd been brainwashed into believing his narcissistic nonsense.

I paced around and around my bedroom while Jamaica regarded me from her perch on the windowsill. I needed to reason with Gabriel, make him understand the mistake he was making. I slid down onto the floor and fought to regain my composure. I had to *think*. He wouldn't listen to me if I were hysterical. Emotions were my enemy right now, even if all I wanted to do was break down and cry.

I crawled across the room. With my ear against my door, I could hear Gabriel talking to Elizabeth, but I couldn't make out what he was saying. Then he called loudly for Luke. More mumbling, some doors slamming, and a sob from Elizabeth, loud and piercing.

"No fucking way," she yelled. "No!"

Gabriel shouted. Another door slammed shut. Another woman banished.

I opened my door a crack, enough to hear what Gabriel was telling Luke. I could only make out every few words. "Walk . . . smile . . . hand . . . box . . . run."

He was sending Luke into the senator's office in my stead.

Before I could do or say anything, the front door opened and shut. I ran down the hall and into the living room just in time to see Gabriel and Luke climbing into the car. I opened the front door and raced down the driveway. The last thing I saw was Luke's face pressed up against the passenger window. His eyes locked onto mine. He made a gun motion with his hand, aiming it, this time, at his own head.

*   *   *

"Give me your phone!" I pushed my way into Elizabeth's room. "Your phone, Elizabeth."

She was standing by the window, looking out at the empty driveway, her hands entwined across her abdomen. Her phone sat on cardboard box that served as a nightstand, with the bed between me and it.

"This is your fault," she said quietly.

"How is this possibly *my* fault?"

"He asked one thing of you, Emma. One thing. The only thing you needed to do to show your loyalty—to repay everything we've done for you, everything *I've* done for you—was hand the senator that stuff."

"The box contains a bomb. A bomb your *son* will now be handling."

She shook her head. "You still don't get it."

"I guess I don't. I thought this was about letting the world know the government had screwed you over, that it had stolen Gabriel's research." I spit out my words. "This was only ever about revenge. About murder."

Elizabeth turned toward me, eyes bloodshot and swollen. "I told Gabriel you weren't worth the risk, and now we'll have to move—again."

"You would have had to move anyway. Once they read those papers, don't you think they'd come after you? You're the one who claims the government is targeting you. How could this possibly fix things?"

"There's fixing things and there's justice." Elizabeth stood still, but her thin mouth twitched and twisted until it had stretched into a macabre smile. I knew then that the envelope I had been about to hand over was not full of nuclear secrets. That the bomb in that box was only part of the weapon. In a flash, I saw Gabriel disappearing into the coal cellar. I pictured the thick gloves and the protective gear and the face masks. I understood why I needed to hand those materials to the senator himself—not an assistant. One way or another, they meant for him to die.

"Two bombs," I whispered. "Gabriel couldn't get a bomb large enough to blow up the whole building, so he made separate explosive devices—one in the box and one in the envelope. If Leffert went for the chocolates first, he'd be blown up, and if he went for the envelope, he'd be blown up." And the box was rigged with a remote detonator, so either way, there would be enough explosives to do some serious damage. Damage that, to the outside world, would have been done by me. *But I messed up their plan, and now they were sending Luke.* "How can you sacrifice your own son?"

"He's just a boy," Elizabeth said haltingly. "He'll show up to get your briefcase, ask to meet the senator, and hand him the materials. Luke is smart. He'll be out of there before anything happens."

"You don't believe that."

Elizabeth's eyes shifted right. "I do."

"What if the senator decides to open the package in his presence, Elizabeth? What then?"

What little color was left drained from her face. "Luke is smart. He won't wait around."

"I guess you're willing to bet his life on it."

Elizabeth turned back toward the window. Taking advantage of the momentary distraction, I launched myself across the bed and grabbed the phone. She spun around and clawed at my hand with surprising speed, but bed rest and inactivity had made her weak, and I was up and out of that room before she could catch me.

I dialed 911. In a barely coherent rush, I explained that someone was on their way to the senator's office with explosive devices.

I hung up before the operator could ask questions. Then I called Gabriel and told him what I had done.

His silence scared me more than any words.

I rushed to my room and gathered my belongings. I'd take my car and get out of there before Gabriel was back. The police could probably trace the 911 call to Elizabeth, although knowing them, that was a burner phone. I wasn't going to wait around to find out. I tossed the phone into the toilet.

"It won't matter, you know," Elizabeth said, following me into the hall. "We'll get him one way or another."

She stood in the doorway while I searched frantically for the cat. I found Jamaica hiding under the bed and scooped her into my arms. I pushed Elizabeth aside and ran for the front door.

"Senator Leffert is the chair of the Senate Committee on Energy and Natural Resources," Elizabeth called after me, her voice eerily calm. "He's responsible for what's happened to us, Emma. He's the reason we have to keep running."

I paused with my hand on the doorknob. Why was she telling me this?

She said, "Gabriel is no fool. He had plan A and plan B."

Plan B? I stood there, struggling cat in one arm, keys dangling from my hand, waiting. Then it dawned on me. "The briefcase."

Of course. I'd been told that inside that briefcase was a fake résumé, books, notes, and a large manila envelope addressed to the senator. The briefcase had been large and heavy, and I'd assumed it was part of the act—something made to look like I was a student. But at some point, Gabriel had placed an explosive device in there too—a device that could be triggered remotely. Plan A was to set off all three devices, ensuring the senator's death and the destruction of his office. Plan B was the briefcase alone.

With growing horror, I realized the danger he'd put me in. Besides framing me for a federal crime, I'd handled that briefcase. What if it had somehow gone off in my hands? What if the administrative assistant or the janitor or a high school intern had opened it while I was still in the building? Surely it had some type of trigger that would cause it to go off if opened prematurely. He didn't care about me. In fact, he probably wanted me dead. I would be called a crazy suicide bomber. He could get back at the senator while making sure I could never squeal. He could get rid of both of us in one messy fell swoop.

This was never about letting the world know what had happened to him. This was always about committing murder.

I'd tossed Elizabeth's phone after calling Gabriel and 911, so I had no way to warn Senator Leffert's office about the briefcase. I needed to get out of there. I would find a phone along the way.

"No one will believe you," Elizabeth said. "In the eyes of the government, *we* don't exist. Only a troubled teen, an invalid wife, and a simple mechanic live in this farmhouse. And you? It's you they'll remember. Your face, your very recognizable clothing, your fingerprints. You're an unreliable social worker who dropped her cases without any warning at all."

I felt frozen to the spot. She was right, of course. I was an unreliable social worker whose father had been a known prepper. An unreliable social worker who'd disappeared for the last month and a half. An unreliable social worker who had managed to fall in love with a madman.

If they disappeared, who would believe me?

Sirens blared in the distance.

As I rushed outside, Elizabeth's voice trailed after me.

"It's too late now, Emma! You'd better keep the lights on. We'll never let you rest. Not as long as we both live."

25

THE DOVE STREET house was empty when I paddled back to the dock later that morning. I'd waited until the electric company showed up on the island to leave, but before anyone arrived, I'd removed the clothes from the mannequin and burned both the form and the outfit in a pit outside. Once the workers were on the premises, I escaped in my kayak, braving the strong currents with hurried paddle strokes. Exhaustion and the currents made me slow. I needed any last bits of adrenaline for what I needed to do next.

At the house, I secured the kayak on the dock and pulled the tarp off the motorboat. I dug around in the dry bag until I found the burner phone and the key to the safe deposit box. I returned the dry bag to its spot. Back in my room, I removed the hidden drawer from the bottom of my jewelry armoire and put the key inside. There were other documents in that drawer—the few items I'd saved that tied me to Emma Strand. I took them out now.

A photo of my parents, arms around one another, before their lives turned forever sour. The last birthday card my mother had ever signed for me. My college diploma. A photo of Jamaica, who'd traveled with me from state to state, identity to identity, until she'd died of natural causes at sixteen. And the frayed and yellowed news article that kept me running. I only needed to look at the headline to know why I couldn't go to the police: *"Explosion Rocks Charleston, West Virginia, Senate Office—Senator Leffert and Two Others Dead in Apparent Act of Domestic Terrorism."*

My briefcase. My image in any security footage. Whether or not I'd known it, I'd carried that bomb into Leffert's office. In the government's eyes, I was a murderer and a terrorist.

I placed the documents back in the false drawer, replaced the drawer underneath the armoire, and refastened the false bottom. After taking a quick shower and changing into fresh clothes, I smashed the burner phone and drove it to a local park, where I tucked it into a dog poop bag and threw the bag into a public waste bin.

My next stop was the Wicker Foundation office.

I wasn't surprised to find that Josh wasn't at work, nor had he left me any messages. After a brief hello to the receptionist and Seth, I locked myself in my office. I called an old friend of mine from New York City, a lawyer I'd dated briefly before marrying Josh. I explained that I was looking for a very sophisticated private investigator to handle a missing persons search—did he know anyone proficient with online PI work? He gave me a name— Evan Blume—and I checked Blume out online. His references and reviews were excellent, but more importantly, he promised discretion.

I called the number my friend had given me. Blume would see me next day at his office in Boston. He set his hourly rate, and I agreed to it.

"I'm not one for bullshit, Mrs. Wicker," he said. "If this is about a suspected marital affair or some other trivial personal matter, I'm probably not interested. I'm long past the days of snooping around bars and seedy hotels."

"It's not."

"You need to be prepared to pay. I require a sizable retainer upfront."

"Of course. Is cash okay?" Better not to have a trail, I thought.

Blume sucked on what sounded like a cigarette. "Everything you want done is on the up and up?"

I said, "I'll see you tomorrow, Mr. Blume," and hung up.

*   *   *

Dinner was a quiet affair. Maya had made baked haddock on a bed of sauteed spinach. The food was good—it always was—but my appetite hadn't returned. I sat alone in the dining room, nursing a glass of pinot grigio and watching the sun go down.

Maya seemed particularly distant. I told her I would handle my own dishes, but she ignored my offer, taking my setting in that quiet way of hers that somehow always made me feel small.

"Do you mind if I leave for a few hours?" she asked later, while I was drafting notes for my discussion with Blume the next day. "I'd like to spend some time with my grandson, Marcus. This kidnapping has my daughter on edge."

"Of course."

"The whole town is on edge."

"I know. It's terrible."

Maya stood there, watching me. "Do you think it's over?"

"I don't know," I said truthfully.

"I have a pain here," Maya pointed to her chest, right below the breastbone, "that I can't get rid of. My daughter says it's stress. I say it's premonition." Maya's mouth worked as though she wanted to say more. Finally, she said, "It's that island. No good comes from digging up the past."

"I'm not sure what the island has to do with anything."

"You'll see," she said. "Josh should have left the place alone."

Once alone in the house, I went outside to sit on the veranda and listen to the sea. A child of the Midwest, the vastness of the ocean remained a wonder to me. I imagined the far-off lands it touched, the secrets it hid, and I felt like just maybe my problems were insignificant. I let myself drift off to sleep, the lapping sound of the surf a sweet salve to my mental wounds.

It was after eight when the doorbell rang. Josh had speakers wired out on the patio, so the insistent buzz reached the outside, forcing me violently awake. I rose to see who was there.

"Thomas," I said, opening the door for Detective Rebelo. "Good to see you."

The detective didn't return my greeting. "Can I come in, Beatrice?"

"Josh isn't here."

"It's not Josh I need to see."

Rebelo's gaze was apologetic but unwavering. I stepped back to let him in, my shoulders tense. Before all of this, a surprise visit from Rebelo would have been a pleasant event. His demeanor made it clear tonight was no social event.

I led him through the foyer and into the living room. He sat down on the couch; I took the chair across from him. "What's wrong, Thomas? You look like you've seen the spirit of serial killer."

"I won't beat around the bush, Beatrice. I need to know where you were the night before last."

Confused, I said, "I was here. Why?"

"You were here, in your bed, sleeping next to Josh?"

I sat back in my seat, contemplating the detective's question. His hands were clenched into fists, his jaw was tight. He was fighting his own demons right now, and I had a hunch I knew what they were.

"I fell asleep in our boat, Thomas. I went out there to be alone, and I must have dozed off at some point, because when I woke up, it was morning."

"Did you take the boat anywhere?"

"I drifted away from the shore for a little while, but I didn't go far."

"Did you go to Ross Island?"

"The night before last? No."

Rebelo waved his hand around, gesturing toward the upstairs. "With a house this big, you needed to sit in a boat to get some privacy?"

"Privacy and alone time aren't the same thing. A person seeks a comforting space when they need alone time. To me, the sea is a comfort."

"But your home here with Josh is not?"

"I didn't say that."

"It's implied."

"Do you always want to be around Betsy, Thomas? Don't you ever need some alone time? I don't understand what you're getting at."

Rebelo sighed deeply. "Josh told me you weren't with him Tuesday night. He said you showed up around six in the morning. You were wet and cold. You claimed to have slept in the boat."

"Yeah, so? I told him the truth, just like I'm telling you."

"He said you were wet, Beatrice. Why were you wet?"

"Some water sloshed over the side while I was asleep."

"I'll ask you one more time: Where did you go?"

I clapped my hands and let out a sharp laugh. "*Go?* Where the hell would I have gone? I was in a small boat in the middle of the fucking night. I sat in that boat, which was tied to the fucking dock. The waves lulled me to sleep, and I slept out there all night."

Rebelo leaned forward. His mouth moved silently under that mustache before he said, "The doctors believe Oliver had been left out in the cold since around four or five in the morning. That means whoever returned that little boy did it by boat. Replays of security cameras in the general vicinity of the bridge to Ross Island show no vehicles moving through there between three and six in the morning. The only way to get there would have been by sea."

"Maybe the doctors are wrong."

"Maybe, but it's not a high traffic area, Beatrice. Boat seems the most likely mode of transportation."

"I'm not the only boat owner in town. Every single person in Cape Morgan has access to a boat. Anyway, you and I both know that calling Ross Island an island is a stretch. During low tide, someone could practically walk out there."

Rebelo stood up. He paced to the window and, his back to me, said, "It's true that most of us have access to a boat, but when I try to think of people who might want to hurt the parents of this little boy, your name is on the list."

Parents. I let the silence hang there between us until it took on a life of its own. Rebelo had hinted at knowing about Josh and Carly when he questioned me the day before, but now he was suggesting that he knew I knew. Worse, he was suggesting that Josh knew I knew. I wondered what else Rebelo suspected.

"I didn't kidnap that child, Thomas. Think about what you're saying. Whoever kidnapped Oliver also set off a bomb. I was with Seth on Ross Island the night the boy was abducted. We were doing a photo shoot for the fundraiser. Before and after pictures. Seth can verify that."

"Do you have his number?"

I texted Rebelo Seth's cell-phone number. "Go, call him now so you know I haven't reached out to him before you could ask your questions. You'll see. I didn't have anything to do with Oliver's kidnapping, Thomas. Whatever you may believe, whatever sick motivation you think I have, it wasn't me."

Rebelo nodded curtly. He disappeared into the kitchen, and I heard him talking, although I couldn't make out what he said. He returned a few minutes later.

"Well?"

"Seth verified that you were with him that day and that the two of you were together in his car when you heard the Amber Alert."

I wrapped my arms across my chest and tried not to look as angry as I was feeling. "Does Josh know you're here?"

"No." Rebelo returned to the couch and sat back down. "He'd be upset if he knew."

Yet Josh had told Rebelo I wasn't home that night. He'd told Rebelo I came home wet. My Josh, the Josh I married, would never have set me up that way. Whether or not Josh would be upset that Rebelo was here, Josh was feeling suspicious himself. I remembered his question from that morning: *"If you knew anything about that little boy who was kidnapped, you'd tell the police, right, Beatrice?"* At the very least, Josh suspected I knew more than I was letting on.

Reluctantly, I said, "You're just doing your job, Thomas." When Rebelo didn't respond, I said, "Do the police have any leads at all? Maybe traces of DNA on the child or the tarp?"

"The tarp is being analyzed, as are the leaves that were stuffed inside." Rebelo chewed on his bottom lip, fussed with his mustache.

"Something will turn up eventually. Criminals make mistakes. They get sloppy."

"I hate to even say this, but have you looked into the mother? Maybe she had enemies. Or maybe something happened with her."

Rebelo frowned. "Are you suggesting Carly staged the kidnapping of her own child?"

Stranger things have happened, I thought. What better way to strengthen a relationship with the baby's father than to cause and then weather a crisis? Especially if the baby's father is pulling away—or already married. I didn't give voice to these accusations, however, because I knew it wasn't Carly. The doll and dress form told me that. Nevertheless, I wanted Rebelo to understand that he needed to widen his search. Looking at me was getting him nowhere.

"No, Thomas, I'm not pointing fingers at Carly Baker. I am suggesting, however, that whoever did this could have been targeting her, not us."

"The baby was returned on your island."

And the baby's father is my husband. I was tempted—so tempted—to acknowledge the giant, fuzzy, lavender elephant in the room, but I knew that would only create more issues. Instead, I said, "Maybe that's because our island is the perfect spot to leave a child. The perpetrator knew construction is happening on the big house and that someone would find Oliver in time. They also wanted a place remote enough that they could get away unnoticed, but close enough to reach easily."

"That person would have had to know there are no security cameras on the project. They would have had to know where to land a boat in the dark and what time the construction crew would be on site." Rebelo's stony gaze was back and pointed at me. "They would have had to know an awful lot about this project."

All paths lead back to me, I thought, and let out a sigh. "Like anyone associated with the Wicker Foundation would. Like anyone who knows someone who works for the foundation or the firm would. Like anyone who reads the papers would. In other words, the whole damn town, Thomas." I stood up. It was time for him to go. "For God's sake, I did not take that child. Give me a lie detector test. Do whatever you need to do to convince yourself of that because while you're busy focusing on me, someone is getting away with these crimes. Someone who could strike again."

Rebelo patted his mustache down absentmindedly with his pointer finger. The coldness in his eyes was gone, replaced with a bottomless, wretched fatigue. "If you find anything, anything at all, on the island, call me."

"I will."

"And Beatrice? Stay out of the boat at night. That's a good way to have a drowning accident, and Josh doesn't need that right now. None of us does."

*   *   *

It was well after midnight when I finally felt Josh slide into bed beside me. He smelled of pipe smoke and lavender. I turned over, letting him know I was awake, but he was curled away from me, a grown man in the fetal position. I inched toward him, wanting badly to feel the comfort of his arms, but I couldn't bring myself to cross that great divide.

26

E van Blume's office consisted of a nondescript trio of rooms in a nondescript building in a nondescript neighborhood north of Boston. Like his professional space, the man was, at best, nondescript. Medium height, graying mud-brown hair, and bushy gray-brown eyebrows. The most distinguishable thing about him was the way he sucked on lollipop after lollipop. I was surprised he still had teeth.

"Come on in," he said, and led me through a small reception room to his office.

The "reception room" consisted of two wooden chairs and a coffee table littered with stacks of *Forbes* and *The Economist*—plus a bowl full of assorted lollipops. His workspace was marginally more welcoming, with an oversized cherrywood desk and three matching chairs. Banks of metal file cabinets lined one wall, and bookshelves lined another. The shelves were crammed full of neatly arranged treatises on everything from international law to philosophy, to Russian poets—plus a handful of framed photos.

"For when I'm bored," he said, waving at the books. "I have a thing for books. The thicker, the better."

"And lollipops," I said, pointing to the jar of candy on his desk.

"Yeah, well, I'm trying to quit smoking." He plopped down on the chair behind his desk and motioned for me to sit opposite him. "You don't smoke, do you?"

"Never have."

"Good for you. Nasty habit." Elbows on the desk, he leaned forward and clasped his hands together. "So, what can I do for you? You mentioned a missing person on the phone. Who's missing and why are you searching for them?"

"I'm looking for a couple. When I knew them, the man went by the name Gabriel Webb. His wife—at least I think they were married—was Elizabeth Webb. They had a child named Luke, although I'm not certain whose child he was."

"Meaning hers or his or whether he belonged to them at all?"

"Meaning hers, his, or both of theirs." I paused. "First and foremost, I need your discretion in this, Evan. If you can locate this family in a quiet manner that doesn't alert them or anyone else, there's additional money in it for you." I slid a piece of paper across the desk to him. On it, I'd written a sizable sum—nearly half my personal account balance, saved from my Wicker Foundation salary over the last ten years. "There's also a confidentiality agreement I'll need you to sign."

Blume read the number I'd written. His furry eyebrows shot up, and he scribbled some notes in a leather-bound portfolio. "Fine," he said, his gaze still locked on the figure. "I'll sign the agreement as long as you understand that it doesn't apply if there's a criminal investigation."

"I understand." I handed him a folder with the agreement and other information I'd put together the night before. I'd left out the gory details of my time with the Webb family, but the basic facts— Gabriel's teaching background, Luke's involvement with social services, their address in West Virginia—were all there. I knew this was dangerous. If Blume found my persecutors, and somehow, connected them to Emma Strand and what had happened at a West Virginia's senator's office all those years ago, and somehow then connected Emma to me, there would be trouble. No confidentiality agreement would protect me. I understood the risks, but I hadn't been Emma in over twenty years. I had no choice but to believe that trail was dead, and I hoped the money would ensure it remained buried.

Blume read through the papers quickly and silently. Finally, he looked up. "This guy was a professor at Michigan State University?"

"Yes—a nuclear physicist."

Blume pressed his lips into a skeptical frown. "Why would a nuclear physicist disappear this way?"

I hesitated. "He claimed to have discovered something very important and potentially dangerous. He said people were after him. He was on the run."

"Was he telling the truth about his discovery?"

"I had no reason to doubt him, but I can't say for certain."

Blume sat back. He studied me with a calm, cynical expression. It was then I noticed the University of Pennsylvania diploma, the multiple graduate degrees. My former boyfriend had been right: Blume was no slouch. Why this career? His lack of wedding ring combined with the photos of four children lining the top of his bookshelf gave me a clue. Perhaps he made more money as a private investigator than in whatever his job had been before, especially if he had alimony and child support to pay. Or maybe he just liked this line of work.

He asked, "Why do you care where this guy and his family have gone? What's it to you?"

I thought about the mural I'd painted in Frida's Cottage—the wild-eyed mermaids and their hunger for vengeance. I thought about the dress form hidden in a creepy annex, the stormy night alone on Ross Island, and that helpless little boy wrapped in leaves and a tarp. I thought about madness, the kind of madness that would drive a woman to leap from a cliff to her certain death.

"They took something from me," I said calmly and firmly. "And I want it back."

*   *   *

I felt eyes on me everywhere now. As I made my way back to Maine from Boston, I glanced repeatedly in the rearview mirror, looking for signs of a tail. Starbucks line, gas station, food counter . . . the hair on my arms would prickle, telling me I was being watched. I saw shadows in the shadows, heard my name whispered down empty hallways.

I wanted to scream.

It had been years since I'd seen Elizabeth, Gabriel, or Luke. Even during those years, they'd stalked me, leaving creepy dolls and ominous messages as their calling cards, I had never gotten a glimpse of any of them. The calls would start first—heavy breathing, long silences—followed by the short, typed notes. The paper and fonts would change, but the messages were always the same: *We know where you are. There's nowhere you can hide. Keep the lights on, Emma.*

They wanted to scare me—and they'd succeeded.

The first day I'd escaped, I'd wanted to go to the police or the FBI. It was my sister, Jane, who'd talked me out of it. Far older and wiser, she'd been convinced the bomb would be pinned on me regardless of whether I'd known what they were up to.

"People died. A senator was murdered. At best, Emma, all they'll see is a lovestruck girl doing the bidding for her manipulative handler. At worst, they won't be able to find this guy, and they'll blame only you. They'll say you made him up. You'll take the fall for the whole thing. That could mean the death penalty."

"I was a social worker. They'd know I would never do such a horrible thing. Not knowingly."

"Not knowingly, perhaps, but they'll say you should have known. Think about Dad, Emma. The local authorities knew he was a prepper. It's not like our family didn't have a reputation. The apple and the tree and all."

The more I'd thought about it, the more I'd known she was right. Gabriel had made sure to stay away from the senator's local office. I'd driven there alone in my own vehicle. Even that last day when he'd sent Luke, there was no contact—my phone call to Gabriel from Elizabeth's phone headed that off. It was the briefcase that caused the crisis. While the name in that briefcase and on that job application had been fake, it was my face they'd remember. It was my face on security footage. Gabriel had seen to that.

When I'd thought about how they'd used me—the perfect naive mule to act out their malicious plans—I wanted one thing: escape. I'd been willing to go along with Jane's suggestion to take on the identities of dead people so that I could run from the authorities and avoid any chance of being sent to prison. Jane worked at the vital records office in Chicago. Finding the right identities to steal was simple enough, and every time Gabriel found me, she'd provide the details of a new identity. It was a risk for her. I knew she did it out of guilt for leaving me alone with my father, and I was too scared and too alone to refuse her help.

Gabriel always found me, though—no matter what my name, town, or occupation. I began to think they simply moved from locale to locale with me, never letting me out of their sights. I had replaced the government as their latest obsession. At first fear drove me, but eventually it was anger. How dare they? Then, when I became Beatrice Bachman, they stopped chasing me. After that, I took odd jobs to make ends meet—waitress, shoe salesperson, ticket taker. One year, then two went by without a single call, letter, or creepy doll. By the third year, I figured something had happened to them, and I was free. Year four without contact, I met and later married Joshua Henry Wicker. I took his name, widening that bridge between me and their insanity even further.

Josh and I had been married for ten years. For those ten years, I had almost been able to believe I was Beatrice Bachman Wicker. I'd given Josh just a few details from the real Beatrice's background— born in Ohio to a nurse's aide and a welder, both deceased—the type of facts that might one day be verified. The rest of Beatrice's background I was free to make up. Josh knew me as an artist with a love of helping others, and that part was true.

For those ten years with Josh, I believed I had become untrace-able, untouchable, and invincible.

I had been wrong.

27

THE AIR IN Cape Morgan was autumn crisp—sun-kissed and cool. I'd been sitting in my office at the foundation, staring at Julianna's initial ideas for the new gallery but unable to focus, when Grace called.

"Come for a walk with me, Beatrice. I haven't seen you in days." Grace's voice was thick with worry. "We'll go to the state park. We can walk along the beach and look for shells like we used to do."

I hadn't been back to Ross Island since the night of the storm. I wasn't scared, exactly—I just felt violated. The Webbs had encroached on every safe space in my life—those I shared with Josh, my job, and Ross Island. That was their intention, I knew, but it didn't make it any easier.

Grace's invitation was a welcome distraction. "Sure. Give me an hour. I'll meet you by the beach entrance."

On my way out, Seth stopped me. "I'm trying to finish up a draft brochure for you and Josh. I was thinking—can we go through the cabins one more time? I heard you finished the mural in Frida's Cottage. I thought we could capture that too."

"I don't know if that's a great idea," I said. "You can use the photos you already have, can't you?"

Seth leaned against his desk, his long legs blocking my way through the aisle. "You want this to be the best it can be, right? If we reshoot, we can show some of the demo progress, and the trees are changing color. That may make for a more dramatic backdrop." He shrugged. "Plus, the island is getting attention ever since that boy was found, so we can capitalize on—"

I held up a hand. The last thing I wanted was more attention. "Look, do whatever you want. You can go back to the island without me." I stared pointedly at his legs. "Can I get through?"

"I need you to let me in the cabins, Beatrice. Remember—I don't have keys to the palace."

"You need *someone* to let you in. Louis, the foreman, can do it, and so can Josh. Now please move."

Josh pulled his legs from the aisle. He let out a long, low whistle. "Someone's in a shitty mood."

I glared at him. "Someone's in a hurry."

I left the office feeling unsettled. Seth was right—we could get more dramatic photos with the autumn foliage, which was becoming more brilliant every day. Had I reacted so negatively because I was reluctant to go back to Ross Island—or was my response rooted in my feelings about Seth? Something about Seth irked me. I couldn't put my finger on it. He seemed well liked by the others in the office. Josh trusted him. Grace's characterization—as though he were always playing a part—seemed right. One thing was certain: I resented his interference, and I didn't want to share my painting with him. I wasn't so sure I was willing to share it with the world either. At least not yet.

* * *

"You seem pretty crabby today." Grace glanced over at me. "When are you going to tell me what's up?" She had rolled her jeans up to her knees and was splashing along the water's edge, grimacing every time a wave of cold water sloshed against her shins. "I'm worried about you, Beatrice."

"I'm fine. Just a little tired." Unlike Grace, I stayed on the dry sand, exploring the deserted beach and searching through the mounds of kelp for shells. The beach stretched for a half mile in either direction. To the right, a rugged peninsula jutted out into the ocean, the small seaside mountains rising up behind the groves of oak, pines, and spruce trees. To the left, the sandy beach meandered, narrowing gradually until it was only a thin, pebbly line between water and woods. The day remained clear, and I peeled off my sweater, enjoying the sun on my bare arms. "I'm happy to be here, with you."

Grace grinned. She threw her head back, face toward the sun, and raised her hands over her head. "I never want to leave!"

I trudged up the sand, toward the dunes—the very dunes we'd searched not long before. I lay down on the beach, my sweater under my head. Grace joined me. She touched the top of her head to mine.

"Have you heard anything about that little boy?" she asked.

"Only that he's okay."

A seagull flew overhead, diving down on the beach in front of us to pick through a pile of kelp. It grabbed a small crab, then squawked loudly, chest puffed, warning away the other gulls. The crustacean's legs waved frantically as the bird took flight.

"Poor thing," Grace said. "Nature is cruel."

"Nature can certainly be brutal." I put an arm over my eyes, blocking out the sun and the image of that doomed crab. "Don't confuse brutality with cruelty, though. They're not always the same."

I leaned up on my elbow so I was facing her. "My father was a brutal man, but he was rarely cruel. I knew another man who could be very gentle, but ultimately, he was nothing but cruel."

"That sucks."

"Yeah, it does. My father was a farmer. My mother died when I was young, and he was on his own. It made him bitter and hard to be around, if I'm honest. He thought the world was an unjust place, and he raised us accordingly."

"Us?"

"Me and my sister."

Grace shifted her head until she was looking directly toward the sun. Her eyes were squeezed shut. I reached over and, on impulse, squeezed her hand. Grace squeezed back.

I said, "You told me before that you have two brothers. Are you close to them?"

"Hardly. I'm estranged from one, and the other is . . . well, the other is dead."

"I'm sorry."

Grace shrugged. "He was a baby when he died."

"That must have been awful for your family."

"My father never got over it. When you said earlier that cruel and brutal aren't the same thing, you were right. My father was cruel toward my older brother. In small ways at first, little back-handed compliments, passive-aggressive snide remarks, pointed comparisons to me. I think my brother reminded my father of my mother and of the brother who never had a chance, and in his own way, my father was really getting back at fate."

Wise words. I listened to Grace talk and thought of me and Jane. Jane had always been the wild child—full of sass and quick to argue. I'd been the silent sister, happiest with the animals and con-tent to wait my turn in life. While my father had not been passive-aggressive or violent, he was rarely kind. When Jane left home at eighteen, right on the tail of my mother's death, it broke his heart. He was left with me, a six-year-old girl he could mostly pretend didn't exist. He sought sanctuary at the bottom of a bottle. I waited for him to see *me*, but that day never came.

I said, "Parents can have special ways of screwing up their kids." We both laughed.

"Leaving was the hardest thing I ever did," Grace said. "I didn't know where I was going or what I was going to do when I got there. I just knew I needed to go." She smiled at me, a warm smile that lit up her violet eyes. "I'm thankful I landed in Cape Morgan."

A dog barked, and we both sat up. I glanced in the direction of the water. A man was walking his Rottweiler along the beach. He waved to us before continuing on his journey, the dog chasing waves in front of him.

"Oh, to be like a dog," I said. "No worries about the future, no regrets about the past," We both laughed again.

"It's good to hear you laugh," Grace stood up and wiped the sand from her backside. "I know what's happened has been hard for you. The kidnapping, I mean."

"It's been hard on everyone."

She held my gaze. "I know it's been especially hard for you."

I searched Grace's eyes for the real meaning behind those words. "Why would that be, Grace?"

Grace looked at the water. "Because that little boy is your husband's son."

I stood up, pulled on my sweater, and walked away from her, toward the sea. I could hear Grace's movements as she followed behind me. "Beatrice, wait!" she called. "Please. I'm sorry."

But the damage had been done. The secret I'd protected for so long was out there, laid bare for everyone to see. I already knew Rebelo and Maya knew. If Grace knew too, then so did others—Seth and Julianna and Mackle and every person at the firm and the Wicker Foundation. I was the brunt of a thousand jokes, the object of twisted, delicious pity. I'd been a fool to think we could keep such a secret.

I waded out into the ocean, ignoring the icy water that sucked at my ankles. Grace ran in beside me and grabbed my arm. "Beatrice, listen to me." She shook me. "Beatrice!"

I spun around. "Yes, he is Josh's son. Is that what you want to hear, Grace? That my husband of ten years is sleeping with a twenty-something and didn't even have the common sense to wear a damn condom?" I kicked at the waves. "That sweet little innocent boy is Josh's. If I had an ounce of courage, I would confront my husband. I would leave him for what he's done."

"Then why haven't you?"

Grace's question was said with such honest interest that it stopped me mid-kick. Why hadn't I? Because of all those tiny little secrets between us? Because of my own big lies? Because of the safety and comfort of being Mrs. Wicker? Because deep down, I really loved him? Because after all these years, I was finally, blessedly not alone?

"I don't know," I said honestly.

Grace took my hand and led me back onto the dry sand. "My mother loved a particular quote from Gandhi. She'd say, 'The weak can never forgive. Forgiveness is an attribute of the strong.'"

"I'm not ready to forgive him, Grace. Not yet."

"I'm not talking about Josh. I'm talking about you. Whatever you've done, Beatrice, whatever it is that makes you feel you deserve how he's treating you, maybe you need to let it go."

"It's not that simple."

"Why?" Grace released my hand. She stepped back, hands on her hips.

I wanted to tell her. I wanted to share the horrors of that summer twenty years ago with this earnest, damaged young woman, but the words were stuck in my chest—a pocket of poison destined to fester there until it was my undoing.

I started walking back toward my car.

"Beatrice?" Grace called.

"I need to go."

"I've never said a word to anyone."

I turned around. "If you know, others do too."

"No one holds it against you. I hear things at the diner. The people here, they know it's their fault—Josh and that woman, Carly. I'm sure of that." Her face contorted, and even from a distance, I could see her eyes were brimming with tears. "I didn't mean to upset you."

I'd never spoken harshly to her, and I felt ashamed of my tone. "It's okay. It's not your fault."

I jogged back to my car. Grace had caught me off guard. I could pretend Rebelo's baiting was a fishing expedition, but if Grace knew, others in town knew, and that put me in a predicament. How would a normal woman react?

How the hell should I know? I thought. I'd lost track of *normal* years ago. At this point, it wasn't even a word I recognized.

28

A POLICE CAR, REBELO's 4Runner, and an ambulance were all sitting in front of my house when I arrived home to Dove Street hours later. *What now?* I wondered. I ran inside, but my entry was blocked by Rebelo, two uniformed officers, and a pair of paramedics. The paramedics were attending to Maya, who was lying on a gurney in the foyer. She wore an oxygen mask over her mouth, and her hands were clasped on her stomach as though in prayer. Josh stood behind her, his hand resting on her shoulder, and when he saw me, he whispered something in Maya's ear before asking Detective Rebelo if he was ever going to let me through.

As I neared Maya, I saw her swollen, wet face. Her hairline was damp, and the tears were still streaming from swollen eyes, with small rivulets of tears pooling around the oxygen mask.

"Maya—" I reached toward her, but Josh took my hand and pulled me into the kitchen.

"Marcus is missing," he said. "When Maya found out, she fainted. I found her in the kitchen. She'd hit her head on the counter." He hesitated. "It's not good."

"Oh God—"

Josh nodded a few times. Exhaustion showed in the shadows under his chestnut-colored eyes, in the gray cast of his skin, and the rounded way he held his shoulders. He said, "Maya's obviously a mess."

I glanced over at Maya and watched as one paramedic measured her pulse and the other shined a light in her eyes, checking her pupils. "Marcus is missing as in . . .?"

"Another pipe bomb, another kidnapping. This time the bomb was small, and it was set off in a dumpster. Thankfully, no one was hurt."

Not again. "Where? How?"

"Marcus's daycare. He was outside at playtime, sleeping in his stroller. His teacher swears she was watching him. She said she left the area for a moment when she heard the bang—she thought a child had climbed into the dumpster—and when she looked back, he was gone. Just an empty stroller."

"Same as Oliver."

Josh nodded.

"No ransom note?"

"Not so far."

Oh, Maya. Her daughter and her daughter's family were her entire world. The only place she seemed to go other than here was to see twenty-month-old Marcus. I wanted to ask more questions, but something in the way Josh was looking at me—guarded, wary—stopped me.

Rebelo had left the paramedics and was on his phone in our living room. I tried to make out what he was saying, but he turned away when he saw me looking at him. A moment later, he clicked off his phone and joined the paramedics.

"They would prefer she go to the hospital," Rebelo said to Josh. "We're headed there anyway to talk with Marcus's teacher. She was hysterical, and the paramedics took her in as a precaution." He said nothing else, concerned, I was sure, about Maya hearing more upsetting news.

"I'd like to join you," Josh said.

Rebelo's gaze shifted from Josh to me and back again. "I don't think that's a good idea, Josh." He turned to one of the uniformed officers. "Stay here, parked outside." To us, he said, "I'll be back in a few hours. Given everything, I think we should talk. Really talk."

* * *

Josh poured himself a double scotch on the rocks. "First Oliver Baker, now Marcus." He shook his head. "This is starting to feel personal."

I peeked outside at the cop car sitting in our driveway. Its lights were off, but I saw the glow of a cell phone in the cop's hand. I wondered whether he was there to protect us—or to make sure we didn't leave.

"This is *starting* to feel personal?" I asked.

Josh gulped down half of his drink before wiping his mouth with the back of his hand. He gave me a halfhearted shrug. His eyes searched mine. There was sadness there—sadness and surprise. "Then you know."

"I've always known."

"And you've never said a word."

"What could I have said?"

Josh rubbed the back of his neck. "Something? Anything? My God, Beatrice, I had no idea." He threw his hands up in the air. "It was never my intention to hurt you."

I backed up until I was pressed against the wall. "I don't want to talk about this."

"What choice do we have?" Josh's voice rose in pitch. "Someone stole my son. Now that same someone has stolen Maya's grandson. There is one thread here, Beatrice. Us. You and me. Got that?" He slammed a hand against the bar. "We don't get to stay silent."

"You're not going to make me the bad guy," I said quietly. "I didn't sleep with someone else. I didn't break our vows."

Josh's eyes turned cold. I saw that wary distrust again, and my mouth went dry.

"I think we're past that, Beatrice. I love Carly. We have a child, and he needs me." Josh's tone was quiet, hard. "I did a bad thing, it's true, but what kind of a woman ignores her husband's affair for *years*? Goes on as though nothing has happened?" His eyes narrowed, his jaw tightened. "I can't believe you've known all along. Holy hell, Beatrice. I'm a bad person. I have to live with that every damn day. But you? What does your silence say about you?"

"Josh, please—"

He threw his head back and groaned. "My God, Beatrice. I don't know you at all."

*   *   *

Josh closed himself up in his study. Although the lights were off, I could hear Schubert blaring through the closed French doors. I poured myself a glass of wine, sat on the back veranda, and watched the moonlight ripple on the water. I thought about escape.

My sister had offered to find me one last new identity. I could take that offer, raid the money and documents in my safe deposit box and personal bank account, and head over the border to Canada or Mexico or even parts south. It'd been twenty years since I'd been Emma Strand. The curvy, naive, doe-eyed girl of twenty-one was long gone. No one would recognize me. Most days, I didn't recognize myself.

Only I didn't really want to escape. I was tired and angry, and so very fed up with those bastards. I didn't want to give up my life in Cape Morgan—Josh or no Josh. I didn't want to leave this community. I didn't want to leave Ross Island to someone else.

Schubert changed over to the pounding rhythm of Stravinsky's *The Rite of Spring*, and I tried to shut out the discordant rise and fall of the percussion and string instruments. Josh was nursing his hurt, but his anger was misplaced. He was feeling helpless in the face of this unnamed, evil threat, and he was lashing out at me. Finding out I'd known for some time about his affair would have been a shock, disrupting his fragile world further. I realized that. I had to give him time.

There were so many things I wanted to say to my husband. I wanted to scream at him for turning this around and blaming me when *he* was the adulterer. I wanted to tear him apart for his stupid, needless unfaithfulness. I wanted to tell him about my life as Emma, make him understand that the mistakes I had made as a young woman were just that: stupid, childish, honest mistakes.

But even if he believed me, those revelations would break whatever remnants of a world we'd built together here. They would wreck his perfect life, and they would take my life away completely.

Stravinsky was whirling, twirling around in my head like a mantel of despair pressing down on me. My chest felt heavy, each breath a chore. I could fight for Josh—another woman might—but deep down, I believed it was hopeless. His betrayal was too great, my secrets loomed too large. And anyway, my shot at keeping Josh had been gone months and months ago—sometime between plucking that platinum hair off his navy sweater and glimpsing Oliver's pinched, placid little face for the first time at the hospital nursery.

Josh was lost to me.

He had a son, and that son needed him.

I could have given him a child. He'd wanted us to have one, but I'd made excuse after excuse until I'd crossed forty and convinced him the risk was too high. I told myself a baby would tie me to Emma—her genetics, her background—and would make me vulnerable. But the truth was, I was scared. Having a child would be an act of faith in my new life here in Cape Morgan, and perhaps deep down I never really believed my journey ended on this piece of rock.

As I nursed my glass of chardonnay and looked out on that endless oceanic abyss, I had to admit that Josh had been right about one thing. He didn't know me at all.

29

Detective Rebelo returned early the next morning. I'd tossed and turned in our bedroom, unable to sleep, and as far as I knew, Josh never left his study. The insistent buzz of the doorbell brought us both into the center hall entryway.

"Josh, Beatrice. Do you mind if I come in?"

"That depends," Josh said brusquely. His eyes were swollen and shadowed, and a rough salt-and-pepper beard sprouted along his normally clean-shaven jawline. "Is this official police business? I noticed that police car was out there all night. What the hell is that about, Thomas? You know we didn't do anything."

Rebelo said, "It was about protection, nothing more."

Josh sneered. "Bullshit."

Rebelo puffed out his chest. "I can make it more official by moving us all down to the station. Is that what you'd prefer?"

Josh grunted, but he moved aside to let Rebelo in before leading the way to the kitchen. Waving his hand dismissively, Josh said, "Coffee?"

"Sure," Rebelo said, as though the confrontation in the foyer had never happened.

"Beatrice?" Josh asked without looking at me.

"Please."

Rebelo settled at the kitchen table, and I sat across from him. We remained silent while the coffee brewed, and it wasn't until Josh placed three steaming mugs down on the table that the detective pulled a small notebook from his pocket.

"I need everyone's whereabouts between two and five yesterday afternoon."

"So much for civility," Josh said.

Rebelo glanced up from his notebook. He looked from Josh to me and back again. "Would you rather we do this individually at the station?"

"No," I said, glaring at Josh. "I was at the beach early in the day. Briar Hill State Park."

Rebelo scribbled that down. "Kind of cold for the beach."

"It was a sunny fall day, and I wanted to be outside."

Rebelo took a long sip of coffee while scrutinizing me over his coffee cup. "Anyone with you?"

"Grace Harding."

One of Rebelo's thick eyebrows shot up. "The waitress at Casey's?"

"Yes. She's a friend."

Rebelo said, "And she can confirm this?"

"Yes."

"Where did you go after leaving the park?"

I thought back to the heated words between Grace and me, to my anger at finding out she knew about Josh and Carly. "I sat in my car for a while. Then I drove around. Eventually I came back here."

"You just drove around?"

"Yes."

"More 'alone time,' Beatrice?"

"As a matter of fact, yes."

Rebelo tapped his notebook. "Anyone see you?"

"I stopped for coffee at Starbucks sometime after three. Otherwise, lots and lots of tourists in cars."

Rebelo frowned, wrote something in his notebook, and circled it. When he was done, he turned his attention to Josh. "And you? Where were you between two and five yesterday afternoon?"

Josh took a deep, audible breath. "You know full where I was because you saw me."

Rebelo said, "I was only there for a short time, Josh. I need to hear it officially from you. I need to make sure all the letters are crossed and dotted. You know that."

"Of course." Josh ran a hand through his hair. He looked at me, then down into his coffee mug. "I was with Carly at the hospital. We were with Oliver."

"For that entire time?" Rebelo asked. "From two until five?"

"Yes, for that entire time. Then I came here and found Maya knocked out on the kitchen floor. And now can you tell me why the hell you're here questioning us when this maniac is still out there? Marcus is in danger—you of all people know that. Oliver could be in danger still. Another child could get snatched. There is something seriously wrong happening in Cape Morgan, and you're wasting your goddamn time questioning me and Beatrice."

"I need you to calm down, Josh."

I placed a hand on my husband's arm, and he shrugged it off. "I am fucking calm, *Thomas*."

Rebelo's face turned pink. "We have our people, the state police, the FBI, local volunteers all searching for Marcus. No one wants to catch this person as much as I do. But facts are facts, and the fact is that both kidnappings seem to connect to you." Rebelo's skin flushed from pink to deep crimson. More softly, he said, "We can do this individually if you'd both prefer."

"She knows about Oliver," Josh said quietly. "She's known for a while."

Rebelo's body stiffened. "Is that true, Beatrice?"

I nodded.

"Let's take this into town." Rebelo's tone left no room for argument.

* * *

The grilling went on for well over an hour. *"How long have you known your husband was unfaithful?" "Have you stalked Carly and Josh?" "Do you resent Oliver?" "Did Maya know you knew about*

Josh?" "*Where were you at such and such hour?*" Rebelo's questions were a transparent effort to decide whether I was a crazy, jilted wife capable of taking her anger out on innocent children or just a victim of a terrible love triangle. I answered as truthfully as I could. My fear, of course, was that he would take it further.

I was sitting in a conference room, sipping watery coffee and trying to stay composed, when a uniformed officer knocked on the door. Rebelo left the room, and when he came back, he let me go.

"Do you need anything else from me, Thomas?"

"No, Beatrice. Not now." The furrow between his eyes had deepened, and he was ruthlessly smoothing his mustache. "You and Josh can leave."

"Did they find Marcus?"

"Not yet."

Confused about Rebelo's sudden shift, I found Josh waiting for me outside the station. We walked to his Volvo together, each of us lost in silent thought. Once we were inside the car and the engine was running, Josh finally acknowledged me.

"Do you know why they let us go?" he asked.

"Because we're innocent."

"Because while we were sitting inside there, someone delivered another doll. This time it was left on the seat of Maya's daughter's car."

I didn't know what to say, so I said nothing at all. I wasn't surprised—the doll was the perp's disgusting calling card. I just hoped the pattern would hold, and Marcus would be returned soon.

I said, "If the doll was in her car, then the kidnapper knew which car was hers. He or she was following her."

Josh nodded. "Or they waited near her apartment for her to park by her home. Small town. Not much privacy."

"For a place without privacy, this kidnapper is sure good at hiding."

Josh bowed his head. "Or maybe they're hiding in plain sight."

It took me a long time to answer, and when I finally did, I hated the pleading in my voice. "I didn't take these children, Josh. Whatever Rebelo may think about a woman scorned, I would never do that. You have to believe me."

"I know." Josh stared out the window. When he turned toward me, he had a certain steeliness in his tired, forlorn eyes. "I'm sorry, Beatrice," he said. "For everything."

I blinked back unwanted tears. "I always hoped maybe you would come to your senses. I kept waiting for it to be just a midlife fling."

We sat in silence until I couldn't stand the sound of my own breathing anymore. I stole a glance at Josh. He seemed so very sad and so very far away.

"Josh?"

"Don't, please." He twisted in his seat. Drops of rain hit the windshield, and I watched them snake across the glass. "I want a divorce."

"Please don't do that. Not now, in the midst of this. Let's take some time to talk and think—"

"It's time, Beatrice." He sighed. "It was time years ago, even before Carly."

"How can you say that?" The tears were streaming now, hot and cruel and relentless. I pressed a fist to my lips. "We were happy."

"Were we? I fell in love with your beauty and your kindness. You came into my life at just the right time—this mysterious, vivacious stranger who somehow made me believe I could be a young man again." He swallowed, caught me watching his hands, which were trembling in his lap, and he clasped them together. "I realize now how blind I was."

"How can you say that? After all we've built together. Expanding the firm, growing the Wicker Foundation. Ross Island."

"That's just it—those are *things*. There's something hard in you, Beatrice. Something unknowable. I don't know quite how to describe it. You latch on to what you want, and you don't let go, consequences be damned. I was one of the things you wanted, I think." He shrugged. "At some point, maybe that changed. Even if it didn't, just wanting all of this, this life we have? It's not enough. We're missing something deeper, Beatrice."

"That's not fair." Only I knew it was.

"You can stay on at the foundation. In fact, I want you to complete the Ross Island project. It's your project, your vision." He glanced out the driver's side window. "We'll figure out a way to work together."

We sat there for what felt like hours, not talking, just listening to the sound of the rain pelting the glass. *We'll figure out a way to work together.* I wasn't so sure.

*   *   *

Later that day, we both joined a community search for Marcus. Once again, I found myself on the beach at Briar Hill State Park, this time with Josh beside me.

A cold drizzle misted the air, and the ocean breeze was harsh and stinging. Despite the tension and the weather, a strange sort of pressure had been released from my shoulders. One secret out there, at least. Losing Josh hurt, but this little taste of honesty was welcome.

As we walked side by side along the sand and dunes, I pictured little Marcus as I'd last seen him. He'd been an infant then, and Maya had invited Josh and me to his christening. He'd been so small and helpless. Why had Elizabeth and Gabriel targeted him? Because they thought they could hurt me by hurting Maya? Maya and I weren't close—although they wouldn't know that. Because they wanted to frame me? They could have chosen times when I had no alibi, but they hadn't. Because they wanted to circle in on my life, getting closer to me each time—tormenting me, warning me?

That sounded like them. Hadn't they always acted unpredictably to keep me unbalanced? They wanted me to be scared. They wanted me to flee, just as I'd had to twenty years ago.

One member of our search party stuck a red flag in a dune, marking the spot where a brass keyring had washed up on shore. It was an irrelevant, insignificant item—we all knew that—but we were hungry for some small victory.

The townspeople of Cape Morgan were wearing down. I saw it in their hollow eyes and vacant expressions. Looking over their shoulders, worrying about their kids, wondering who was next—it was all taking its toll. They could only sustain this for so long. But I knew Gabriel and Elizabeth had infinite patience. They could play this game forever.

As we headed back to the parking lot, I felt the weight of someone's stare. I glanced back to see Josh's intern, Julianna Kent, watching us from behind. She looked away quickly when I caught her eye. We were a curiosity now. The couple at the center of the tornado destroying Cape Morgan.

If they *were* circling, like vultures who become braver with each go at their prey, who would be their next target? I glanced over at Josh, whose hands were red and chapped from the icy, damp air. He was focused, applying the same dogged drive to the search as he did to his job and his golf game.

Would they go for him next?

Or would they come straight for me?

30

THE HOUSE ON Dove Street that had once felt like a safe haven now seemed suffocatingly, relentlessly empty. Maya, released from the hospital, was staying with her daughter in town, and Josh was staying with Carly and Oliver, so I wandered the halls alone. My first night solo, I drank an entire bottle of chardonnay and fell asleep on the couch. My second night, I graduated to vodka and passed out on the bathroom floor in a pool of my own vomit. On the third evening, I left.

I hadn't been back to Ross Island since the storm. I took my car this time, and the first thing I noticed as I drove over the bridge that connected the island to the mainland was the change to the outer structure of the big house. The ramshackle, dilapidated line of additions that loomed from above had been reduced to rubble. The rear of the house was already boarded up, and piles of construction materials sat unattended and covered with heavy plastic tarps.

The sun had started to dip beneath the western mountains, and in the hazy gloom, the house looked misshapen and foreboding. I'd come prepared this time, though, and I pulled two sleeping bags and pillows from the trunk of the car and trudged up the path to the porch. I'd work in the upstairs rooms, clearing out the remainder of Miles Ross's belongings. Grace had agreed to help me, and once Grace arrived, the two of us planned to sleep in Frida's cabin. We wanted to catch the sunrise over the ocean before she had to leave for work in the morning. Sunrise from the eastern edge of the island was a sight to behold, and right then, I needed a sight to behold.

The workmen had locked the house up tightly, and the exterior and interior lights were off. I fumbled my way around the wall, found the switches, and let out a breath of relief as the sweet golden glow flooded the interior. I threw my gear on the floor in the gallery area, pulled a flashlight and notebook from my purse, and started up the sturdy U-shaped staircase that led to the second floor. The wooden steps squeaked, their tops worn and warped from years of use. Windows faced the stairway, and the last vestiges of light glistened through the old leaded glass, casting shadows along the high center ceiling.

Miles Ross had used the room at the end of the hall as his own, and because his body had been found there, it had been the first space we'd cleaned out. Like the rest of the house, we'd had to wade through stacks of books, papers, neatly arranged garbage, and piles of old clothes. Miles had been a hoarder, but there'd been a method to his mess. Other than a few family portraits and a dozen first-edition books, we'd discarded or donated nearly everything.

The upstairs contained more than Miles's bedroom, though. There were seven more rooms that needed to be sorted, cleaned, painted, and decorated. The second floor of the inn was going to serve as offices as well as two en suites for visiting speakers and artists. I'd volunteered to go through the few boxes that sat stacked along the rooms' walls, a task I was anxious to finish. It would at least keep my mind occupied.

I passed Miles's old room and paused to look inside. It was the smallest of the second-floor bedrooms, a mere hundred and forty square feet, plus a small, attached bathroom. According to his nephew, Eli, Miles had lived in this room for twenty years, rarely going beyond these walls and even more rarely venturing off the island.

The room itself was an anomaly. The floors throughout the upstairs—random width white pine that had mellowed to a pumpkin-colored patina—were etched with scratches and gouges, but the scars were absent in Miles's room. The floor and walls and even the bathroom were immaculate. Despite the organized chaos in which he'd lived, Miles's room, unlike the rest of the house, had been well maintained.

I moved on to the next room, which shared a wall with Miles's bedroom. This one was considerably bigger. The floors were scuffed and water stained, and the doors to the small closet at the back of the room—an afterthought to the original construction—gaped open. Inside were stacks of plastic bins, each filled with papers.

I pulled the first of these bins out and placed it in the middle of the bare floor. Expecting Ross family records and mementos, I'd brought a garbage bag and a box so that I could sort trash from things we could frame and keep—or give to Eli. The top box contained old photos, mostly 1970s- and 1980s-looking snapshots of what looked like Ross family gatherings. I set these aside.

I was well into the third box when I heard a shuffling noise coming from the direction of the steps. "Up here!" I called.

When Grace didn't respond, I stretched my way to standing and went back into the hallway. "Grace, I'm upstairs!" Still no response. I'd left the front door open for her. If someone had driven across the bridge, I'd see the headlights, but I thought perhaps I'd been too engrossed in the containers' contents to notice.

I hustled down the steps, calling her name. No answer. A quick check outside told me I'd been hearing things. Her car wasn't in the lot. *Ah, well.* I was walking back upstairs when I heard the sound again. *Shuffle, shuffle, thump.* I sprinted up the rest of the stairs. The noise was coming from Miles's old room. It was faint but unmistakable. *Shuffle, shuffle, thump.* I pushed opened the door, half expecting a ragged doll or a dress form or an angry spirit. Instead, the room was empty.

A mouse, I thought. The little guy was probably scurrying inside the walls. I made a mental note to have Louis set some humane traps.

You're letting the stress get to you, I told myself. Old houses were noisy. I returned to the second bedroom, but I couldn't shake the feeling of being watched.

*   *   *

I was in the middle of the sixth box when I heard the front door open. This time when I called Grace's name, she answered.

"Up here," I yelled.

I followed the sound of Grace's progress up the stairs. She popped into the room, her purple-dyed hair tied back in a short ponytail. She carried a brown paper bag in her arms. The scents of ginger and garlic wafted ahead of her.

"This place is seriously creepy at night," she said as she placed the bag on the ground. "Veg lo mein for you, chicken for me. I figured it was the least messy thing we could eat while sitting on a floor."

"Thank you." I put the storage container's lid back on and pushed it aside, grateful for the food. My stomach was growling. How long had it been since I'd had a full meal? I couldn't remember. Perhaps shedding the weight of Josh's affair had brought back my appetite.

Grace settled in across from me, sliding down onto the hard floor with an ease I envied. She handed me a cardboard box of lo mein.

"Thanks for the invite." She stabbed at a piece of chicken with a set of chopsticks. "It's been a day."

"Coming right from work?" I pointed to the round stain on her gray top.

"Ugh." She wiped at it with a napkin. "I'm a hopeless mess." She looked up, and, catching me watching her, smiled shyly. "I was painting. I'm working on a new project."

"Oh! Tell me about it."

"It feels silly talking about it in the midst of what's going on in town. You know—that poor child." She put down her chopsticks. "Are you feeling any better today?"

"I'm worried for Maya and her grandson." I told Grace about Maya's fall and her trip to the hospital. "We're all worried."

Grace nodded. "Understandable. Marcus's mother must be a mess. And poor Maya."

"I know." I swallowed some noodles and placed my chopsticks on the top of the container. "Maya hasn't been around all week. I think she blames us."

"That's silly. Why would she blame you?"

"The police believe that whoever is doing this is targeting me and Josh. Maya works for us, and Oliver—" I swallowed, still not ready to say the words aloud. "Maya has to feel like her loved ones have been caught in the crossfire."

Grace shook her head. "Listen to yourself, Beatrice. I'm sure she doesn't blame you. How could she? You no more wanted this to happen than she did. And anyway, who would possibly be targeting you or Josh?"

"Maybe someone who was turned down by the Wicker Foundation."

"Why not go after Josh directly if that's the case? Hurt him, not these kids?"

I shoved my half-eaten food away, no longer hungry. "Because whoever it is wants to play with us. They don't just want to hurt him; they want to ruin our life together. Take away his business, the respect he's earned in Cape Morgan. Maybe even hurt the town itself." *Destroy our marriage, however tenuous. The life I've built here. My sanity.* I balled up a paper napkin and tossed it across the room, in the direction of the trash bag. It missed completely. "We're being punished, and they've done a damn good job."

Softly, Grace asked, "Do you think Marcus is in danger?"

I took a deep breath. "I don't know. Oliver was returned unharmed, but if someone is crazy enough to pull a second kidnapping, then they could be demented enough to hurt Marcus."

"I heard from one of my customers at the diner that the FBI is involved."

"It's a nationwide hunt, Grace. As I understand it, the FBI is always involved when a child is taken. Either this person is a very good criminal, or they're very lucky." *Or they're very, very used to hiding.*

I busied myself cleaning up the small dinner mess before returning to the storage containers I'd pulled from the closet. I didn't want to think about Marcus or the FBI. Not tonight.

"These all seem to contain Ross family materials. The foundation technically owns this stuff, but anything super personal I'd like to return to Eli Ross, the prior owner's nephew. The rest we can discard once we catalog what we find." I pointed at the notebooks and the pile of white plastic containers. "We have five more containers to get through in here. I haven't looked in the other bedrooms. There may be more."

Grace nodded. "Happy to help."

I pulled the next bin in front of me, opened the lid, and stared at the contents. Old bills, postcards, a few photos. I sighed. "I have to wonder if Miles Ross ever threw anything away."

* * *

We finished sorting through the containers in the first room by ten. "Onward to the next?" I asked. It was nice to be doing something productive that had a concrete outcome. Each box we cleared felt like a small win.

"Sure." Grace's face looked drained of color. "Whatever helps."

"Are you okay?"

She rubbed her stomach. "I don't think the chicken agreed with me."

"Why don't you go home? I'm fine here, and—"

Grace held up a hand. "I'm okay—it'll pass. You shouldn't be alone, and I'm enjoying this. Let's keep going."

Like the second room, the third room needed repairs. The wood floors were scuffed and warped in spots, the gold striped wallpaper hung in tattered strips, and the windowsills were peeling. A mildewy board sat propped against one wall. The room stood empty except for an old walnut bureau. The scent of mildew was overpowering, and we hung back in the doorway.

Grace stepped into the room first. She wrapped her arms around her chest and let out a low moan. "Do you feel the chill?" she asked as I stepped beside her.

"It's definitely colder in here."

"They say this place is haunted."

"You don't say." I smiled and pointed to the windows, around which there were gaps. "I think it's poor construction, not ghosts." I figured those gaps were the only thing keeping the mildew smell at bay. "The ghost stories should help bring in customers, though. Everyone loves a good ghost story."

Grace didn't smile. "I don't like the feeling I get up here, Beatrice."

"You look a little pale. Maybe it's the chicken you're reacting to, not the house."

Just then, there was a deep rattling sound from somewhere below us. Grace jumped. I felt my breath constrict in my chest before letting out a sharp laugh. The rattle was a familiar sound, one I'd grown up with.

I said, "It's only the old radiators gurgling away. Come on. We're scaring ourselves."

Satisfied that rooms three, four, and five were completely empty, we moved on to the room at the end of the hall. This room was the largest on the second floor. At six hundred square feet, it contained a large dressing room and its own bathroom. The floors were scratched and rutted in spots, and the wallpaper was peeling in broad, stained strips, but the windows were airtight.

"No ghostly cold spots," I said, spinning around in the center of the room. "Just a perfect, warm location for a guest suite."

"*Uh-huh*. Let's finish up so you can show me your mural. The sooner we leave this part of the house, the better." Grace frowned. "I really don't like it up here."

I wanted to laugh, but one look at her surly expression and I knew she wasn't joking. It wasn't like Grace to be this sensitive, so I chalked her fears up to stomach upset and recent local events. With everything going on in Cape Morgan lately, a little late evening jitters were understandable.

I said, "I don't think there's much to see in here. You check the bathroom, and I'll check the closet."

While Grace rummaged through the cabinets in the dated bathroom, I went through each of the built-in drawers in the dressing room. The generous walk-in was lined from floor to ceiling with shelves and drawers. They had been painted a soft avocado green and were adorned with ornate glass pulls. Other than a moth-eaten scarf and a few random socks, the drawers were empty.

"Anything?" I asked Grace when she reemerged into the bedroom.

"Not a thing."

We were about to leave when Grace pointed to a particularly large crack in the wall in one corner of the room. "What's that?"

"Poor maintenance."

She walked over to the wall and ran a hand along its surface. A few feet from the crack was a circular hole. The edges of the hole had splintered. The hole looked like a bull's-eye. "I don't think this is a crack, Beatrice." She put her finger inside the hole and pulled. After a few tugs, a section of the wall opened up. "Oh, wow."

"Oh, wow" was right. Inside the wall was a hidden closet.

"Stinks like mothballs." Grace waved her hand in front of her face. "And look at those cobwebs. Come, take a look."

The closet contained a safe—unlocked and open—and two vintage metal file boxes. Each file box was lightly dented and discolored, and each had a latch and a small metal handle.

Grace said, "Someone must have forgotten this stuff was here. I bet it predates the last owner."

I took a photo of the find. "Miles lived here for over seventy years, his father and mother before that. This stuff could be old. Very old—late 1800s old." I made some notes in the book. "Want to see what we have?"

"I do," Grace held her abdomen and leaned over. "Right after I use the bathroom."

Worried about her, I said, "The closest working bathroom is in Miles's old room. I'm afraid it's the only one up here that's functioning."

While she was gone, I took out the first box. It was heavy. The latch was rusty, but it opened with some serious coaxing. I pulled up on the lid, and eventually it gave way too. Inside were piles of old documents—black ink on parchment-like paper, now yellow and brittle with age—some from the late 1800s. I dragged out the second box. More of the same, although the documents were younger—1900s, some with photographs attached.

I sat on the floor and had begun to sort through the documents when I heard a door slam and then Grace scream. I scrambled to my feet and darted into the hallway. I found her in the hall, staring down the stairway, her shoulders heaving.

"Grace? Are you okay?"

Grace pointed toward the steps. "I saw someone down there. I swear I did. Tall, thin." She gulped. "I couldn't see his face."

"*His?*"

Grace nodded, pressed her fists to the sides of her head. "A man."

I went back into the bedroom in which I'd been working and grabbed a heavy metal flashlight and my phone. "Stay here." I walked down the steps slowly, listening intently and watching for movement. The lights were on downstairs, but I didn't hear or see anything—just the dusty, empty rooms.

"Hello? Who's there?" I called. My voice echoed in the cavernous gallery space. "Hello?" I called again, forcing a confidence I didn't feel. With the metal end of the flashlight raised over my head, I moved from room to room, throwing open cabinets and closet doors, until I was back where I started—by the central stairway.

I locked the front door, checked the back entryway. There was nowhere else on that floor to hide.

I climbed the steps, looking back over my shoulder every few seconds. I half expected to feel that bitter coldness against my skin or icy hands grabbing my neck, but I made it to the top unscathed. Grace stood in the hallway, her back to the wall. She looked dazed.

"Hey," I said. "Are you okay?"

"I know what I saw, Beatrice. He was right there, on the steps."

"Well, if someone was here, they're not here now. I looked everywhere."

Grace rubbed her hands the length of her arms. "I'm sorry, Beatrice. I don't think I can stay here tonight. My stomach is off and—"

"And this place is creeping you out."

She nodded before dropping her chin to her chest. "I'm really sorry."

"It's okay." I kept my voice bright. "I'm just sorry you're not feeling well. I'll walk you out."

Her eyes widened. "You're not going to stay here alone."

"I am, indeed. The faster I go through these old documents, the faster this place will be ready so people like you will have a place to paint."

"Do it in the daylight, Beatrice. Not now, when it's dark and you're by yourself."

I shot her a reassuring smile. "You're letting the ghost stories get the best of you. Besides, I'm not in the mood to go home. There's nothing for me there."

A pause. "Come to my place."

I reached out and touched Grace's hand. "You're sweet, but you worry too much."

"I don't." Grace scowled. "Oliver was found here. You told me someone broke in last week. Whoever is doing this is still out there. They're targeting you and Josh—you said so yourself."

I started down the steps toward the front door. "I'm fine, Grace. This place is a second home to me. I don't believe in ghosts, and as you saw, there is no one here."

I walked quickly, my back to Grace, so I couldn't see the fear and disapproval in her eyes. We went out into the brisk night air, and I walked her to her car, the flashlight still in my hand.

"Go in and lock the door," Grace said once her engine was running. "I'll wait."

I hugged her through the window, then ran back up the path to the front door. After a quick wave, I ducked inside, double-locked the door, and watched as Grace drove across the bridge.

As I ambled back up the grand staircase, I sensed a change in the old building's atmosphere. The air felt charged, and the creaking, settling sounds of its mature skeleton clanked around me. I pulled my sweater tight and hugged the flashlight to my chest. The slap of my sneakers against the wooden treads echoed against the high ceilings. I focused on my breathing, willing my heart to slow down its pace.

I told myself there was no one here—no stalkers, no ghosts. Grace's fear was contagious.

I was simply alone.

31

Try as I might, I couldn't relax. I went from room to room, checking closets and bathrooms. I found no tall, lanky mystery man, no evidence of ghosts. I stood for what seemed like an hour at the bottom of the attic steps contemplating whether I wanted to check the third floor as well. I hadn't been in the attic since we had first toured the old house. I knew I needed to go up there again eventually, but Grace's warning to do this in the daylight seemed a good idea.

But if someone was up there, I needed to know.

I took the attic steps one at a time, mindful of weak treads and the broken banister. At the top of the stairs, I turned the knob slowly, my pulse pounding. I told myself there was nothing to fear. I'd seen the face of my devils already—there could be no real surprises lurking here.

I pulled the attic door open. The air was stale and dusty, and I choked and coughed on my own breath. A corded light hung near the entryway, and I pulled the rope. Three bare bulbs illuminated the middle of the vast attic, but it was enough. As my eyed adjusted, I braced myself for what I might find.

But the attic remained largely empty.

I saw an old-fashioned child's rocking horse, its metal cradle rusty, the horse's once-festive paint chipped and faded. I saw a few cardboard boxes stacked in the center of the room. I saw an old bureau and a half dozen dining room chairs. Other than that, just dust and cobwebs. No tall man hiding. In fact, there was nowhere for him *to* hide.

I pulled the light cord and closed the door, my hand shaking violently on the knob. I made my way back down those steep steps, still on edge, still waiting for Grace's ghosts to push me from behind.

* * *

Eventually, I sat on the floor in the large bedroom, with the intention of sorting through the boxes once again, but the joy of discovery had disappeared with Grace's exit. At 11:14, Grace texted me that she'd gotten home. I felt a slight loosening in my neck muscles. At least she was alright.

The air upstairs was still old-house chilly despite the gurgling radiators, and I decided to take the metal boxes downstairs. I lugged them in two trips before returning upstairs to close the doors and turn off the lights. The thought of traipsing across the island to Frida's Cottage in the dark made my throat ache, so I set up my sleeping bag and arranged the pile of pillows in the gallery. The chimneys weren't fixed and inspected yet, so I couldn't light a fire, but at least the ground floor was warmer. I'd sort there until I grew tired enough to sleep.

I began with the box that held the older materials. I placed the residents' records in one pile along with any corresponding photographs, and the assorted bills and receipts and other materials in a different pile. The records read as one might expect: terse summaries with words like *hysteria*, *melancholy*, and *epilepsy* were common, as were prescriptions for rest, sun, medication, and even bloodletting. I reminded myself that this island had been billed as a sanctuary, not a hospital, but despite the fluffier sound of the word *sanctuary*, these records certainly seemed medical in nature *and* official.

One resident caught my attention. Her name was Maria Luisa Dennison, and her file consisted of one sheet of paper and a photograph dated September 19, 1894. The woman looking back at me from the photograph was pretty in a somber way. Her black hair was parted in the middle and pulled behind her head in a smooth bun that stuck out in gentle puffs behind her ears on either side of her head. Her full cheek rested lightly on an elegant hand, and her long, slender neck rose from a cascade of ivory lace. Her eyes captivated me. Sable colored, mournful, and heavy lidded, they seemed to be pleading silently and longingly with the photographer—in sharp contrast to the rest of her emotionless face.

Her records were meager. Some notes about diet, the need for fresh air and routine, a diagnosis of melancholy. Underneath the paragraphs describing her treatment were the words "deceased, October 31, 1895."

She had lived here for more than a year and died at the youthful age of thirty-one. I stared at those pleading eyes, wondering what it would have been like to be a resident here for so long. Had she checked in voluntarily, looking for a much-needed respite from her everyday life—or had her parents or husband or brother shelved her here like a worn or unread book? Had she been one of the women to jump from the cliffs to her death? Or had she passed some other, more mundane way—misdiagnosis of disease, tuberculosis, the flu?

I would never know.

The rest of the first metal container read the same way. Short histories, diagnoses, directions for treatment, discharge dates, a few photographs. I was able to follow the fashion of the time by the way the women's hair and dress changed as I got down toward the base of the metal box. At the very bottom were two files, both women, seemingly related in some way. Sarah and Mary Bolton, ages twenty-five and thirty-nine. There were no photographs, but their medical notes described them as temperamental and obstinate. They'd arrived on June 12, 1938. Both were diagnosed with hysteria, Mary with deviant sexuality, and young Sarah with recurring mania. They'd died on June 17, 1938.

Two names, two diagnoses, two deaths—all within a week.

I placed their papers in the "to keep" pile and put my head back on my stack of pillows. The house had gone quiet, as though in mourning for these women, and I breathed deeply into the silence. I was, of course, fictionalizing these women's lives, but I imagined them to have been held against their will, holed up on the island and forced to undergo whatever treatments were in fashion at the time and ordered by men. *Sexual deviant.* Maybe the Boltons were lesbians; maybe that was a label given to two unmarried cousins who simply didn't want or need the company of men.

My thoughts wandered to Elizabeth Webb, the way I would catch her looking at Gabriel, and the way I would catch her glaring at me. Looking back, I knew she would have done anything for him. Indeed, she *did* anything for him, believing, as I once had, that he was being persecuted. Elizabeth had made the ultimate sacrifice, letting Gabriel dictate her life and her son's life, and even allowing him to take a second lover to be used for his cause. Only I'd had a limit. Ashamed as I was of my past, I also knew that she, apparently, had no limit.

Perhaps Sarah and Mary Bolton had possessed more courage than either Elizabeth or I did. Perhaps they, too, had escaped a controlling man, an uncle or husband or grandfather, and in doing so, the world had labeled them crazy.

Outside, an owl hooted. The sound roused me from my thoughts, and I opened the second box. On top of the pile of ivory-papered records was a photograph of a little girl. Unlike the other pictures, this one was more modern and in color. It had been taken in the 1980s. The child had wild, curly brown hair, an upturned nose, and stormy green eyes. Her sweater-clad arms hugged the neck of a large goat. Her bright red galoshes, worn over brown tights, were mud covered, as was the edge of her frilly pink dress. On her head was a crooked tiara. My temples began to throb. I squeezed my eyes shut and opened them quickly. The photograph was still there. Hands trembling, I picked it up and turned it over. On the back I read: *Emma, 1986—at the farm.*

My breath came in gasps, my pulse pounded in my ears. My mind spun with the implications of what I'd found. How had a photo of me, taken so long ago and hidden in a box along with my family albums, gotten into this box of dead women? This photo had been in the Sparrow, West Virginia, farmhouse. Had they kept it all these years and then placed it in Ross House when they left the dress form? Impossible. I would have seen it when I first opened the metal box upstairs. Plus, the closet itself had been undisturbed, the inside musty, the door nearly painted shut.

Someone had put this in here later.

Someone tall and lanky. Grace had been right. We hadn't been alone.

I had been out of the house for five minutes to say goodbye to Grace. That meant someone could have remained in here the entire time, hiding in the basement or some other dark corner when I, in my arrogance, had searched the place. They must have gone upstairs while I was outside or in the attic and tucked this in the metal file box on the floor in the big bedroom. They'd been listening to me. They had heard our conversation.

That could mean they were still here.

I could call the police. I should call the police. But calling Rebelo now would only cast more suspicion on the connection to Josh and me. There was no way I could tell him about the photo without disclosing it was a picture of me. No, it was too big a risk. And simply calling him to report a sound or a suspicion was out of the question—he would label me hysterical. I could hear Rebelo's admonitions now: *"Why would you stay there alone in the first place, Beatrice? Are you crazy?"*

The only thing I could do was go back to Dove Street. Slip out of this house and leave my stalkers alone here with the night sounds and the roaming ghosts.

32

I AWOKE IN MY car to the sound of my phone ringing insistently. I was huddled under my sleeping bag on the back seat. I needed to pee. The caller identification said it was an unknown caller with a Boston area code. I hit "Accept."

"Beatrice? Evan Blume."

I rubbed my eyes, cleared my throat. My head throbbed, and I fought to think through the painful fog. "Yes?"

"I found your people."

I sat up, feeling a tiny tickle of something I recognized as hope. "And?"

"We should discuss it in person. Can you come in today?"

"Can't you tell me over the phone?"

Blume was silent for a moment. "The bottom line is that your people are dead."

"Dead? I don't understand."

"Elizabeth Mansfield and Gabriel Webb are dead."

"That can't be right."

"Please come to my office. There's more, but I'd rather tell you in person. I can meet you somewhere closer to you, if that's better."

Dead? Impossible. I struggled to find my voice. "No, no, your office is fine. I can be there by noon."

After I hung up with Blume, I rang Rebelo. I wanted to tell him about the inn's visitor last night. Only Rebelo didn't pick up. I left him a message and headed inside.

* * *

Josh showed up while I was drying off after my shower. I heard him rustling around in his walk-in closet, and I entered our room, naked and damp, with just a towel wrapped around my torso. He glanced up at me, wide-eyed, before focusing his full attention on his loafer-clad feet.

"Beatrice—"

I smelled the lavender. It emanated from him like the stench from a dumpster. Revolted, I grabbed my robe. "What?"

"I don't think you should be in here like that—"

"You don't think it's appropriate for me to be undressed in your presence? Does it feel like cheating?" I pulled on a pair of black pants and a black turtleneck sweater from my closet. They seemed like mourning clothes, and I felt like I was in mourning. "Yeah, cheating sucks."

Josh shook his head. "I don't know what to say to you."

"'Hello' is a good start."

"You don't need to be so—"

"Agitated? Angry? Sensitive?" I pulled a pair of black boots from my closet. "How would you like me to be?"

"Civil."

I sat on the bed and pulled on my boots. Josh watched me, looking like a confused little boy.

Softly, I said, "How's Oliver?"

"Is that really what you want to know?"

I zippered my boot. "That's the only thing I want to know."

"You're making this harder."

"Believe it or not, I do care how he is. He's your *son*." I paused midway through the second boot. "Ask yourself whether it's me making this harder. Did you expect me to welcome your new woman with open arms? Bow down gracefully to the younger generation?" I stood up, feeling rushed. I wanted to get to Blume. "It's complicated and you know it."

"You've known for months, years maybe. You don't get to act like the victim now."

I checked myself in the mirror. Same long, curly brown hair, now peppered with gray. Same strong jaw and broad cheekbones—handsome, maybe, but never classically beautiful. Same faint, jagged scar over my left eye, a leftover from an argument with the large goat in that picture. But other than my reflection in the mirror—a liar, surely—nothing about me seemed remotely the same.

"Listen to yourself, Josh. I've known for years, and that makes me the bad guy? You've let it go on for years. I think you win that award."

"Beatrice—"

"I need to leave, and now isn't the time for this conversation." I sighed, turned. "I don't want to fight with you. You win, okay? I'll give you a divorce. Is that what you want to hear? Go back to your baby and his mother. Drown in her damn lavender bodywash, for all I care. I'll move past the anger eventually, and someday I'll remember why I made the choices I did. You will never understand them, though. I can't expect you to." I grabbed my purse and keys off the bureau.

"Where are you headed?"

"To take care of something I should have handled years ago."

*   *   *

Blume met me at the door to his office and led me back to his desk. He seemed preoccupied by something on his phone, and he left me sitting in his office for nearly ten minutes while he made a call in the reception area before returning. His absence gave me time to think about what he'd said. Gabriel and Elizabeth dead? How could that possibly be?

When Blume returned, he sat opposite me, sucking on a red Tootsie Roll Pop and regarding me with guarded curiosity.

"Who did you say this man, Gabriel Webb, was?"

"A nuclear physicist."

"And how did you meet him?"

"With all due respect, Evan, I'm the one asking questions—remember?"

Blume steepled his hands, sighed. "Elizabeth and Gabriel are dead, as I told you. She died fifteen years ago. He died almost two years ago."

"That's impossible."

"Why is that impossible?"

Because they're kidnapping children from my town, I thought. *Because they're planting warnings on my property and undermining my sanity.* Instead, I said, "You'll just have to trust that I have reason to believe they're still alive."

"Well, they're not." Blume passed me two papers, both printouts of death certificates.

While I studied the materials, I felt a tightening in my chest. They certainly *looked* official. I said, "As I explained in the background materials I gave you, both were good at living off the grid. They assumed different aliases. He was a nuclear physicist running from the government. Paranoid, angry. Maybe these death certificates have been faked."

Blume's eyes narrowed. "How do you know this man was a nuclear scientist?"

"Because he told me."

Blume shot me a sardonic smile. "And I have land to sell you on Mars."

I felt my face heat up. "What are you trying to say?"

"Is this the Gabriel Webb you knew?" Blume passed me a photograph.

I swallowed, hard. His hair was gray, and the skin around those chiseled cheekbones had started to sag, but those perpetually amused, cruel eyes were the same. "Yes."

"That's Gabriel Robert Webb. He was sixty-one when he died of a self-inflicted gunshot wound to the head."

"He killed himself?"

Blume nodded. "Gabriel Webb wasn't a nuclear physicist, Mrs. Wicker, and he didn't have a doctorate. He was an IT specialist with an associate degree from a community college in California."

"That can't be right. He knew things about nuclear energy and fusion. He had proof—diplomas, papers, notes. He worked for

Michigan State. I saw a news article with his photograph." I shook my head, felt the queasiness in my gut. *If not them, who?* "Whatever you found, it's wrong. It has to be."

"I have no reason to deceive you."

"Is it possible they faked their own deaths?"

"Possible? I suppose. Probable? Hardly. Everything was in order, Mrs. Wicker. I'd bet my professional reputation and the few belongings my ex actually left me on the fact that he's dead."

"This just doesn't make sense. Not a scientist? He was so confident, so convincing."

"He was a con man." Blume pointed at me with his lollipop. "Your man had a history of petty crimes. Check cashing fraud, shoplifting, embezzlement. He *did* work for Michigan State, as an IT specialist in their science and engineering departments. That was years ago. From what I could tell, he was fired for using their systems to embezzle funds."

"Did you confirm this with the university?"

"Of course." Blume slid some papers across to me—lists of towns and addresses, dates of jobs. "Here's what I was able to piece together with public information."

All those discussions, all those notebooks, all those stories. Could Gabriel have been full of crap about all of it? I thought of our nights together. His gentle lovemaking, the way he made me feel like the only person in the entire world who understood him. The only person who mattered. Had he been lying that whole time? *Wake up, Beatrice,* I thought. *He set you up for a felony.* Why should I believe he would have been honest about anything else? The notebooks, the diplomas, the letterhead—all of that could have been faked. Even the photograph from that university dinner hadn't actually stated that he was a chair of any department. Maybe it had simply been a departmental dinner to which he'd been invited.

I said, "He told me he'd changed his name. Was that at least true?"

"Gabriel Webb had aliases, yes, but nothing official. He never actually changed his name, if that's what you mean, which is why I was able to find him pretty quickly. He moved around a lot, though.

Looked like he and his wife were grifters. Didn't stay long wherever they landed. He'd take odd jobs as a mechanic or farmhand or janitor, and she very occasionally worked as a waitress or clerk."

"Where did their money come from?"

Blume shrugged again. "Those odd jobs? Handouts? More embezzling perhaps? I couldn't say."

I thought of those monitors, the blinking lights, the sophisticated computers. Was it possible he'd been using them for something other than monitoring nuclear power plants? I glanced down at the papers Blume had compiled. The towns corresponded with my own movements—at least for the first few years. After that, I had no idea why Gabriel went where he went, but their nomadic lifestyle made sense. I flipped through the papers, skimming the dates. "His last known address?"

"Seattle."

"And Elizabeth? How did she die?"

"Brain aneurysm. She was only thirty-eight. Death certificate listed Atlanta as her place of death."

Atlanta. I'd lived in Atlanta as Kira Gray sixteen years ago—until Elizabeth and Gabriel found me and started again with the dolls and the notes and the threats. I got out of Atlanta quickly. It sounded as though Elizabeth had never left. Her death wasn't a surprise. Elizabeth had always seemed so sickly. Her death in Atlanta was a shock, though, especially because Gabriel had continued their quest for revenge on his own.

"Where is she buried?"

"I don't know. There was no obituary. Maybe wherever she was born? I can't even say for sure she *was* buried." Blume cleared his throat. "Elizabeth was unwell. I don't just mean the aneurysm. She had a criminal history going pretty far back. Petty theft, shoplifting, identity theft, stalking. She was ordered to get counseling on multiple occasions."

"Before or after she married Gabriel?"

Blume stared at his computer monitor. "Before. After, she was quiet. Lived on the down-low, as we say in the business. Maybe Gabriel reformed her."

Hardly. I closed my eyes, pictured Elizabeth as she was all those years ago. Her mental health issues were also no surprise, although I wondered whether I would have noticed them had I been better trained, less zealous, less infatuated with Gabriel. A small part of me felt sad for Elizabeth. Despite what she and Gabriel had done to me, dying in a strange city, so full of hatred and spite, seemed a terrible way to go.

I said quietly, "Elizabeth and Gabriel had a son. He was included in the materials I gave you."

"*She* had a son. Gabriel adopted him when they married. Lucas David Webb."

Luke. I pictured his slight, almost frail build. The high cheekbones and dark, questioning eyes. His small kindnesses. "He looked like Gabriel. I originally assumed they were related, but Luke did tell me Gabriel was his stepdad." Afraid of the answer, I said, "He's dead also?"

"Actually, he's the reason I wanted to talk to you in person. He's MIA."

"You couldn't find him?"

"There's information out there on the parents. Not a lot, mind you, especially for her, but the son remains a mystery. I found birth records, some evidence he was involved in the social services system in a place called Sparrow, West Virginia, as a young teen—which you had already told me in your notes—and then when he was around fifteen, just *poof.* It's possible he was homeschooled and kept under the radar, but he would be in his thirties now, and normally there'd be information out there on the Web—social media accounts, address listings, credit information, the normal stuff people should pay attention to but don't."

"Did you try searching under Elizabeth's maiden name?"

"Mansfield? I can, if you'd like."

"Is it possible Luke is dead?"

"I suppose. I checked death records, though, as well as missing persons databases." Blume leaned toward me, plucked a green lollipop from a jar on his desk, and started to unwrap it. "It could also mean he managed to change his name or he left the country or who knows. But I can tell you he doesn't have a criminal record or a listed address or social media accounts in his name." He plopped the lollipop in his mouth.

"Then he's probably out there somewhere, living under the radar. Is that a reasonable deduction?"

Blume's eyebrows shot up. His lips were stained green. Under different circumstances, I would have laughed. "It's possible, especially if he uses cash and knows how to manage the system."

I felt welded to the chair beneath me. All this time, I'd thought it was Gabriel and Elizabeth who'd discovered me in Maine and renewed their chase, but she'd been dead for years, which meant that during the additional time I'd endured their sick blood sport, it had only been Gabriel hunting me. *Why did he stop?* I wondered. And where was Luke?

Luke.

I felt a sudden, urgent coldness spread from within my body. Gentle, sweet Luke with his love of cats and his childish code books and his tree fortress. Could it be *he* was my tormentor? Could it be that Luke was snatching children, sending me warnings?

"Mrs. Wicker, are you okay? You look like you've seen a demon. Do you want some water? *Mrs. Wicker?*"

I looked up, blinked. "Can you keep searching for Luke Webb?"

"Of course." Blume stood. "Seriously, Mrs. Wicker. You don't look well at all. I don't think you should be driving."

I touched my hand to my face. *Luke?* The thought stabbed at me somewhere deep and tender, somewhere I had believed was immune to further hurt. "I'm fine," I said. "Just find Luke. Please."

CHAPTER

33

ROSS ISLAND SEEMED benign in the daylight. I drove across the bridge and into the parking area, my chest aching. Luke as the kidnapper? The thought had plagued me as I drove up Route 95 and back into Maine. I just couldn't reconcile the young boy I'd worked and lived with twenty years ago with a man who could kidnap *children*.

It didn't make sense.

And yet someone was stealing toddlers, and that person was leaving those dolls and had planted the dress form and my child-hood photograph. I sat in the car, staring at the old house. The construction crew were working on the exterior of the house, trying, I knew, to button up the framing before winter. They looked like large ants, crawling around the exterior of the big house. I couldn't see the cottages from my vantage point, but they would be empty—vacant and largely forgotten until the spring. What a wonderful place for someone to hide.

I didn't fully believe Luke, the Luke I had known, would hurt a child, but a lot could happen over twenty years. If there was a chance it was Luke—and who else could it be?—Rebelo should know he was looking for a man.

There was at least something I could do. I rang Rebelo's cell phone, but my call went to voicemail. Disappointed, I left a message asking that he return my call.

I climbed out of the car, up the path, and started toward the cottages.

"Mrs. Wicker? *Mrs. Wicker?*"

I turned to find the foreman looking at me from across the churned-up lawn. "Yes?"

"Do you want to walk through our progress? It'll be time for another payment installment soon, so I'd like you to understand what we've done and what's next."

It took me a moment to understand what he wanted. All I could think about was Luke. "Not now, Louis," I said.

"Tomorrow then?"

"Sure." I started my trek again and stopped. I called after the foreman. When he turned toward me, I asked, "You've lived in Cape Morgan your entire life. Do you know any history about this island?"

The foreman shrugged. "Not really. Just the old ghost stories. Stupid stuff."

I nodded, disappointed. I was thinking of the metal boxes full of old records, thinking of Mary and Sarah and the women who had died here. I heard him say my name again, and I turned around, a mean, biting wind blowing my hair behind me.

He said, "There's a professor in Portland. Herman Hanes. My daughter knows him. Fascinating fellow, she says. Medical guy. Kind of a legend around here. Anyway, he knows all the local history."

"Herman Hanes." I made a mental note. "Thanks."

"Are you okay, Mrs. Wicker?" The foreman asked. "I hope you don't mind me saying, but you look kind of pale."

I hurried up the path, away from him and his unwanted concern. "I'm fine, Louis," I said over my shoulder. "Just a little tired."

* * *

I was sitting in Frida's Cottage, gazing out at the surly sea, when Rebelo called me back. "There's another search for Marcus underway," he said. "Thought maybe you'd be there."

"I didn't know. When and where?"

"The dogs picked up a scent near Bruner Wilderness Preserve. It's getting late, but you could still make it. Search parties are underway."

I knew the area. It wasn't far. "That's good news, I guess. I'll head there now. Thanks, Thomas."

"That's not why you called me," the detective said.

"No, it isn't." I tore my eyes away from the view and walked toward the door and my mural. In the daylight, the mermaids seemed even more agitated, even angrier. "When Grace and I were at the inn last night, she thought she saw a man roaming around the place."

"Did you see him?"

I hesitated. "No."

"Any evidence of a break-in?"

"No, but the door wasn't locked, so—"

"Seriously? With everything going on, Beatrice, don't you think—"

"Thomas, please. I wasn't going to tell you for exactly this reason. But with everything going on, you should know. I can't prove it, but I believe her. There were . . . certain noises. I chalked them up to old house aches and pains, but maybe it was something more sinister." I squeezed my eyes shut, hating to contribute even more to the goddamn palace of lies.

"I'll send an officer over to check it out."

"The construction crew have been here all day, and I checked the place last night. I think he's long gone."

"Then why are you telling me?"

"Because it may be worth another search. And because Grace said he was tall and thin and male, and that could be helpful information." I paused. "In the search for Marcus's kidnapper, I mean."

Rebelo grumbled something unintelligible into the phone. I imagined him jotting a few things in his ubiquitous notebook. He sounded exhausted, his voice rough and low. Sleep was probably not a priority. "I did tell you to call me if you noticed anything unusual."

I was about to hang up when Rebelo said, "Did Josh mention the drugs?"

"Drugs?"

"The doctors at the hospital found nothing wrong with Oliver. No cuts or bruises. No signs of sexual abuse. He had an evil case of diaper rash, was a few pounds thinner, and was a little clingy with his mother, but in general he seemed to be in okay shape. The labs came back positive for certain sedatives, though."

"The kidnapper kept him drugged?"

"They must have kept him quiet by keeping him sedated. Removed the need for any other kind of . . . restraint."

"Are you looking at doctors, pharmacists, nurses? The type of people who would know what to give a child?"

"Of course, although that stuff is available on the internet for anyone to find. Wouldn't take a medical professional."

I paced back toward the window. Below, about a half mile from the island, a lobster boat was running parallel to the coast, its cabin painted a cool Mediterranean blue. I watched its frothy wake snake across the water. "Why are you telling me this, Thomas?"

"Because that little boy was found on Ross Island. There's a lot of empty, abandoned real estate up there. If someone wanted to keep a baby in, say, an old cottage, and that baby was properly medicated, no one would notice."

"Your people searched the island three times, twice for Oliver and once for Marcus. They found nothing. By all means, feel free to search again."

Rebelo cleared his throat. "There's no need to sound defensive, Beatrice. I'm telling you because you're there. Josh tells me you've been sleeping on the island on and off. If someone *is* roaming that place, someone who has the knowhow to reach it by boat, it could be the same someone who is kidnapping children. It could be the same person Grace saw inside the inn." He paused. "I'm simply asking you to be on the lookout."

I am. "I will."

"I'll see you at the preserve?" Rebelo asked.

"Yes, Thomas. I'm on my way."

*   *   *

The search at Bruner Wilderness Preserve had begun more than an hour before, but the scene there was anything but orderly.

A small park about twenty minutes from town, the preserve was beloved by tourists because of its miles of intertwining walking trails. It was easy to feel far from civilization even if you were fifteen minutes from downtown Portland. Just as the wooded paths lent themselves to reflective nature time, they were also a haven for youthful transgressions, sexual exploits, and the occasional drug deal. Locals had a love–hate relationship with the park, which had no noticeable security. The local police just plain hated it.

I counted two ambulances and heard the wail of sirens as emergency vehicles traveled the access road toward us. Dozens of civilians wearing orange safety vests were making their way from the trails toward the parking lot, many carrying flashlights and red flags on posts. Some chatted animatedly among themselves; others walked with an air of somber concern. I spotted Josh by the ambulances with Maya, and I headed in their direction.

Maya's face was tear stained, her eyes bright and locked on Josh. He turned when he saw me but quickly returned his attention to Maya. He took her hand. To me, he said, "Volunteers found Marcus. He was in one of the utility sheds off the access road, sound asleep."

"Is he okay?"

Josh squeezed Maya's hand. "Yes. We were asked to clear the area so the experts could tend to him."

Maya eyed me warily. "My daughter is with him."

The parking lot was buzzing with activity. Volunteers huddled in groups. More police arrived and began directing traffic. I heard the whir of propellers and looked up to see a helicopter hovering overhead.

"They must be flying him to Boston." Maya's almond eyes rounded in panic. She pleaded with Josh: "Why Boston? That's not good. Find out something, please."

"Don't worry, Maya. This is good news. He's safe. I'll see what else I can find out." With a curt nod to me, he left.

"I'm sure it's just a precaution," I said to Maya. "The helicopter, I mean."

Maya pressed a hand against her throat. The other held a cell phone so tightly that her knuckles were white. She turned away from me without speaking.

"Maya?"

Maya spun around. Her black eyes blazed with hurt.

"Maya, what's wrong?"

Maya's mouth worked, but nothing came out.

"Maya?"

"For ten years, I've tried to reach you, Mrs. Wicker. *I mean Beatrice.* No matter what I did or said, you rebuffed me. I tried to feed you, and you didn't want the food. I tried to look out for you, and you pushed me away. I tried to make your life easier, and you wanted none of it." She shook her head. "When Oliver was taken, I thought, 'This is it. She will finally confide in me, see me as someone on her side.' But you didn't. Still, you pushed me away."

"Maya, I always thought—" But even as I tried to form the words, I realized how hollow sounding they would be. Perhaps I'd transferred my guilt and shame onto my relationship with Maya, believing she was the judgmental one when all the while I was judging myself.

Maya held up a thick-knuckled hand, fingers swollen and bent from arthritis. "But this"—she motioned toward the helicopter, now in the process of landing on the access road—"this affected *my* family. While I was busy attending to yours, a monster invaded mine."

I stood there, mute and still. She was right, of course. Not in the way she thought, perhaps, but right, nonetheless. "Maya, I'm sorry for what you're going through. For your family's pain."

Like that, the anger seemed to drain from her body. She nodded a few times. "I know." She slumped forward, grabbing the ambulance to steady herself. I reached toward her, but she shook her head. "I'm fine." We both looked up to see Josh coming toward us with Thomas Rebelo.

Maya said, "I will be giving notice to Mr. Wicker. Once this is over, once Marcus is home safe, I will be leaving Dove Street."

"We'll be sad to see you go."

"I'll be sad to go. I've been with Josh for many years. But times change. People move on."

Rebelo joined us by the ambulances. "Ms. Delapena," he said to Maya, "Marcus seems to be fine. They're taking him to Boston as a precaution. Your daughter will travel with him."

Maya's quiet sobs racked her body. Josh put an arm around her and began to lead her away, toward his car. I was about to follow when Rebelo held me back.

"Do you have a minute?"

"Sure."

Rebelo led me through the maze of cars and emergency vehicles to a small, shaded area near the picnic pavilion. "We think Marcus will be okay. Like Oliver, he has some diaper rash and was clearly drugged. Time and tests will tell. We found him in the same condition—wrapped in a tarp, only this time the tarp was stuffed with leaves and hay."

I waited for more, for the reason he'd singled me out.

"Have you ever seen this?" Rebelo handed me a clear plastic evidence baggie. "Don't open it. Just look at the image."

I turned the Polaroid over. It was a photo of the dress form with the plaid miniskirt and blouse I had worn all those years ago. The same dress form I had found in the annex at the inn. Across the Polaroid were pasted the words "E knows" in letters cut from magazines.

I fought to stay present, calm, but panic and reason were at war, and panic was winning. "No," I said finally. "Should I? 'E' could be anyone."

Rebelo looked at me pointedly. "True. But all things considered, I thought I would ask."

I stared at the photo again. The backdrop was different from the annex. Plain boards, like those you'd see in a New England barn—which did nothing to narrow down the location. I shook my head. "I'm sorry I can't help you." I handed him back the evidence bag.

Rebelo brushed his mustache down with his finger. "It was worth a try."

"Maybe there are prints on the photo or some fibers or hairs in the leaves and hay? Anything the police can use to find this guy?" I sounded ridiculous—of course the police would search for forensic evidence—but I needed words to fill the void, and that was all my frantic mind could come up with.

"We're trying. Whoever it is seems to know the area—what's surveilled, what's not. They seem to float about unnoticed. Not so easy to do in a small town."

"Maybe they don't live here," I said. "Maybe it's a vagrant, someone invisible."

"Perhaps."

I watched Rebelo walk back to the circle of law enforcement agents and wondered once again where Luke could be hiding.

* * *

I was climbing into my car when I felt the weight of someone's stare. I turned just in time to make out a man sitting in a large, black GMC truck. He wore an orange volunteer vest, and in that second, I remembered his name as Len someone or other—the dock worker I'd met at Oliver's search party. But something else was niggling at the back of my mind, and as he pulled into the line of traffic leaving the park, I realized what it was.

That truck had also been parked at the diner over a week ago. Then, like now, I'd found him watching me. I snapped a photo of his license plate. Perhaps it was time for another call to Evan Blume.

* * *

I slept in Frida's Cottage that night, awash in moonlight and accompanied by my vengeful mermaids. My dreams were vivid and terrifying, and I awoke at first light, sweaty, sore, and stiff. Gulls shrieked. I watched the birds flying overhead through the picture window, swooping down and circling the jagged cliffs, fighting over whatever fresh kill had washed up on the rocks below.

34

WITH MARCUS SAFELY at the hospital, the town seemed to take a momentary, collective sigh of relief before the reality of the situation sank back in. The kidnapper was still on the loose. All area schools and daycare had increased security, and the added tension was visible on parents' faces. Cape Morgan tried to go back to normal, but we had lost a sense of what normal even was.

At the Wicker Foundation, Josh and I danced around one another, vacillating between frigid politeness and open hostility. Our professional battle lines had been drawn—I would remain in charge of the Ross Island project, and he everything else—but our personal lines remained muddled. In the meantime, Frida's Cottage became my home, and I settled into the four-hundred-square-foot space with as few belongings as I could manage.

By Monday of the next week, when no more children went missing, I had convinced myself that Luke had played all his moves. To be on the safe side, in addition to paying Evan Blume for his searches, I used my own funds to have Frida's Cottage quietly wired with security cameras, and I put alarms on its doors and windows. No one knew about the added measures. If Luke returned with more memorabilia from my prior life, I didn't want the foundation involved. And if someone from the foundation was involved, I didn't want them to know about the added security.

But I couldn't stop looking over my shoulder.

Thankfully, the Ross project kept me busy. As September drew to a close, and the tourist season stretched toward its climax, our window of opportunity to get work completed at the Ross House dwindled. Interior work could happen over the winter, but the cold weather, snow, and harsh winds from the Atlantic would prevent much exterior work after November. My job was to get the interior ready for the construction crew to switch gears once that bad weather hit.

The containers of old medical records presented a problem, though. Most of the records, logbooks, and correspondence were dated before 1950. Most of these women were dead, but some were the mothers and grandmothers of people who still lived nearby. My inclination was to donate the materials—there was so much rich information about women's mental health treatment in the nineteenth and twentieth centuries—but the foundation's lawyer said HIPPA protections could still apply. Her suggestion was to talk to a researcher at the university first, and she gave me the name of a professor in Portland, one Herman Hanes. It was the same professor our foreman had mentioned. I made an appointment for that afternoon.

While I loaded the containers in the car, I thought about the picture of me as a child, stuck on top of the other documents. There were probably fingerprints, smudged or gone now from my repeated handling. And that was what my stalker was banking on—that I would be too afraid to say anything, to do anything.

He knew me well.

The thought angered me, and that sense of rage stayed with me on my trip into Portland. I parked in the visitors' lot, loaded the containers into a cart, and walked up the pathway to the professor's office. Hanes met me at the door. He was a short man, with small wire-rimmed glasses and cropped white hair. His face was slightly skewed to the right, and when he spoke, the muscles on the right side of his face hung slack.

"Stroke," he said as we walked back toward his desk. His right hand was curled into a claw, and his right arm was cradled to his side. He walked with a pronounced limp. "It's a damn good thing I'm a lefty or I'd be in trouble. This is five months of physical and occupational therapy. I'm getting there." He sat, smiled, and said, "What have you brought me?"

I explained who I was and what the foundation was doing. "These documents were found during construction."

"I'm well aware of the project. A little jealous, truth be told." He held out his left hand. "May I?"

I placed the first file box on his desk. Hanes put on a pair of gloves, carefully opened the box, and removed the documents, placing them gingerly on the desk in front of him. He took a few minutes to scan them, taking particular interest in the physician letters and the photographs.

A smile played with the edges of his lips. "These are something."

"I thought they might be of interest to the university."

"They are, of course, but their medical nature gives me pause."

"Yes," I said, "our lawyer thought it might."

Hanes sat back down and motioned for me to so the same. "The problem is the pesky medical privacy laws. Many believe they would apply in a situation such as this, even though most of these documents are much older than the law itself." He picked up a photo, turned it over, and said, "Of course, certain online websites put up similar material. It really becomes a question of how much trouble you want to go through."

"What do you mean?"

"Researchers who want to share this type of information—meaning make it open to the public—have to decide whether to redact names and other identifying data. Alternatively, they could simply bear the risk that someone could sue, or they could decide to keep the material private altogether."

"And what would your organization do?"

"I'm not sure. Perhaps we would redact names and any identifying information. That would seem the safest route." Hanes looked up at me, meeting my gaze with an intelligent, blue-eyed one of his own. "I guess you have the good fortune of working at the old sanitorium. Rumor is it's haunted."

I smirked. "Gee, no one has mentioned that."

"Ah, a cynic." He laughed. "No ghosts for you?"

"Not of the supernatural variety."

Hanes's smile was mischievous. I liked him on the spot. "Come now. There must be something good you can share. I heard the prior owner died in his bedroom, right there on the second floor. Maybe his spirit still haunts the old place."

"Actually, Professor, I was hoping you could shed some light on what happened to the women there over the years. I've heard you're very knowledgeable about the local lore."

"Is that so?" Hanes sat back. The action seemed to pain him because he grimaced and repositioned himself before saying, "That island has quite a history, but I'm sure you know that. It was a so-called 'relaxing' retreat for women suffering from mental maladies." He put finger quotes around *relaxing*. "Such an unfortunate euphemism for what went on there."

I thought of Sarah and Mary Bolton and the unfortunate ending to their *relaxing retreat*. "And what was that?"

"If you've read these files, I'm sure you got a flavor for it. The retreat was started innocently enough. The owner's wife suffered from postpartum depression, and he put her up there so that the sea and fresh air could help her heal. Of course, as we know now, with time often comes hormonal balance, so sometimes women's postpartum issues resolve on their own. He credited his wife's improvements with the island, and a business idea was born."

"Then he hired staff and built the cottages and the bridge."

"Yes." Hanes skimmed through ones of the sheets in front of him. "Hysteria. Sexual deviation. *Idiocy*. That's a particular favorite of mine."

"I heard that women killed themselves there."

Hanes's eyes narrowed, his mouth tightened. "I imagine more often than was disclosed. Pretend for a moment you're a strong-willed woman in an unhappy marriage. Maybe your husband is a bore, but maybe he beats you or sleeps with other women or rapes the maid. What recourse do you have? If you fight back, you could be labeled as difficult or hysterical. Then shut up in a place like that. Even in a nice place like the retreat, you would have no say over your own treatment."

"That's awful."

Hanes nodded. "Maybe they're shoving sunshine and eggs down your throat, but maybe it's antipsychotic drugs with serious side effects. Or maybe even electric shock."

Horrified, I asked, "Was that done there?"

"They had treatment rooms, but I can't say with certainty what treatments were received." He lifted a stack of records. "Maybe the answer is in these files." Hanes grew quiet. "We can't go back and fix things for these women or the thousands of others who suffered across the nation, but we *can* learn from our mistakes."

I wasn't so sure we, as a species, were always so good at learning from our mistakes.

"What are you going to do with these?" Hanes asked.

"I could burn them."

"You could, indeed, but I hope you won't."

I rubbed my temples, thinking. On one hand, these women's families might want the option of claiming these documents. On the other hand, would these women really want their families— two, three generations later—to know the humiliations they'd endured? Once you knew someone in a certain way, learning new information—especially after their death, when they had no ability to set the record straight—could be damaging. In my brief perusal of those documents, the only women mentioned were the residents. I didn't think they should have their histories told only by those men who'd treated them and written the reports. Seemed to me they deserved more say in their own stories.

I said, "Would you like them for the university, Professor?"

"Very much."

"They belong to the Wicker Foundation. I'll need their permission to donate them, but if they say it's okay, we'll make arrangements to get them here. I would, however, request that anything that will be public be redacted."

"Of course. And thank you, Mrs. Wicker."

Hanes walked me to the door of his office. As I was leaving, he held out his right hand and I shook it. His grip was limp, his hand clammy. "I need the practice, or so my therapist says." He gave me a tight smile. "I know you and the Wicker Foundation will do every-thing you can to preserve the history on that great island."

"We're trying."

"And if you see a ghost—"

"I'll send them your way."

Hanes laughed. He looked past me, into the wind-swept court-yard beyond. "My family has lived in this area for generations. We've seen the changes—to the people and the landscape. Some-times, though, the more things change, the more you realize noth-ing changes."

"Are we still talking about the island and psychiatry, Professor?"

Hanes winked at me. "We're talking about life, my dear. Just life."

* * *

Evan Blume called me as I was driving to the foundation office. "I have a hit on the license plate you sent me."

I pulled over into a Shaw's parking lot so I could write the infor-mation down. "Go ahead."

"His name is Leonard Ronald Kalchik. Thirty-three years old. Lives in South Portland. Was employed as a dockworker. Lost his job in April, and now he does janitorial work part-time at a hospital."

Hospital. Drugs. Both boys had been drugged. I knew it was a tenuous connection, but still, it was worth looking into.

"Does he have a record?"

"Assault, battery, one DUI. Angry, drunk bar stuff. The guy is a hothead."

"You're sure Leonard his real name?"

"Are you wondering whether this man is your Luke Webb?"

"Maybe."

"Seems unlikely, Mrs. Wicker—"

"Please, call me Beatrice."

"Beatrice." He paused, and I heard the sound of a lollipop clicking against his teeth. "I'll do some more digging into his background, but I would be very surprised if this man is your fellow. In the meantime, do you want his address?"

I jotted down his street address, and hung up, disappointed but not surprised that Blume didn't think Len and Luke could be the same person. Luke had never been hotheaded, and whoever was carrying out these kidnappings was methodical, not impulsive. It didn't sound like forethought and planning were Kalchik's strengths.

But if Len Kalchik wasn't Luke Webb, why did he seem to be following me?

35

L EN KALCHIK AND his role in the kidnappings continued to plague me through the night and into the next day at the office. I was deciding whether to drive by Kalchik's home when I looked up to see Julianna Kent, Josh's young intern, standing over my desk. Her long blond hair was pulled away from her face with an oversized tortoiseshell barrette, and she was wearing dark denim jeans with a white blouse and red blazer. She sat on the edge of my desk uninvited, crossed her arms, and sighed.

"Yes?"

"The gallery, Beatrice. We were supposed to go over my plans, and, well, that got disrupted."

Ah yes. The gallery plans. It seemed like months ago that she and I were supposed to meet, and instead she'd found Oliver outside Georgia's Cottage. "Right. Sorry about that."

"I was thinking we could review the plans today. That will give me time to go through the material with Josh and make any changes you want before we hand the plans to the contractor."

"Good thinking."

Julianna stood up from my desk. She was tall, with broad shoulders and slim hips—a model's build—and she clearly knew the power of her appearance. It wasn't her looks that captivated me; I envied her confidence. Perhaps if I'd had that confidence as a young woman, my life would have been much different.

"I took the liberty of scheduling us for a few gallery and festival tours as well," she said. "I hope that's okay."

My mind had wandered, and I asked her to repeat what she'd said.

"I thought we could discover some local artists and include their work in and around the Ross House. You know, visit a few Maine galleries, scout for talent at local fall art festivals, that sort of thing." She shrugged. "As a scholarship kid myself, I love the idea of giving someone a boost, discovering new talent." She slid a file onto my desk. "Here are my initial thoughts. I included a color schematic as well."

I glanced down at the file, thinking of new talent. *Grace.* This would be a perfect way to give her some exposure. I said, "I didn't realize you were a scholarship kid."

Julianna smiled. "Oh yeah. That's how Josh found me— through a program that helps young women in traditionally male fields, like architecture. I owe him a lot."

"Josh can be very selfless when it comes to helping young women."

If Julianna heard the sarcasm in my voice, she didn't let on. "He's the best. Everyone here is. We never stayed in one place long as a kid. You're lucky to live in a town like Cape Morgan. I saw the way the town supported the families affected by that kidnapper. I never had that kind of community growing up."

I took a fresh look at Julianna. The jeans were generic, the blouse and jacket off the rack from some big box store, the jewelry fashionable but inexpensive. My first impression had been of another rich girl taking advantage of mommy and daddy's connections to improve her career, but I'd been wrong. It wasn't the first time my first impressions had led me astray.

Just look at Maya. And Luke.

I decided I *would* go see Len Kalchik after work. Perhaps I'd been mistaken about him too. And then I rang Grace. Julianna was right—I had the power to give a starving artist a real start, and no one deserved a leg up more than Grace. I tried her number twice. Grace didn't pick up. *She must be working,* I thought, and left her a message.

* * *

I was studying Julianna's proposed plans for the main area of the art gallery when the door to my office opened. Seth came in holding a set of files and a poster board. He put the files on my desk and leaned the poster board on a bookshelf against the wall.

"When you have a chance, take a look at the layout for the fundraiser brochure and let me know what you think."

I glanced up at the posterboard. On it, Seth had arranged the pages of the brochure in order, with photos of the main house and several cottages juxtaposed against renderings of the final product. Pictures of Frida's Cottage—without my mural—and the island views were also included.

"There are spaces for you to include written information as well—on the history, the types of artists you hope to attract, and whatever else you think is pertinent."

Seth's demeanor was crisp. I figured he was still annoyed about our last interaction, when I had refused to go with him to the island. I thanked him for his work. The brochure *did* look good, and I didn't need more tension in the office.

"No problem." He moved closer to my desk, and I smelled woodsmoke and musky aftershave. "What are those? The gallery plans?"

"Julianna's renderings. Would you like to see them?" I handed him the file and watched as he perused it.

I placed another document in front of Seth. "Here is the color scheme. As you can see, Julianna provided a few alternatives. We can go traditional—with warm whites and creams. Or we can use one of the more colorful options."

Seth placed all the materials on my desk and bent over the proposals. Julianna's color palettes were attractive, and any one of them would work.

"I'm thinking of the traditional," I said. "I rather like the crisp whites against pumpkin flooring and the artwork we'll bring in. Let the color in the art be the focal point."

Seth handed the materials back to me. "I like the maritime palette. Seems appropriate for the location, and the blue is pretty."

I took a second look. The maritime palette had the walls done in a soft yellow, with ocean hues of green and blue as accents. "The blue doors *are* nice. Very nautical."

Seth's gaze locked on to my own. "'Haint blue. It will keep the ghosts at bay too."

I blinked, fighting to keep my face expressionless. All the while, shock coursed through me. Seth left my office, but as I watched him go, I thought of Luke. Was it possible?

Seth was in his early thirties. He was tall and handsome, with cheekbones that could slice a tomato. Wouldn't I recognize him, though? Maybe. But it'd been twenty years since I'd seen Luke last, and the skinny boy I'd known would have become a man. Seth certainly knew the ins and outs of the Ross Island project, and my schedule was just an admin conversation away. I picked up the phone and called Blume.

"Evan," I said, "I have one more person for you to check out." I gave him Seth's name.

*   *   *

At 5:14, I left the foundation and headed north, toward Portland. The address Blume had given me for Len Kalchik led me to the ground floor of a house in the Valley Street neighborhood. I pulled up in front of the building and killed the engine. A mix of homes, apartments, and professional offices lined Kalchik's street. His house was three stories, beige, and run down. An old wheelbarrow, rusty and broken, lay on its side in the front yard beside a small pile of overstuffed black garbage bags. An elderly man in gray sweatpants sat on the first-floor porch, watching me. He was so small and bent that I didn't see him at first. I waved. He didn't wave back.

Kalchik's GMC was parked on the street, cattycorner to the house.

I got out of my car and started up the stairs, heading for the door to Kalchik's apartment. "Excuse me," I said to the older man, "I'm looking for Len Kalchik. I understand this is where he lives?"

The elderly man used his cane to stand. With an annoyed glance in my direction, he shuffled to the door, opened it, and disappeared inside just as I reached the porch. I knocked loudly on the door, calling Len's name while I did so.

No one answered. Curtains moved in the window to the right of the doorway, and I tapped on the window glass. I couldn't see anyone inside, and no one responded to my additional knocks.

"*Damn,*" I muttered under my breath. But I couldn't force Kalchik to come out.

I'd try again another time.

* * *

Blume called me while I was pulling into the parking area on Ross Island. "I have some preliminary information on this Seth fellow. Ready?"

I cradled my cell between my chin and my shoulder while I rooted around in my purse for paper and a pen. "Go."

"Pretty straightforward. Seth Andrew Miller, thirty-two. He's originally from Arkansas. Moved to Maine a few years ago."

That didn't sound right. "From Arkansas to Maine?"

"Based on what I could find."

"Any college education, Web presence, that sort of thing?"

"I didn't want to dig too deep if it was a dead end. Costs you money, you know, so next steps are up to you."

I put the notebook down on the passenger seat and unfastened my seat belt. "Seth told me he moved here from New York City. He said he had a big job there but preferred small-town life."

"Hmm." Blume shuffled around some papers. "Based on public records, he's lived in Maine for three years now. Before that, he was in Little Rock."

"Are you sure?"

"I am. Let me give you his address. You can check it out yourself."

I listened while Blume rattled off an address in Gorham. "I thought he lived in Cape Morgan?" Although I couldn't remember if Seth had told me that or whether I had just assumed that's where he lived.

"Look, I haven't followed this guy or anything. Surveillance is extra, if that's what you're looking for—especially because you're two hours away. I'm telling you his registered address is Gorham, Maine. Do you want me to dig further?"

"I'll call you back," I said. "My husband will have his résumé somewhere. I'll want you to confirm it."

"Sure thing."

"Anything more on Len?" I asked before hanging up.

"Not yet. Looks like he lives with his father. I'm digging around a little. Still don't think he's your guy."

I thanked Blume and ended the call. Len Kalchik might not be a good fit, but Seth was interesting. Grace's description of him returned to me: a man who was always playing a role. If Blume was right, not only had Seth lied about his background, but he'd been living in Maine—not New York—these last three years. That meant he could have been watching us from afar. Learning, planning, waiting.

Luke would have had years to learn the art of deceit from his parents, and who knows what kind of rage they'd ignited and fueled in a teenage boy. If Seth *was* Luke, he was playing his new part well. But not well enough.

Haint blue.

It was a slip. A small slip—but as Rebelo had said, often a small mistake was enough.

The sun had set, and dusk was quickly turning to night. I gathered my belongings, pulled out my flashlight, and climbed out of my car. The exterior of the inn was unlit, and cloud cover would hide the moon. I took a deep breath, steeling myself for another evening alone. One thing was certain: I wanted to be in the cabin before the darkness was absolute.

* * *

Morning light painted the cottage in creamy yellows. The evening had been blessedly uneventful, and I stood up, stretched, and
stepped into the shower. The hot spray warmed me, and for the
briefest moment, I felt something akin to happiness. I could live
here. Maybe, just maybe, if I could get to Luke, convince him that
his parents' vendetta need not be his, we could let this all go. Oliver
was fine, Marcus would be fine. Luke could make his escape back
into oblivion, and I could stay here on Ross Island—a permanent
caretaker.

I stood naked at the picture window and stared out at the sea. A
lapis-lazuli sky, untouched by clouds, stretched out to the horizon.
The ocean was calm today, and I watched two seagulls bob on the
water. The clock read 6:44. The workers would be here in an hour,
but that gave me time for a quick swim.

Excited by the idea—it had been weeks since I'd swum in the
ocean—and energized by the sunny morning, I threw a robe on,
grabbed a towel, and slipped on a pair of flip-flops. The air outside
felt cool and refreshing. I nearly skipped my way down to the small
beach, and before I could talk myself out of it, I tore off my robe
and dove into the water. The first cold plunge stole my breath. My
bare skin prickled and tightened, and I threw my head back and my
arms upward, reveling in the sweet pain. I felt alive.

As my head crashed up through the water and into the air
again, I caught my breath, laughing out loud at the absurdity of it
all. A few more dolphin dives, and I was ready to get out. Too long
in this water and I'd be an actual ice cube.

The towel, heated lightly by the sun, felt rough and warm
against my body. I wrapped it around me and started to make my
way up the trail to the cabin, when movement caught my eye. It was
only a gray squirrel running from the cottage to a nearby tree, but
as I got close to the door to Frida's Cottage, I saw a bouquet sitting
near the walkway, propped against the tree.

Lavender.

A large, generous bouquet of English lavender wrapped with
a silver satin bow. Except the tops of the blooms were cut off so
that it was nothing but a macabre, mutilated bunch of stems. Even

without the flowers, its sickening smell funneled toward me, swirled and curled and coated my tongue until I wanted to yell and vomit and tear at my own face.

Fuck you. Fuck you. Fuck you.

The security footage showed nothing—the bouquet had been placed just out of its reach. Nevertheless, I knew damn well what this meant: he wasn't finished. What else could he take? My marriage was gone. The town was rocked to its Cabot Cove core. This island was becoming a prison. I had no one else for him to steal.

But I did.

Grace.

36

I CALLED GRACE THREE times, and each time it went straight to voicemail. I raced across town to the diner, but the manager told me grumpily that Grace hadn't shown up for work that morning or the morning before. I drove to her home, but her apartment was locked up tight, and her landlord wasn't home—hadn't been home for weeks. I had no choice but to call Rebelo.

I spoke quickly, my words tripping over themselves in muddled run-on sentences.

"Slow down, Beatrice."

I slammed my head against the seat of my car, forcing my mind out of its warp speed spin. "Grace is missing."

"Grace?"

"Grace Harding. The woman who works at Casey's." More quietly. "My friend."

"Ah, okay. I remember. And you think this is somehow related to what happened to Marcus and Oliver?"

"I'm sure of it."

Rebelo's tone changed. "Why are you sure of it?"

"Because she's my friend, Thomas. You said yourself that this person seems to have some obsession with Josh and me. First his child, then Maya's grandson, and now Grace."

"Grace is an adult."

"She's twenty-four. *Twenty-four, Thomas.*" I gulped at the stale air in my car. "What if he hurts her. He spared the babies, but a young woman?" I shook my head, pushing the thought away. "Please find her."

Thomas took his time responding. "Do you know whether she's absolutely missing, Beatrice?"

I explained that she hadn't answered my calls, nor had she turned up at work.

"When was the last time you saw her?"

I thought back to our last time together. It had been at the Ross House. The night of our Chinese dinner, when she saw the man in the stairwell. I gave him the date. "We had takeout at the island. She didn't feel well and left."

"Did she return home that night?"

"Yes. She texted me when she arrived."

"There you go. She had food poisoning. She's just recuperating."

"Her car's gone. She hasn't returned my calls."

"Then she went on a trip, Beatrice. She's an adult. She's allowed to move about freely. You're letting your imagination get the best of you."

I slammed my hand down on the dashboard. "She always answers my calls, Thomas. I'm telling you—something's happened."

"Get a hold of yourself, Beatrice. You sound hysterical."

"Because my friend is missing!"

"You seem awfully sure of this. What aren't you telling me?"

"Seriously, Thomas?"

"Listen to yourself. Grace is an adult. This kidnapper has been taking children. There was no pipe bomb, and that's the perp's MO. Look—" He paused, and I could almost hear him playing with his goddamn mustache. "If she's not back by tomorrow, I'll personally call the landlord to let us in, and we can check her apartment. Okay?"

I hung up. I was wasting my time with Rebelo. He'd already decided I was unstable, and nothing I said would be taken seriously. In a fit of resolve, I stormed up to the garage door that led to the

stairs to Grace's apartment. It was locked, and a few pulls told me
it wasn't going anywhere. I walked around the side of the garage.
There was a back entrance. It was locked too, but the metal handle
was broken, and the door flimsy and splintered. I looked around,
and spying a pitchfork on the ground by one of the abandoned
barns, I wedged it between the door and the frame and pushed
down. With my full weight on it, it eventually gave way. I went flying and landed on my hands and knees on concrete.

Good going, I muttered to myself. The garage smelled of engine
oil. I flipped on the light and meandered through a maze of sport-
ing equipment—paddleboards and rafts and oars and life jackets
and soccer nets and bicycles with flat tires—until I got to the steps
that led to Grace's apartment. Unlike the exterior entrance, the
door to her apartment was unbolted. I knew it would be—it didn't
even have its own lock.

"Grace?"

I flipped on the lights and searched room by room. It didn't
take long—there were only three. I checked the closet and the
shower. No Grace—and no sign of a struggle. Her paints were
stacked neatly on their shelf, her bedroom was free of clutter, and
her bathroom had recently been cleaned. Shoes were lined up
next to the door, and her umbrella was missing. A quick inspection of her small kitchenette was a different matter. A loaf of
bread sat on the countertop, the twist tie off. A half-eaten piece of
toast sat on a plate next to a glass of orange juice and a crumpled
paper napkin.

Grace was a neat freak. Clearly, she'd left in a hurry. She would
never purposefully leave her kitchen in this state.

Could Rebelo be right, and she simply went away somewhere?
I thought back to our recent conversations. I'd been distracted;
maybe she'd mentioned something, some trip, and I'd missed it.
But the kitchen mess . . . Grace would never leave food out like
that, not without a reason. Had someone tricked her into meeting
them, convinced her there was an emergency, and then abducted
her? I looked around for her phone. No luck. In fact, her purse,
keys, phone, computer . . . all were missing. But she'd left her art

supplies. If she'd gone away, she would have taken them. I walked back into her bedroom, and there, under the bed, was her lone red suitcase.

I took a deep breath. If Rebelo wasn't going to help, I was on my own.

* * *

A call to Joan, the Wicker Foundation administrative assistant, landed me a copy of Seth's résumé and confirmation that Seth was at work. The résumé stated he had a master's degree in photography from a small university in California and that most of his work experience was in New York City.

I sent the résumé to Blume and used the opportunity to drive out to the address Blume had given me. If I was right, and Seth was Luke, then maybe I would find Grace at his place. I pictured a cabin in the woods—somewhere spooky and isolated.

Instead, I found a small, pristine Cape Cod in a neighborhood of other neat Capes. The house was a blue clapboard colonial, simple and tidy, with a straight row of purple and white flowers out front and an actual white picket fence. A silver Honda Pilot sat in the driveway. I knocked on the front door and was met by an eager-looking woman wearing a pink polo shirt and pressed jeans.

"Yes?" Her expectant smile died as she took in my appearance. I'd left the cottage that morning without a thought for what I looked like, and I realized now how mismatched and disheveled I must appear. "Can I help you?"

I pushed my curls away from my face. "I'm looking for Seth Miller."

"And you are?"

I glanced around, saw the "Eat More Kale" sticker on the back of the Pilot, and said, "I'm from the local organic farmers' coalition. I was hoping to talk with Mr. Miller about doing some work for our organization's holiday calendar."

The woman's well-waxed brow crinkled. "I don't understand. What would my husband do for your calendar?"

"The photography."

She shook her head and started to back away. "Look, there must be some mistake."

"Your husband is a photographer, right? That's the only reason I stopped by."

"He certainly likes to think he's a photographer. He is always taking photos, but if you're looking for a professional—"

"Doesn't he work as a professional for the Wicker Foundation?"

More confusion twisted her delicate features. "He's the vice president of the Wicker Foundation, not a photographer. I mean, he could probably take some photos, if that's what you need, but I doubt he'll have time with the project he's overseeing right now."

"Project?"

The woman pulled her shoulders back, thrust her chest out. "The new art gallery on that island by Cape Morgan. Ross Island. Maybe you've heard of it? That's his baby." She grinned, clearly proud of her husband's accomplishments. "So you see, there's no way he'll have time for your calendar. Maybe we can make a donation instead? If you want to leave me your card, I can have him reach out to you."

I nodded, momentarily speechless. Seth as vice president? Seth as the brains behind the Ross Island project? "To be clear, we're talking about Seth Andrew Miller from Arkansas, right?"

The woman clapped. "Well, that's why the confusion." Scents of cinnamon and cloves wafted from within the house and mingled with something acrid and burning. Woodsmoke rose from the chimney and disappeared into the blue sky above. "My Seth is from California. Wrong guy!" She turned toward the burning smell. "My cookies are burning. Thanks for that." She closed the door in my face.

Whether or not Seth was Luke, one thing was obvious: the man was a pathological liar.

37

I REACHED BLUME ON my second try. "Any news?"

"You sent that résumé an hour ago, Beatrice."

"Right, so what's the verdict?"

"The verdict is that I don't know yet. The college in California is real, but I haven't been able to confirm his attendance. I can tell you that he seems to have a real live family in Arkansas. Parents, aunts, a few dozen cousins. I don't think he's your boy."

I was parked down the road from Seth's Gotham house. The neighborhood was quaint and quiet. Wasn't that the kind of environment where serial killers thrived? His house had no outbuildings, though, so if he had abducted Grace, it was with his wife's knowledge, or he was hiding Grace in some hidden part of his basement. I had to admit, in a house that small, it seemed unlikely.

I said, "He's the right age, and he's a big fat liar." Vice president of the foundation? Manager of the Ross Island project? "Maybe he took on the identity of the real Seth Miller."

Blume sighed. "I can send you his high school graduation photo. Will that help?"

I waited until the photo hit my inbox. Skinnier, pimply, and pale—but that was the same Seth. It was my turn to sigh. "That's him."

"Beatrice, you know I'm happy to take your money, but I think we both have to acknowledge that this isn't going anywhere. Short of an all-out manhunt for this Luke Webb—"

I sat up and gripped the steering wheel. "That's it."

"That's what?"

"Can you work backward, Evan?"

"It depends on what you mean by 'work backward.'"

"Clearly Luke doesn't want to be found—assuming he's alive. But it's impossible not to leave some imprint in today's world. Even sites like WhitePages.com list other people in a household. Maybe you can find Luke by looking for his social circle."

Blume was quiet, and I thought he'd hung up. I heard the unmistakable sound of a cellophane wrapper being opened before Blume said, "Interesting. That could work. What can you tell me about him?"

I rattled off what I remembered. "He loved the mountains and woodworking and animals, especially cats. He was smart. He was into writing codes—"

Codes. Of course. What if all of this was some crazy code? The dolls were obvious, but there could be other clues as well. Oliver, Marcus. *Oliver.* Oliver was found at the Georgia O'Keefe cottage. *Georgia.* Elizabeth had died in Atlanta, Georgia. Coincidence?

"Beatrice, are you still there?"

"Yeah, I am. Look, something has happened that makes this more urgent. I think Luke is in Maine, somewhere near Portland. You could start there and work your way out. Maybe try with his mother's maiden name, Mansfield. Luke is out there, I'm certain of it. Please find him."

"If you're willing to pay for the time, I'll do my best."

I thought of Grace, that empty, sad apartment, her beautiful artwork. "Whatever it takes, Evan."

When we disconnected, I stuck my phone in the center console and put the car into drive. I knew my next destination. Maybe it would tell me something.

* * *

I made it to Bruner Wilderness Preserve forty-five minutes later. I thought perhaps I'd find the park overrun by thrill seekers—people hungry to see the spot where Marcus had been found—but the lot was nearly empty. I drove through the parking area and continued down the access road to the northern entrance. I wanted to see the spot where Marcus had been recovered. I wanted to see if my hunch was right.

It didn't take long to find the utility shed where he'd been hidden. The vegetation around it was trampled, and deep, muddy tire tracks crisscrossed the narrow lawn in front. I parked along the access road and climbed out of the Subaru. The building was padlocked, and there were no windows. Nevertheless, there was nothing extraordinary about the shed—just a small, rectangular outbuilding built to hold lawn and snow-removal equipment.

How could that possibly provide a clue? Perhaps I had it wrong.

I hiked along the road a quarter mile in either direction. Other than the walking trails, which crisscrossed the access road with cute names like "Eagle Path" and "Beaver's Run," there was nothing here. No buildings, no placards. As I approached my car, I noticed the trail sign for the path nearest the shed. It had been hit, probably by an emergency vehicle, and its wooden post stood cockeyed. Feeling discouraged, I closed the distance between me and the path until I could read that twisted sign.

"Sparrow's Way."

I tried to catch my breath. Luke and his parents had lived in Sparrow, West Virginia. That's where I'd met them.

Georgia. Sparrow. Luke, ever the coder, was drawing me a sort of map.

Wherever he'd taken Grace, it would be somewhere with meaning to him. I leaned against my car and thought about all the possibilities. Mountains, codes, animals, haint blue. His father had been fired from Michigan State, which was in East Lansing. Could that be a clue?

Would Rebelo believe me now?

As my brain spun with a whirlwind of chaotic possibilities, I caught my reflection in my car window. My curly brown hair stuck out every which way; my bare face was lined with worry lines; and the outfit I'd worn that morning, put on distractedly after finding those lavender stems, didn't match. If I went to him now, he'd label *me* crazy and move on.

I slipped into the car, ready to go to him anyway—let the chips fall where they may—when my phone buzzed. It was Blume.

"I think your crazy backward method may have worked."

"Okay—"

"I can't say for certain, Beatrice, but we may have a match. There's a little town in northern Vermont called Lyndon, in the Northeast Kingdom. I found a man who lives there named Bruce Walden. He owns a furniture shop. Handcrafted furniture."

"And?"

"And his partner and master craftsman is listed as Luke Mansfield."

I struggled to find the right words. Was it possible we finally found him? And living in nearby Vermont? "You're sure this is him?"

"Like I said, I'm not sure at all. I used the information you gave me and did an extensive number of searches. I still couldn't find anything much on this Luke Mansfield, but the name seems right, and the occupation seems right, so, it's worth checking him out in person." Blume waited a beat. "If you want me to go, there will be an additional travel charge—"

"No need," I said, cutting him off. "Give me the address, Evan. I'll go."

* * *

Under different circumstances, this would have been a perfect fall day. Cool air, plenty of sun, glorious foliage, and enough breeze to rain down brightly colored leaves. Today, though, the brilliant sky seemed unfriendly and vast, the canopies of golden- and orange-topped trees seemed somehow toxic, and the cold September air chilled me to my core.

As I drove through Maine, across New Hampshire, and entered the Northeast Kingdom of Vermont, I wondered what I would say.

I was tired—so tired. I didn't have the energy for subterfuge, but nor could I walk in and ask whether this Bruce Walden was harboring a kidnapper and domestic terrorist.

It turned out I didn't need subterfuge.

Walden Woodworking inhabited a refurbished train station on the outskirts of Lyndon. The exterior of the building was dark green and cream, and a large wooden sign advertised the name of the business and a phone number. I opened the door to the showroom and breathed in the scents of wood and polishing oils. The business was divided into two parts: the showroom and the workshop, which was visible behind a glass wall. The showroom furniture was beautiful—handmade tables and chairs with interlocking joints and contrasting dovetails—and so was the man in the workroom.

Despite twenty years and the physical changes those years had wrought, I recognized Luke instantly. He stood as tall as Gabriel, taller perhaps, with broad shoulders and a tapered back. His dark hair, always shaggy as a boy, was combed back from a startlingly handsome face. Sharp cheekbones; hungry, dark eyes; and a mouth set in the same determined line. It was those eyes that did it. He looked up from the table he was sanding, glanced back down, and looked up again. His eyes grew wide.

"Luke?"

Luke covered his mouth, shook his head. I studied him, searching for panic or shame, but I only saw surprise.

A man entered the showroom from a back room. "Can I help you?"

I felt reluctant to turn from Luke, afraid if I did, he would somehow disappear. Without looking at the man, I said, "I'm here to talk to Luke."

"I see."

Luke's gaze met mine. "Please," I mouthed to him.

The stranger tapped my arm. "Luke is busy, so—"

But Luke put his hand up to stop him. He pulled the door to the showroom open and walked through. Up close, I could see the signs of age—the fine lines around his mouth, the crow's feet etching the corners of his eyes, a few stray gray hairs—but if anything, he'd grown into himself in a way I'd never imagined.

"Luke," I said.

"Emma."

"Do you know her?" the stranger asked.

"I do, Bruce, and it's fine."

I finally glanced at the other man in the room. He was shorter than Luke, with thinning auburn hair and a goatee. He had kind eyes, though, and those eyes were focused on Luke with loving concern.

"Emma, this is my business and life partner, Bruce."

"Nice to meet you, Bruce."

Time seemed to stand still. The absurdity of being in a furniture store with Luke, three hours from home, and saying things as mundane as "nice to meet you" when Grace was in danger was not lost on me.

"I need to talk to you," I said. "It's important."

"How did you find me?"

"You've clearly changed, but maybe not as much as you think."

Luke's smile was wistful. "Bruce, give me fifteen minutes." He led me into the workshop, where a small table and two chairs sat beside a pile of hardwoods. "Can I get you some coffee or water?"

"No, thank you. I know what you've been up to, and I'm here to ask you to stop." Tears welled in my eyes, and I resisted every urge I had to scream for Grace's return. "Whatever beef you still have with me, that was years ago. These others have nothing to do with you or your parents. Just let it go."

Luke's eyes narrowed to slits. "What are you talking about?"

"The babies, Grace. The pipe bombs." When his expression didn't change, I said, "Luke, I know you've been stalking me, leaving me warnings." I swallowed. "The dolls."

This time, Luke's face reddened. "I don't know what you're talking about, Emma. Those dolls never came from me. You have to believe me. None of it was me."

"The kidnappings—"

"The children in Maine? You think that's me?" Luke shook his head violently back and forth. "My God, Emma. I didn't take those babies."

"Why now? Why after all this time?" But even as I spoke, I realized what he was saying. And looking around at this shop, and Bruce, I realized I believed him.

Luke sat staring at me for what felt like hours. "You don't know, do you? How could you?" He took a deep breath. "My parents are dead."

"I heard."

"My mom died when I was seventeen, but I was long gone already. I ran away from home. Somewhere around Charlotte, North Carolina, I decided I didn't want to live that way anymore. I hitchhiked to my grandmother's house in Louisiana. She was . . . well, she was already dead . . . but I had an aunt there, and I took her name. Luke Mansfield. I learned woodworking, and the rest— well, the rest is history."

I watched his face, the open way he was staring at me now, and I saw the kid he'd once been. That Luke had been wounded but sensitive and caring. It seemed to me that the man was as well.

Luke said, "I don't know who's doing this, but it's not me. You have to believe that. Go talk to Bruce, check whatever records you need to. When I left home, I swore all I wanted was a drama-free life. No lies, no moving around. I don't even have a cell phone."

"Why did you run away?"

"I think the real question is why didn't I run away sooner."

I nodded. He could be connected to what happened in Charleston all those years ago too. In some ways, he had as much to lose as I did. "Your dad. Those things he told me—the nuclear secrets, the cold fusion. He didn't have a PhD in nuclear physics. He had an associate degree in IT. Did you know that?"

Luke smirked. "Eventually I realized he was crazy. I think it was the dolls. That day after . . . well, you know, he beat me up— bad. He blamed you for the fact that we were on the run again. Had things gone as planned, they would have gotten their revenge and blamed it all neatly on you. But after things went awry, he blamed me too." Luke rubbed his face. "Gabriel was mentally ill. He was delusional. All that stuff about the government and cold fusion and running for our lives? All bullshit. He believed it, though, and he was so convincing that he made my mother believe it too."

And me as well. "How? Why?"

Luke shrugged. "I've seen a therapist for years, and the best I can tell you is that he had what they called shared delusional disorder, or folie à deux. It's rare, but it happens."

"All those monitors, the secrecy, the notebooks and—"

"All part of the delusion." Luke stood and paced the room. He ran a large, calloused hand over the top piece of hardwood. "Somewhere along the line, Gabriel convinced himself that he was being persecuted by the government. He was fired by Michigan State— that I know. I don't know if the stress of losing his job triggered some psychosis, but he became convinced my family was being persecuted and that he held the key to our country's energy needs." Luke shook his head. "Bizarre, I know. My mother had her own issues—my therapist called her codependent—and she bought into his nonsense. That's the shared part of the delusion. I'm sorry you were caught up in it too."

"Why me? Why of all the people in West Virginia did he target me?"

"I don't know. Your finding the computers was an accident. I think maybe Gabriel was a little in love with you, and that was his excuse to pull you in. He convinced my mom you were a crucial part of the plan. That we could pin it all on you. And then when you called the cops"—he shrugged—"he redirected his anger toward you. You betrayed him. If it hadn't been for you, he would have gotten his life back, that kind of stuff."

"Why did he stop?"

"Why did he do anything? Who knows."

"Absurd."

"That was my childhood, Emma. Absurd."

"Haint blue," I said. "It never saved you."

"You remembered." Luke's voice was flat. "Those were unhappy times." He sat back down on the chair across from me. "I can't help you any more than that. I only know Dad died because my sister told my aunt."

A shock ran through me. *"Your sister?"*

"You didn't know? Mom was pregnant back in Sparrow. Why else would she have been so sick all the time?"

My mom says we don't need another mouth to feed, he'd said about Jamaica all those years ago. Elizabeth's nausea, the irritability, the constant tiredness. Illness had been the obvious answer, but a rough early pregnancy made sense too.

I slouched back in my seat. "I had no idea."

Luke nodded. "The twins were born almost five months after we ran from Sparrow. Mom had a tough pregnancy and refused medical care. She never fully recovered. The boy died. Gabriel blamed you for that too."

The dolls. No wonder. I'd always wondered why they left me those horrifying dolls. Now I knew.

Luke said, "Gabriella would be about twenty now."

Gabriella. "Twenty? Luke, I hired a PI and he didn't mention more babies. He never said you had a sister."

"That's because the twins were born at home. No birth certificates, no Social Security numbers. My brother is buried in a backyard somewhere west of Virginia Beach. For all intents and purposes, those twins were ghosts."

I let that sink in. A daughter. Twenty years old. "What does Gabriella look like? Do you know?"

Luke frowned. "Last I saw her, she looked like my mom. Blond, thin, tall for her age. She was a spirited kid. Never took no for an answer. I haven't seen her in over a decade, though." His eyes darkened. "I should never have left her there. Gabriel killed himself, you know. She found him. I left her with him to deal with all of this alone." Luke shrugged. "And now you know why I need therapy and have no electronic connection to the world."

Thin and blond. *"I'm a scholarship kid."* An underprivileged twenty-year-old student who lands a job at the Wicker Foundation. Coincidence? I had to face it: if it was Gabriel's daughter doing this, it was possible she was someone I'd never met or seen. Someone lurking only in the shadows. But Julianna Kent was an interesting possibility. The figure Grace had seen at the Ross House the night I found my photograph was tall and thin. She'd thought it had been a man—but maybe it had just been an unusually tall woman. And Julianna had conveniently been on Ross Island the day Oliver was discovered.

I asked, "Did your sister go to college?"

"She was homeschooled, like me. What she did after my dad died, I couldn't tell you. She contacted my aunt and let her know about my dad's suicide. It was my aunt who told me. I don't have any contact with Gabriella. For my own sanity, for Bruce, I don't want any either."

"Even though she's your sister?"

"She's Gabriel's daughter." He ran a hand through his hair. "I should get back to work."

She's Gabriel's daughter. The thought sat with me the entire trip home.

38

Ross Island was quiet that night, the sounds of the waves breaking against the rocks a gloomy soundtrack to my thoughts. I sat on the edge of the cliff behind Frida's Cottage, stared out into the darkness, and considered my ghosts. Seeing Luke had brought up a host of regrets—about how I had left my home all those years ago, about how I had fallen for Gabriel's nonsense, and about how I'd lived my life since I'd left, always running, always just a little afraid that I was being hunted, by the Webbs or the government or my own sense of self-loathing.

The irony was not lost on me.

I straightened my legs so they were hanging over the side of the cliff. It would be so easy for someone to come at me now—push me off the ledge to join the women who'd died here over the years. "Do it!" I screamed into the wind. Was she—whoever *she* was—watching me now? It was hard to believe a twenty-year-old girl could cause this much havoc and pain, but misery knew no age boundaries. Hadn't history taught us that?

Tomorrow I would speak with Julianna. If she was Gabriel's daughter, there would be some tell. An amused twinkle in her eye, a quick temper. I hadn't cared enough before to look, but now I would dig beneath the surface.

And tomorrow Rebelo would take a missing persons report on Grace. He had no choice. I was at the end of my line. It was time to lay it all out for Rebelo—my past, my connection to the kidnapper—and accept whatever punishment was meant to be. I should have turned myself in years ago. If we could find Grace, prison would be worth it. She, at least, could have a life.

The wind was picking up, and I lifted my face to feel its full force. I could stay out here all night, huddled on the rocks, listening to the breakers, thinking about the past, but I had other things to do. The kidnapper had given me clues—Georgia, Sparrow. At first, I'd thought they were Luke's codes—related to events in his life. But on learning about the existence of his sister, I started to see things differently.

Georgia was where Elizabeth had died.

Sparrow was where she had conceived Gabriella.

The lavender was what had grown in Elizabeth's West Virginia gardens, where Elizabeth had been betrayed by Gabriel and by me.

The dress form represented my act of treachery against Gabriel.

The dolls and the children and the picture of me—they represented the fragility of parenthood and revenge for what they thought I'd stolen—their baby.

I had no children, so there was no one to steal that could have quite the same impact. Grace was my friend, but she was *like* a daughter, and whoever did this knew that. Grace would be found somewhere significant to Gabriel's daughter. But where? Moving a grown woman would be harder than moving a child. The kidnapper, barely more than a kid herself, would leave Grace where she'd imprisoned her—that would be the only way to keep her drugged. If I could figure out the final clue, I would find Grace.

Of that I was certain.

* * *

"Where's Julianna?" I asked our admin, Joan, the next morning. "I need her."

Joan eyed me warily. I'd made sure to shower this morning, and my hair was tamed into a bun, and my clothing matched. Still, I could see hesitance in the other woman's eyes.

"What's wrong?" I asked.

"Nothing, nothing. Josh was looking for you, is all."

"I'm going to grab coffee. After that, you can tell Josh I'll be in my office, waiting for Julianna."

As I walked past Seth's desk, toward the kitchenette, I felt the weight of his stare on my back. "Beatrice," he said.

I spun around, cocked my head. "Yes, Seth."

"About yesterday." All his bravado was gone. He was a popped balloon, visibly deflated.

We stared at one another. I knew I had the power. Seth wasn't Luke, and he had nothing to do with what was going on, but he was a liar and maybe even a fraud. At the very least, I could make him lose his job. Still, what possible right did *I* have to judge?

I said, "Just tell me why."

He was silent for a moment. I watched as his expression changed from fearful to resolute, to defiant, all in the space of a few seconds. He said, "I like this Seth better."

I nodded. I wasn't sure he actually knew what compelled him to tell so many lies, but I felt like his response was, at least to him, honest. "I'll be in my office. Maybe we can discuss the brochure later."

Seth's nod was perfunctory, but I saw his jaw relax, the relief in his eyes.

I didn't need to take it further. Eventually, his lies would catch up with him. And even if they didn't, he'd always have that fear. The ever-creeping, everlasting panic that someone would find him out.

*   *   *

I made it to my office six minutes later, coffee in hand. I didn't see Julianna, but there was a note and a package on my desk. I opened the note:

Beatrice—You stood me up yesterday! No worries; I went to the art fair without you. Ran across these. If you're interested, I'll connect us with the artists. —JK

The art fair. I'd forgotten all about it. I placed the package on my desk. The last thing I wanted to think about right now was the art for the gallery and retreat, but after another ten minutes of waiting, my restlessness won out. I opened it and flipped quickly through the contents.

An eight-by-ten print of an abstract painting by someone named Henrique Moulet. I tossed it aside. A five-by-seven reproduction of a nude by an artist named Shawna Jones. I tossed that aside too. I was about to toss them all aside when the third one caught my eye.

Bold, saturated colors. Slightly impressionistic. Anachronistic. A mother and a baby—the mother staring out into the desert, the baby swaddled to her breast. The painting left me feeling lonely and melancholy and uncomfortable, as though I was witnessing something deeply private. I recognized the subjects, the style, the feeling. This was Grace's work. Only when I turned the print over, her name wasn't on it—it was signed by an artist known simply as Maude.

Maude's website included a photograph. In the picture, Maude was in her sixties and had gray dreadlocks and wore a pink kaftan. The bare-bones site also included photographs of her previous works. I recognized all of the art Grace had passed off as her own.

Feeling ill with the implications, I called the Bar Harbor gallery listed on the site as the only gallery carrying Maude's work.

"How can I help you?" asked the woman on the line.

"I'm looking for work by an artist named Maude, and I understand you carry some of her paintings?"

"Yes! Maude. We have two of her pieces left. She's a street artist who recently received some positive attention. Lovely woman, beautiful work. Are you looking for anything in particular?"

"I think I've met the artist, but I want to be certain before I drive north. Older woman, dreadlocks, colorful character?"

"That's Maude." The woman laughed. "We discovered her at a local craft fair. Amazing artist. Stunning paintings, really."

Amazing alright. I thanked the woman and hung up the phone. Why had Grace lied to me? I thought back to our relationship, forged over that pottery wheel more than a year ago. Grace had a story that had touched my heart. Rough family life, living on her

own, trying to make a go of it in a brutal world. Art was her passion. Yet had I ever actually seen her paint?

On impulse, I called Blume. To my relief, he answered
immediately.

"Good thing you called. I've got some news for you. That Len
Kalchik? Relative of the Ross family. Len's great-great-grandfather
and Eli's great-great-grandfather were brothers. When their dad
died, he left the island to the last surviving offspring. I think they
call that per capita. Anyway, Miles's side of the family got everything, and Len and his dad got nothing. When the island sold, he
must have been pretty unhappy he didn't get a cut. I guess that side
of the family has been harboring resentment for a lot of years."

Well, that would perhaps explain why he was stalking me.
"Evan, I appreciate that—I really do—but I have a more urgent
question. You mentioned that Gabriel Webb used fictitious names.
Do you have a list of them?"

"Sure. Hold on; I'll need a minute." I heard Blume pecking
away at his keyboard. "Ready?"

I didn't need to write down the list. The third one was what I
was looking for. Gabriel Harding.

Grace Harding.

Grace wasn't missing because she'd been abducted. Grace was
missing because she was the kidnapper. Suddenly all the missing pieces clicked into place. Grace always had an alibi—almost.
She was supposed to have dinner with me the night Oliver was
abducted. She met me at the beach—her suggestion—the afternoon
Marcus was taken. Neither of these events would have precluded
her involvement in the crime; they were just convenient enough
to remove any suspicion. After all, why would the police suspect a
twenty-something with no obvious connection to the victims?

All the taunts left on Ross Island. Grace knew my schedule, she
knew the names of the cottages, and she could have easily gotten
access to the buildings at any time. The garage where she lived was
a treasure trove of old boating gear, so getting to the island would
have been simple enough. And the night we had Chinese food?
It was Grace who placed that photo in the box while I was busy

searching for her mystery man. She would have had time to sneak it in there when I was searching for her phantom invader.

Oh, Grace.

I left the foundation office with a brief goodbye to Joan.

"What about Josh?" she called after me.

"I have a cell phone ," I said. "Tell him to call me."

CHAPTER

39

I SAT IN MY car, too stunned to move, too upset to focus. Grace as Gabriella Webb? Grace as Elizabeth's daughter? They didn't even look alike. Grace was round and sturdy, not tall and willowy. But genetics were always a gamble.

Grace had been my friend. More than that, she had been a mentee, a daughter. She'd even lied about her age.

I couldn't decide if I was angry or heartbroken. All the while she and I had shared stories and meals, the whole time I had introduced her to the art world, it was all a lie—a diabolical series of lies to get me to trust her so she could seek her own sick revenge. Even our time in the pottery studio had been a lie. She must have followed me, enrolled when I had, arranged to sit near me. She had fabricated our whole relationship.

Only it wasn't *all* a lie. The late-night chats, the concern I'd sometimes see in her eyes when she thought I wasn't looking, the easy laughter—underneath the facade, something was real.

I needed to end this once and for all. For both our sakes. And to do that, I needed to turn us both in. That is, if I could find her.

I went back to the clues. Georgia. Sparrow. Elizabeth's death.

Of course—*and Elizabeth's birth*. Elizabeth was from Louisiana, but I had no idea what town. I dialed Blume again, but this time he didn't pick up. I searched for Walden Woodworking and tried that number.

Luke's partner, Bruce, answered. "Look, your visit was hard for Luke. It might be better if you just left him alone."

"I have one question only—I promise. But it's important." I took Bruce's silence as acquiescence and requested that he ask Luke where his mother was born.

"That's easy," Bruce said. "Oak Grove, Louisiana." Bruce put a flourish on the word *Louisiana*. "She's dead, though. They all are. Luke lost his aunt last year."

I mumbled a thank-you and ended the call. Oak Grove, Louisiana.

There was an Oak Grove Cemetery in Bath, Maine. Could that be where Grace was? I was tired and cranky and heartsore, but I put Bath in my GPS and headed the hour to Oak Grove.

* * *

Oak Grove Cemetery in Bath was a bust. I walked around its perimeter and its interior, and I checked out any buildings near the property. Other than a sense of foreboding so deep it felt like someone was walking on my own grave, nothing unusual occurred. I drove back to Cape Morgan, feeling like an idiot. Grace had left town. Her empty apartment was proof. She'd accomplished what she'd set out to do—unwind my life, undermine my sanity—and then she'd disappeared.

Her apartment. When I'd last been there, I'd been looking for *Grace*, not evidence that Grace was involved with the kidnapping. Maybe I'd missed something. There was only one way to find out.

* * *

Grace's apartment was just as I'd left it. Her landlord's house was deserted, and the garage—both her living quarters and the downstairs—remained dark. The back door to the garage was still broken. As I let myself in and crept up the steps toward Grace's apartment, I felt fear and sadness envelop me. Suddenly, I saw these quarters in a new light. The shabby furniture and decor, the neat boxes of art supplies, the chipped china dishes and teacups—antique store finds—once viewed by me as sweet, were all attempts by a deranged young woman to carry on her father's sick legacy.

Shared delusion disorder.

I went through Grace's drawers, her closet, the cabinets, but I found nothing out of the ordinary, and certainly nothing indicating she had been holding children hostage. The wind had picked up, and it rattled the rickety windows. I felt a prickle on my scalp like I was being watched. I needed to get out of there.

Outside, the wind tunneled in the narrow courtyard, and bits of hay and golden leaves were swirling around the rundown farmland like mini tornadoes. *Hay.* Ignoring the prickle, I made my way to the first of the two barns. The door was ajar, and inside the one-story building, stacked bales of hay sat against the wall in four horse stalls. The stalls were long empty, and the hay was mildewy and discolored. I backed out of the barn and eyed the second building.

This one was taller, with a sliding barn door that remained structurally sound. I pushed it aside, grunting with the effort, and blinked, trying to adjust to the darkness inside. Unlike the other structure, this one housed more than hay. An old tractor, a plow, and boxes of what looked like bridles and other horse paraphernalia littered the hard-packed dirt floor. A set of steep, questionable wooden steps off to the right led to a second-floor storage area. There was no light switch that I could find, so I turned on the flashlight app on my phone.

I eyed those steps, the tightening in my gut giving way to a hard ache.

One foot over the other, I told myself. *You got this, kid.* My senses were on high alert—for sound and movement. The fourth step wiggled under my weight, and I hopped quickly to the next. At the top, I looked back. No one was in the barn. I swung my leg up over the small rail that divided the storage area from the stairway, and I shined my weak light around the tight space.

The floors were swept clean—too clean. Unlike the musty leather scents from downstairs, this area reeked of chemical disinfectant.

The noise from I-95 could be heard through the thin barn walls—insurance that the children's cries would never be noticed. No clutter filled this space, and as I walked across the wooden boards, I spotted something on the other end of the room. My head grew light, and my vision narrowed. In the corner, propped against the wall, was a doll. Not an old, dirty baby doll like the others. This one was made of dried corn husks with a skirt of preserved lavender. A ribbon connected the neck of the doll to an oversized craft paper gift tag.

"For Emma" was written on the tag in big, ugly, bloodred letters.

*   *   *

I drove from Grace's to the house on Dove Street, with a stop at a convenience store along the way. I had three missed calls from Josh, but I ignored them. The Dove Street house was empty, and I ran upstairs and threw some clothes and other belongings into a duffel bag. I had purchased a new burner phone, and I took it and the bag downstairs. The duffel bag I left by the front door, but I took the phone outside with me.

I walked across the veranda, past my gardens, and down to the gate that led to the small dock on the bay. I pulled the tarp off the boat and climbed inside. When I'd motored the boat about an eighth of a mile from shore, I called my sister. One more name, she'd said before. I would take her up on that offer. I would leave the facts for Rebelo—Cape Morgan had been good to me, and the town deserved the truth—and I would head as far from this little corner of the States as I could go. I had one other stop to make—back to Grace's apartment to take the inflatable raft and one of the oars stored in the garage. No one would miss them. It was a perfect plan.

Only Jane didn't answer her phone.

I sat there in the boat and let the bay waves try unsuccessfully to calm my nerves. Looking toward the shore from this distance, I could see the stately Dove Street house rising up from the water's edge, surrounded by flowers and red maple trees. I knew deep down that I'd never see this place again. The grief was sudden and stabbing.

I was heading back toward shore when my phone rang. I was expecting Jane's raspy, irritated voice, but instead it was a masculine voice that said, "Emma?"

My brother-in-law. "Hello, Jake. Is Jane okay?"

"I'm sorry," Jane's husband said, and his voice broke. "It took her quickly in the end, at least."

My sister was dead.

And in that moment, I knew where Grace would be.

I hung my head and cried.

CHAPTER

40

I ARRIVED ON Ross Island at the golden hour. The trees were on the cusp of their brightest show; gold, orange, and crimson leaves teased against the green backdrop of their stately evergreen cousins. The windows, roof, and exterior walls of the main house had been repaired, and scaffolding was up for the scraping and painting that would occur next. In a flash, I saw the house as it would be: tall and regal and welcoming—a sanctuary for creative people to leave the stressors of the real world and reconnect with nature and their inner artists.

They would love it here, as I had.

The last of the construction crew were just finishing, and I stood on the lawn and watched them pack up their belongings.

The foreman joined me. "What do you think?"

"I think it looks spectacular."

"We should be finished before temperatures are an issue."

"You'll do your best."

The foreman raised his eyebrows, started to say something, and stopped. He nodded goodbye, and I watched him drive away.

I'd been waiting for him to leave. I'd been waiting for them all to leave.

*   *   *

I finally listened to Josh's voicemails.

The first: "Beatrice, call me."

The second: "Beatrice, where the hell are you? Thomas called me and said you were raving about your friend Grace. You claimed she's missing now. Look, just call me, okay? I know things aren't great between us, but . . . just call me back."

The third: "Beatrice, seriously. Joan said you've been acting weird. You never called Thomas back, you missed an appointment with Juli-anna, and now you're ignoring me. I'm in Boston tonight, but I'll drive by when I get back. If you're staying at the island, I'll come there." A pause. "I'm worried about you, Beatrice. Really worried."

*   *   *

The smallest marked gravestone wasn't much bigger than a brick. Smooth and flat, the words "Baby Girl Fletcher" and the year 1812 were engraved on its face. Like the other grave markers, a fine coat-ing of moss had turned the stone the faintest green. I had planned to scrub and bleach these stones next spring. I hoped someone else would do it in my stead. These ghosts deserved better.

Next to Baby Girl Fletcher rested Betsy Arrent, a "fine wife and mother" who died in 1913. Betsy's stone was larger, vertical, with intricate flowers carved beneath the year of her death. Grace was sitting on the ground, her arms wrapped around her knees, and her back against Betsy Arrent's grave. Grace's body was shadowed by the grove of oaks that called this area of the island home. A tire iron lay on the grass beside Grace.

I sank down next to Grace. From here, I could see the big house, Frida's Cottage, and the ocean beyond. It was a perfect place for introspection. It was a perfect spot for spying.

Grace spoke first. "You came."

"You thought I wouldn't?"

"I wasn't sure you'd figure it out."

A small dead branch had fallen from one of the oaks, and I picked it up, rubbing along the loose bark with my finger. "Why, Grace? Why me, why here, why those children?"

"I never hurt them."

"That doesn't change what you did."

"What *I* did?" Grace shook her head. "How about what *you* did?"

"What did I do? Tell me, please."

"You ruined my father, tried to turn him in to the authorities. He would have been imprisoned for life. Or worse. You made my mother ill. You betrayed us." Angry tears glistened in her eyes, and she pushed them back with an impatient swipe of her hand. "It's your fault we had to run. Always somewhere new, always people chasing us."

"Like your family was always chasing me." I watched a red squirrel run across the graves, using them as stepping stones to get across the brush and branches. "How did you find me?"

"Photos from your wedding. My father identified you before he died. In a way, you killed him."

I put a hand on her shoulder, and she shoved it away.

"You have no idea what you're talking about, Gabriella."

The use of her birth name seemed to irritate her, and she glared at me with wide, hard eyes. "Then tell me the truth."

I laughed sharply. "The truth?" What the hell *was* the truth? Did I even know anymore? "It's late and getting cold. How about if we go into the cottage and I tell you a story instead."

I turned to study her. She seemed so young and so tiny and so very, very vulnerable. I saw neither Elizabeth's frail beauty nor Gabriel's cruel strength—just a very hurt and confused young woman.

She nodded roughly. I followed her inside.

*   *   *

"Once upon a time, a young girl left home at sixteen. She said she was seeking adventure, but in reality, she was seeking escape. Eventually she found both—and love, or what she thought was love—with a family on a small farm in West Virginia."

We were sitting in front of the mermaid mural, in the soft light of Frida's Cottage, looking out through the picture window. The sun had dipped below the horizon, and alternating bands of yellow, pink, and orange hovered just above the sea.

I continued, "The young woman came to believe this family had her best interests at heart. She came to believe the family was being unfairly persecuted." I paused, remembering. "Most importantly, she came to believe she was part of something bigger, exciting, important."

"And then she destroyed it all," Grace said.

I held up a hand. "And then she realized the parents weren't telling the truth."

"You're calling my father a liar," Grace said.

"I said they weren't telling the truth. Sometimes there's a difference." I breathed deeply, steadying myself. "Your father and mother were using me, Grace. Did your father believe he was a wronged scientist? Luke seems to think so—"

"You talked to Luke?"

I nodded. "I did, and he shared the reasons he left. Your father and mother may have convinced themselves that they were being persecuted, but it wasn't true. I got caught in their crazy plot for revenge, and you got caught up as well. And for that, I'm sorry."

Grace picked up the tire iron and balanced it in one hand. Her gaze traveled from the iron to the mermaids to the picture window, now black as the night sky.

"My father said they never would have found you. You ran for nothing, Beatrice. All these long years. The explosion destroyed anything linking you to what happened in Charleston. Anything linking us too."

"Maybe. Maybe not. It was a chance I was unwilling to take."

"My father said you were evil."

"You came to Cape Morgan to kill me," I said. "And yet you've had every chance to do it, and here I am. Somewhere inside you know I'm not evil. And you know I'm telling you the truth. That I care about you, the real you—not this twisted, enraged version of you."

"He had diplomas and notebooks and books and knowledge. So much knowledge—"

"I know."

"He was so angry *all* of the time." Grace let out a low moan. "At you, at the government. *At me.*"

"I know."

· "He planned this. He said you would never see it coming. That I should get close to you, destroy what mattered to you just as you had destroyed our family. Never let you rest." She paused. "He killed himself. I found him."

"I'm so sorry, Grace."

"He said it was your fault. That if you hadn't turned on them, they could have stayed in West Virginia. I could have had a normal life there, Beatrice. Luke would have stayed home. My mother would be alive. My father would have been a prestigious scientist once again."

"Do you believe that, Grace? First the government stealing his secrets, then my betrayal?" I asked softly. All these years, and the only story Grace had heard was theirs. She was a child with no other past and no other present. Just the endless lies. "According to Gabriel, the problems you endured were always, always someone else's fault."

"What if he was telling the truth?" Grace stood up. She was gripping the tire iron so hard her entire arm was trembling. "How do I know *you're* telling the truth?"

"You don't. And that's the horrible reality of all of this." I put my hand out. "Grace, you have to trust me."

"I'm going to go to prison anyway." She raised the iron over her head. Tears streamed down her face, and she was shaking her head from side to side. "Nothing matters now."

"There's another way."

"It's not fair!"

"No, it isn't."

Grace threw her head back and howled. She brought the tire iron down, turning at the last second so she destroyed the half wall and my mermaid mural. The screaming continued until it morphed into high-pitched wails and, eventually, sobs. She fell to her knees in a pile of colored plaster and tossed the tire iron to the side.

"Those little boys," she said, phlegm running from her nose. "They were so helpless." She looked up at me. "I never hurt them."

I crawled over to her and wrapped an arm around her heaving shoulder. This time she didn't pull back.

CHAPTER

41

WE DIDN'T HAVE much time before Josh would come looking for me. I left Grace in the cottage and ran back into the Ross House. Inside, I grabbed a piece of paper and wrote the university's name on it, along with Herman Hanes's contact information. Before fastening the two metal file boxes containing the old medical records, I selected two sets of records from the pile—Sarah and Mary Bolton. Their ages were about right, and based on their histories, no family would ever come forward. Somehow using their identities seemed apropos.

In the light of the moon, I pulled the inflatable raft I'd found in the garage where Grace had lived and placed it on the shore. Into my drybag, I added a flashlight, a headlamp, and a pack of matches. I pulled two hoodies from my duffel bag and left the towels and dry clothes inside. I placed the duffel bag on the beach.

I found Grace lying prostate on the floor of Frida's Cottage. "Get up," I said.

She blinked at me, unmoving. I shook her, hard.

"Grace, get a hold of yourself. There is one way out of this mess that doesn't land us both in prison, and this is it. Put on the hoodie, gather your belongings, and come with me."

Grace stood up. She seemed shaky and bleary-eyed, but she listened. She was clutching a canvas satchel. I took it from her. Inside, I found a wallet, some cash, a baggie of tampons, and a stash of documents tethered with an elastic band.

"Open them," she said.

As I unfastened the elastic, I felt my insides start to quiver. I recognized Gabriel's handwriting, slanted and unreadable as the man himself. Inside these pages were his notes. Page upon page of scientific calculations. They meant little to me now. Once upon a time, I'd believed they were some kind of gospel.

"What are you doing with these?" I asked.

"I need to know," Grace said. "I'm going to take them to a university in Mexico. See if they make any sense to someone who understands physics."

I placed the band back around the documents and handed the package back to Grace. "And then what?"

Grace remained silent. I understood her torment. I had only lived with Gabriel for a few months, but I felt it too. Blume had been adamant—there was nothing in Gabriel's record supporting his version of the story. No PhD, no awards, no lofty career. Of course, if the government could steal his secrets, they could also cover up their tracks after the fact as well. But how far would such a conspiracy have to go to leave absolutely no trace of his supposed life?

Finally, Grace said, "I just need to know."

"If the equations in those letters are real, if Gabriel was who he says he was and agents of the government really were after him, having them could be dangerous. If they're not"—I frowned— "your father was a sick man, Grace. He needed help."

"If they're real, or even if they *could* be real, I'll know he wasn't lying. This"—she waved her hand back toward the inn—"wouldn't have been for nothing."

"It was still for nothing. Sometimes you have to accept that and move on. Don't let regret be the anchor that holds you back forever."

Grace's face was twisted in a mask of indecision and hurt. I was afraid, for her, there would never be peace.

"Where does it end?" I whispered. "Even if the equations are real, that doesn't mean they're his original work. He was employed by a university. Maybe he copied the equations or compiled them from things he'd read on the internet." I touched her arm lightly. "You may never know the truth. Sometimes we just have to live with the gray."

Grace wrapped her arms around her knees and buried her face against her legs. She stayed that way, cocooned against her body, until I finally left her, to finish getting ready.

* * *

It was after midnight by the time things were set. The inn, the cottage, the beach—they all had to give the appearance of one last excursion out into the sea, with no evidence that Grace had ever been here with me.

I left the boxes for the university.

I left a simple note for Josh: *I did love you, Josh. More than you will ever know. May you find what you're looking for. XO —Beatrice*

I erased any contacts and email exchanges with Blume—he'd signed the confidentiality agreement, which I'd written to apply after my death, and I believed he'd honor it if he could. Then I left my wallet and my cell phone behind.

This time, I found Grace in the oak grove, near the unmarked graves. She was standing over a small fire, her back to me.

"He was never buried," she said. "I never claimed his body. Neither did Luke or my aunt. We just left him with the government." She glanced at me, her eyes liquid and round in the soft glow of the fire. "The state of Washington cremated him. I don't know where he is now."

She tossed the bundle of his papers on the fire. Together we watched them burn.

* * *

On the shore, I loaded the raft and our bags into the rowboat. I didn't dare turn on the headlamp, so we rowed beyond the island in silence. When we were past the jutting rocks, I pulled the ring on the raft and prayed it would inflate.

It did.

I flipped on my headlamp and slipped from the boat into the raft in silence. Grace handed me the bags. When I held out my arms for her to join me, she sat there, silent.

"Grace," I hissed. "Come on."

"How will this be better?"

"It can't be worse," I said quietly.

Grace pulled the black hoodie up, over her head, and stared down at her hands. The ocean was calm for now—a kindness, for sure—and as Grace floated there in that rowboat, I wondered how this would go. Was I bringing my past with me, or would I finally be able to escape it once and for all?

With a sudden surge that rocked both boats, Grace sprang forward and into the raft. I righted the craft, and she handed me her oar. Together we tipped the rowboat over until it capsized. I tossed the rowboat oars in the sea too, along with my orange dry bag.

If we hugged the coast and were mindful of rocks, the raft was in good enough shape to get us back to shore north of Cape Morgan, where we could discard the raft and the kayak paddle and catch an early bus from Portland. I had the money from the safe deposit box in case we decided to cross a national border. Getting out of the United States wouldn't be a problem. Getting back in could be. I didn't think that mattered.

Grace was staring out, over the ocean, her eyes focused straight ahead. I looked back, toward Ross Island. All I could see was that orange bag, drifting alone on a black sea of nothingness.

ACKNOWLEDGMENTS

F OR HER ENDLESS patience, helpful critiques, and constant advocacy, I'd like to thank my fantastic agent, Frances Black, of Literary Counsel. To Faith Black Ross, my wonderful editor at Crooked Lane Books, and to the entire tireless Crooked Lane team, including Rebecca Nelson, Madeline Rathle, Dulce Botello, and Melissa Rechter, I offer grateful acknowledgment. Many thanks to my early readers, Sue Norbury and Kim Morris, and to my family—especially Angela Tyson, Ian Pickarski, Mandy Pickarski, Matthew Pickarski, Jonathan Pickarski, Greg Marincola, and Marie Fulmer—for always being my champions.

I've been fortunate enough to be part of a truly unique book club, and I'd like to acknowledge the members for their friendship, enthusiasm, and genuine love of learning and reading. Pat Meulemans, Lauren Roppolo, Mimi Wright, Carol Cantwell, Marilyn Donovan, Mary Kathleen Butera, Ellen Deweerdt, Amy Hekker Peckel, Patty Eisenhaur, and Lois Schram Osnow, I leave every gathering feeling energized and inspired. What a gift. Most of all, thanks to my husband and travel partner, Ben Pickarski, whose love and support keep me going.